PINNACLE CITY

PINNACLE CITY

A SUPERHERO NOIR

MATT CARTER &
FIONA J. R. TITCHENELL

TALOS PRESS

Talos Press books may be purchased in bulk at special discounts for sales promotion, corporate gifts, fund-raising, or educational purposes. Special editions can also be created to specifications. For details, contact the Special Sales Department, Talos Press, 307 West 36th Street, 11th Floor, New York, NY 10018 or info@skyhorsepublishing.com.

Talos Press is an imprint of Skyhorse Publishing, Inc.®, a Delaware corporation.

Visit our website at www.talospress.com.

10 9 8 7 6 5 4 3 2 1

Library of Congress Cataloging-in-Publication Data in available on file.

Cover illustration by Corrie Phillips
Cover design by Jason Snair

Print ISBN: 978-1-945863-16-5
Ebook ISBN 978-1-945863-17-2

Printed in the United States of America

For all those fighting the never-ending battle for truth and justice.

PINNACLE CITY

CHAPTER 1: THE DETECTIVE

O f all the cities in all the world to be thrown through a plate glass window into a rain-soaked gutter swirling with garbage, Pinnacle City's gotta be my favorite.

I'm sure there're gutters in other cities that'd do the job in a pinch, but they wouldn't have that feeling of home.

I also got my doubts any other town could have such storied windows to be flung through.

Take the fine piece of glass I was just forced to use as an impromptu emergency exit, for instance.

Though I didn't touch any of its shards long enough for my superpower to give a solid history (thank God), here's the highlight reel of what led up to my exit:

- An hour ago: a drunk put a CARD FOR SENATE sticker on the bar's window before skipping the alley and just pissing right outside the door.
- Three hours ago: a dealer cheated some junkies on a badly cut batch of Montage, ignoring the bloody, badly beaten gene-job trying to crawl away.
- Four hours ago: three skinheads beat a gene-job to a pulp at the base of the window, yelling some damn vile (and inventive) slurs at him.
- Four hours five minutes ago: the same gene-job tore a CARD FOR SENATE sticker off the window, pissing off the skinheads.
- Six hours ago: a nicely dressed woman who didn't belong in West Pinnacle City put a CARD FOR SENATE sticker on the bar's window.

Like I said, a storied window.

Storied until Harold Berryman decided to throw me through it, though some might say *decided* is an exaggeration since I did everything possible to encourage him to do this.

Him taking a shortcut to the street by smashing through the barroom wall after me—tearing through bricks and wood like gift wrap, followed by his friends whooping and cheering him on—that I didn't encourage.

The way his fists are glowing green at this moment, this is also something I didn't intend to encourage.

Unfortunately, his friends—plus about eight or nine beers—offer all the encouragement he needs.

"Get 'im, Harry! Fuck his beaner ass up!" one yells.

I'd share what the others say, but it's more of the same with only slight variation, mostly in their choice of ethnic slurs and level of drunkenness.

I stumble to my feet, rain pouring down around us. Old aches take over as pain rockets up my left arm, from the middle finger all the way up to my ear. It's a fire, almost paralyzing.

Shakily, I toss a couple pills from the bottle in my pocket into my mouth and crunch down on them.

According to the docs at the VA, they shouldn't kick in yet, but I feel instant relief.

Doctors. What do they know?

When everything feels like it oughta, I'm relieved that Harriet's still in my left hand. While she may not look all that impressive as most wooden baseball bats go, she's got a hollowed-out core with a couple pounds of solid lead inside. Being that I'm not legally allowed to have a gun, she's helped me out of a few tight spots.

Probably not this one, though.

Berryman tears off his shirt, revealing an upper torso glowing with green light. He might've looked impressive about ten years back, but his beer gut (about the only part of him not glowing) and thinning hair covered in a ratty Santa hat do him no favors.

"You're the one's been following me, aintcha?" he taunts, cracking his knuckles.

"You workin' on a point?"

"Don'tcha got nothin' better to do than follow honest people 'round, spyin' on them and shit?"

"Don't you have anything better to do than beat your wife in a piece of shit bar?"

"FUCK. YOU!"

Well, at least he's a sucker for the classics.

More people exit the bar, some filming on their phones, some egging the fight on, others trying to break it up.

They don't try to stop *him*, of course. A glowing green drunk with superhuman strength, that's a job you leave for the superheroes—when and if they decide to make an appearance at this end of town. Until then you enjoy the show, post it online, and hope you don't get too hurt.

Icy rain sizzling off his glowing skin, Berryman yells and runs toward me.

One thing's for sure: If I survive, I'm charging extra.

✷

The name's Eddie Enriquez, Edgar if you wanna get formal (don't get formal), and I'm a private investigator, primarily working out of the Crescent in glamorous Pinnacle City, California.

It's not a sexy job like the old movies wanna make it out to be, and mostly means me following people around, watching them cheat their insurance companies on disability, but I gotta knack for it.

By which I mean I sneak into a place I know a target was, use my powers and implant to record their past dirty deeds, get the job done in a couple minutes, and pad out the rest of my invoice for a gig with some reasonable-sounding expenses and hours close to what a norm would bill.

At the end of the day, I still charge less than everyone else and get the job done, so everyone walks away happy.

Well, almost everyone.

It's not exactly the future I dreamed of growing up, but for a former henchman to a terrible (as in incompetent, not evil) supervillain, it pays the bills.

I like the gig . . . mostly. Not having anyone looking over my shoulder telling me what to do and not to do, setting my own hours, working with clients I chose instead of ones some boss wants to make nice with, that's a life I can live.

But like anything else, it's got its drawbacks. For instance, being an ex-con with my skin color and trying to not look suspicious in a lot of the places I need to be is next to impossible. The cops, the DSA (Department of Superhuman Affairs), and, less frequently but still enough to be a problem, the pro-heroes enjoy hassling me to no end. I show them my paperwork, my PI license, my DSA-issued R-SAL (Registered Superhuman Ability License) card, and, though that should be enough, the moment they run my name and see I've done time, my day gets a whole lot longer.

That's bad enough as it is.

Then there's days like this when things get rough, and working solo is more dangerous than convenient.

When your back's against the wall, you gotta decide if the fight's worth it or if it's safer to run. I usually run—especially when my arm's flaring up like it is now.

But there's times, like right now with Harry Berryman, where I just can't do that.

For the past year, Berryman has been collecting disability on a supposed back injury. While no one's doubting the construction accident he was in, with an R-SAL stating he's got superhuman strength and a low-grade regenerative power, his insurance company had doubts and called me in to verify just how bad his "constant, debilitating pain that keeps him in bed most days" was treating him.

Three days in and I'd collected enough footage of him playing softball, moving furniture, and hitting up some pretty active strip clubs to prove he was gaming the system. I could've cut it off after one day, easy, but something in what I'd seen made me stay on. A kind of anger and tension I've seen too much in this line of work.

Something I knew I had to keep an eye on.

Tonight, I'm glad I did.

He wasn't any drunker than usual tonight, and nothing out of the ordinary happened. It was just a night out with the wife and his boys.

But then a disagreement became an argument, an argument escalated to shouting, and shouting became him glowing and punching his wife to the floor.

Standard protocol's not to interfere in cases like this—let others intervene or, if you're feeling really proactive, call the cops.

I've never been much for standard protocol.

That probably explains why me introducing Harriet to the back of his head ended with being thrown through a window.

Still, I'd rather be his punching bag than her.

Which brings us back to the present; him charging, hitting me like a freight train, and sending me through the air and onto the hood of a parked car.

Believe it or not, this isn't the first car hood I've ridden. One thing I've learned from experience is that, no matter how much you think it's gonna hurt, it always hurts much worse.

I roll, and my trench coat takes a lot of the impact, but it still sucks.

I'm hardly able to get my feet beneath me—something the rain's not making any easier. Sliding off the hood, my shoe catches on the decorative Rudolph nose on the front of the car. Kicking free, I rip the sodden, fluffy red toy loose and toss it at Berryman.

He laughs. I do too.

He charges and swings for me, but I dodge, with the car taking most of the impact.

The clumsy kick he spins at my back, however, hits home and I'm sprawled out in the middle of Fuerte Street. Harriet rolls from my grip and I crawl for her, but another kick flips me onto my back.

Then there's a boot on my chest, and all I can see is that glowing green beer belly and Santa hat. He's staring down at me, rivers of rain still streaming down his chest, steaming from whatever makes him glow.

"Had enough? Had enough, you scrawny piece of shit?" he says while grinding his boot into my chest.

If he wants an answer, he's gonna have to let off the pressure, but I'm guessing his question's more of the rhetorical type.

A bolt of lightning lights up the sky. A figure, dark and indistinct with a billowing cape, is lit up. By the time the thunder cracks she's already off the roof and coming toward us.

Well, this should be fun.

A small explosion lights up Berryman's back. He screams and is immediately surrounded in a fast-expanding foam, hardening around him like cement. His boot lifts off my chest and I crawl away.

Berryman breaks out of the foam quickly, but the dark figure is on him in a flash, tossing blinding, disorienting explosives. The figure charges before Berryman's eyes can clear, bashing at his weak spots—knees, lower back, temple—with a pair of twin, foot-long clubs.

He's down at once, and soon bound tightly by a thin yet powerful net from the dark figure's utility belt.

A few of Berryman's buddies look like they want to take her on, and the dark figure welcomes them. When they get a good look at her, at her slender physique bulked out with heavy body armor, utility belts full of weapons and ammunition that criss-cross her chest, the billowing cape, the glistening black helmet that covers her head, two glowing white eye pieces piercing the darkness, they recognize her and stop in their tracks.

"Boo," she says softly, her voice distorted by digital filters in the helmet to sound like a computerized nightmare.

This gets the desired response.

"It's Dissident!"

"She'll kill us all!"

"Let's get the fuck outta here!"

With most of the crowd dispersed, Dissident looms over to me.

"Hey."

"Hey."

"You look like hell, Eddie," she says, reaching down for me.

"I feel it." I take her hand and let her help me up. "You seen Harriet?"

Without even looking, she flicks her wrist, shooting a small grappling hook out and pulling it back, Harriet in hand.

"You really like showing off your toys, don't you?"

"Yes."

"Can I have her back?"

"Say it."

"Do I have to? I've really had a helluva night."

"Say it . . ."

Sigh. "Oh thank you, Dissident, for saving me from this dangerous rogue, I don't know what I would do without you."

"You're welcome."

"Harriet?"

She tosses me my bat.

Dissident's what the media calls a "non-powered vigilante," being that she doesn't have any powers aside from a bunch of cool (read: expensive) toys, and isn't legally licensed for heroing.

However, given what the cops are like and that the heroes don't make it into WPC (West Pinnacle City) or the Crescent unless there's something happening that'll get their faces on the news, Dissident's about all that keeps the peace on the streets most nights.

As a rule, I hate heroes, but Dissident's reason enough to make an exception.

"So what brings you to my neck of the woods?"

She aims one of her gauntlets at a nearby alley and illuminates its wall.

Fresh, rain-streaked graffiti reads:

MILGRAM TERRITORY

"Same old, same old," she says.

I hadn't heard Milgram had expanded his territory this far; I thought Little Lemuria was as far south as he went.

"He's here?" I ask.

"Already took down two of his dealers just four blocks from here, and I'm following a lead on his human trafficking operation working out of one of the old hotels on Miller Street. He's a cockroach, but all cockroaches die eventually with the proper boot."

"Town's going to hell," I mutter, rubbing my aching head.

"Not if we stop it first."

"Not if *you* stop it first," I correct her.

She sighs, which through her helmet's digital filter sounds like a growl. "I keep telling you, the city needs good people to fight for it. There aren't enough vigilantes to keep the people safe, and the *heroes* couldn't care less. You could make a major difference if you worked with us."

This isn't the first time I've heard this speech, and I know it's not gonna be the last.

"Pass."

"Then why keep doing this?" she asks, putting one foot up on Berryman, who moans in pain.

"He was beating on his wife. Dick had it coming."

"No doubt," Dissident says, stomping down on Berryman's crotch and making him cry out. "But there's a lot of bastards out there who have it coming even more, and for even worse reasons."

I've had a long night and an even longer day trying to work off the hangover my pills only put a moderate dent in; I don't have time for this shit—well-intentioned though it may be.

"Look, Dissident, until vigilanteing pays enough to cover my bills and bar tab, I won't—"

Lights overhead, bright enough to cut through the storm. This time not lightning.

People.

Superheroes. The Pinnacle City Guardians.

I only expected cops, but people must've called in Berryman's power, and anytime you got a power that dangerous involved . . .

Motherfucker.

Dissident's already gone, hiding in the darkness and putting as much distance as possible between her and the pro-heroes who'd treat her no better than a common minion.

Every instinct tells me to do the same—to run before they find a convenient enough misunderstanding to take me in or kill me. After all, I'm just another ex-villain from the Crescent. Why shouldn't they kill me too just to be on the safe side? What kind of world would miss a guy like me?

I nearly bolt, but then I see her.

Berryman's wife, staring at me with two of the saddest damn eyes you'll ever see (even if one's swollen shut). She stands beneath the bar's faded awning along with the last few looky-loos who didn't bolt when Dissident intervened. Pulling her coat tight, her lip quivers—whether from the cold or from fear it's tough to say.

But I know that look. I know the confusion in her eyes. The anger, the hurt, the love she still feels for the bastard tied up by my feet for what he did to her, has done to her, and may do again if he doesn't get locked up for this.

I know the slight nod she gives me is all the thanks I'm gonna get, and more than I need.

I also know it's the best possible reminder to play this by the rules, since it's the only way it'll go on record.

As the superheroes circle in for their landing, I pull my necessary paperwork from my trench coat, hold my hands over my head, and hope this won't take too long.

CHAPTER 2: THE SUPERHERO

The grand ballroom of the Rose Terrace Hotel never looks more inviting than it does when you're sneaking in.

I touch my heels down on the holly-decked balcony with a muted *click* and, as usual, Mason instantly releases his death grip on my hips, straightens up, and adjusts his black and crimson body suit to look as if he didn't need me to fly him up here in the first place.

Cory and Derek run and parkour their way up to join us, while Leah drifts intangibly up through the floor.

I can hardly wait for her hands to become solid before grabbing one to lead her inside, into the delicious aromas of cinnamon and sage, the chords of the live string quartet playing "God Rest Ye Merry Gentlemen," and the sparkling light of the crystal chandelier across the polished tiles of the dance floor.

We aren't gatecrashing; technically this gala is in *our* honor, my mom and my uncle's thank you to the Justice Juniors for last week's successful containment of the gas main explosion down in the Seaside Shopping District. If Uncle Ethan had his way, we'd remain mysteriously unseen until prime entrance-making, speech-giving time, and then become mysteriously unseen again after convincing the guests to double their donations to the Seaside Economic Relief Fund.

I don't mind helping to remind everyone that we're partying for a purpose here, other than to celebrate Thanksgiving's end and Christmas's approach, but I don't see why that has to mean missing out on half the fun.

My friends follow me more hesitantly into the mingling crowd of donors in their tuxes and jewel-bright gowns.

"Bloodhound!"

A teenage girl in a blue chiffon frock notices Mason as we creep not-so-covertly toward the bar.

"Oh my gosh, do you think I could have your autograph?"

"Um . . ." Mason grunts. "Sure, I guess. Do you have a pen?"

"Always! I have the complete Bloodhound stationary set!"

The greetings snowball from there.

"Makeshift! Remember me?" Derek poorly feigns a look of recognition for the excited young man accosting him. "I helped you foil that bank robbery a few years back? You asked if anyone had an inhaler and some mustard packets? That was me!"

"Oh yeah." Derek forces a slightly more convincing look of recollection. "Good work."

"Gothique?"

Leah tries to hide behind her hood, which doesn't do her much good, considering that her hood is at least as famous as her face, if not more so.

"I've been trying to get in touch with you," says an older man I recognize from the board of Pinnacle City's premier news station. I believe he goes by Rickie Maroon. "I've got a killer idea, completely groundbreaking, for a celebrity investigative journalism program, and I think you'd be perfect . . . both of you!" he adds as an afterthought, passing me one of his cards over Leah's shoulder.

I palm the card and slip away quickly, then have to wait up for Mason, Derek, and Leah to stumble for polite exits to their conversations.

Gala attention is a little different from the regular kind of attention. Fans who call out our names on the street usually just want to be able to say they've met us. Guests at functions like this one want to be able to say they *know* us.

Instead of *I love your new costume* or *I named my pot-bellied pig after you*, we get a lot of *Remember me from that one time?* or *When are you going to take up my invitation to go waterskiing?*

It's like a mad memory game of names and faces. Names and faces of people we matter to. It's weird, but always a bit awe-inspiring.

The first person to pull me in for a hug, a tiny older woman with bottle-red hair and cat ear spectacles, is one of my favorite regulars at these sorts of affairs.

"Glitter Girl! I swear, you get more beautiful every time I see you." She squeezes me with all the surprising strength in her boney arms.

"Then I'll have to make sure we see each other more often," I joke, squeezing back. "You're looking great too, Aggie. How are the boys?"

Aggie doesn't spare a single glance to check whether the other guests noticed that I know her name.

"Little Brad's sounding out words now!" she exclaims, releasing the hug but keeping hold of my hands. "He loves reading his picture books for his old granny."

After Aggie spilled my code name out loud, someone in the crowd must have taken a census.

"Brisk Boy isn't with you?" someone asks us, and I turn to look at where Cory was standing last.

It doesn't take long to find him across the ballroom behind possibly the most delicious-looking refreshment table in the city, waving mischievously back at us, his hand a blur of superspeed.

"Oh, darn, did we lose him again?" says Leah dryly. "Guess we'd better go looking."

She turns translucent and intangible again, drifting straight through the still-pitching Rickie Maroon and then through the rest of the startled gathering toward Cory. Mason and Derek follow at crowd-shuffling speed, impatiently beckoning me.

"Save me a dance, yeah?" I call to Aggie as the tide of mingling cuts between us. "Something fun!"

Derek's made a gyroscope out of pretzels by the time I reach the refreshment table, spinning it between his fingers.

"Well, *I* for one sure am glad we decided not to be fashionably late." He directs a teasing gaze at me.

"You guys didn't want to bother blending in until show time," I say. "You have no one to blame but yourselves."

I twirl until the skirt of my new, shimmering violet ball gown bells out around me. My Glitter Girl outfit is fully concealed beneath it, its accessories jammed into my purse. The others are already prepared for speech time, dressed in the same old super suits they wear every day.

"There should be laws against having to change clothes more than twice a day," says Derek.

"Totally. Intolerable waste of time," adds Cory, who can change his clothes in one one-hundredth of a second.

"There should be laws against *those* clothes," Leah whispers, nodding at a passing dress with a runway collar twice as high as its wearer's head. "You ever think about how much more we could raise at these things if everyone chipped in their wardrobe budget for the night?"

"We'd raise zip," says Derek. "If they didn't get the chance to show off their threads, no one would show up."

"Be nice," I bump his elbow and catch the pretzel gyroscope in my mouth. "Everyone here bought tickets." I swallow. "Every bit helps . . . ooh!"

The quartet's broken into a warbling cover of "All I Want for Christmas Is You."

It's my favorite, so naturally I pretend not to check whether Mason's pretending not to check whether I'm pretending not to check whether he's going to ask me to dance.

He broods predictably against the wall, so I lift the top layer of my skirt and groove to the strings by myself, because to hell with Mason and his moods and his slouching and how his creepy Bloodhound super senses make me want to bathe in Febreze.

I mean it this time.

Cory smells the awkward in our little circle faster than Mason ever could, and in half a blurry second he's gone and back again with an entire tray of the harmony juice known as champagne, probably leaving a very confused waiter empty-handed somewhere.

Another blink and the glasses are in our hands, sloshing precariously. I slow down to let mine steady.

"To the Seaside Shopping District," Cory proposes. "And to its mostly un-explodedness."

"Cheers!" My glass clinks on contact with Cory's, in spite of how even my reaction-enhanced brain insists that he's currently several feet away, toasting Leah.

Before I met Mason, I'd have said it was impossible to brood and drink champagne at the same time.

I'd have been wrong.

He looks at me piercingly over the rim of his glass, which seems exponentially more delicate in his not so delicate hand, and leaves me wondering what he's thinking about so hard.

"Miss Kline, could I trouble you for a dance?"

Mason's slightly open mouth snaps rigidly shut when the question comes from my other side.

I hardly turn to see the asker before saying yes. Lucky for me, it's not that producer wanting me to put in a good word for him with Leah.

I'm halfway across the dance floor holding Quentin Julian's pleasantly fluffy hand before realizing I'm still holding my glass as well.

Quentin doesn't seem to mind the impediment. There are maybe fifteen years between us, and he puts his hand on my shoulder instead of my waist as if I'm five. We've often spoken for a few minutes on occasions such as this—he asks about the team, I ask about his work running the shelters across town—but the dancing is new.

"Slim pickings for partners tonight?" I ask, trying to gauge if there's a shortage of dresses among the tuxes around us.

"What? Oh, no, everyone's been perfectly friendly," he says, watching the dancers behind me distractedly. His pointed bobcat ears, relic of his mother's rebellious years of self-splicing, back before all those supervillain DNA bombs set off the gene-job panic and put a stop to the trend, are perked up and twitching in all directions.

"Are you waiting for someone?"

He shakes his head and then, apparently satisfied with our surroundings, leans abruptly closer and whispers, "Have they asked you yet?"

"Have who asked me what?"

"Nothing," he says quickly.

"Woah, no way. Don't you open that door and leave me hanging. Who's going to ask me what?"

"You'll know soon enough." He shakes his head, and like waiting to open my Christmas presents, I allow myself a couple seconds of pouting and then try to let it go.

"You're going to have a chance to do a lot of good for a lot of people," he goes on, whispering faster. "It won't be easy, or safe, and you're not going to like hearing it."

"I like what I'm hearing so far."

He looks dubious and relieved all at once.

"I wouldn't ask if I didn't think you could make all the difference. We'll need to speak confidentially . . . trust doesn't come easily these days."

I get invitations to discuss mysterious subjects with strange men in private places several times a week, but I know Quentin well enough, and I know what he does. He not only funds those shelters for the involuntary gene-jobs; he's out there almost every day giving free legal counsel, helping them build résumés, apply for housing, you name it. If he says there's helping to do, I'll bet he knows what he's talking about.

The song ends and the quartet announces a short break, leaving the dance floor to disperse around us.

"Kimberly!"

I try not to look too sheepish when my mother's voice cuts through the music's absence.

Quentin drops my hand.

"Kimberly, I can see you," she says, gesticulating in my periphery as wildly as her red velvet sheath dress allows.

"Email me," I tell Quentin, backing away. "Whatever I can do to help, I'm in."

I prance innocently over to my mother. Now that I'm here, she can't possibly kick me out and tell me to come back later . . . or so I hope.

As soon as I come within reach, she makes a point of brushing invisible bobcat hairs off of me and confiscates the champagne glass from my hand.

"Mom, I'm twenty-three," I protest, reaching to take it back.

"Shh!" She holds it out of reach, or out of reach without the use of my super reflexes or flight, and looks over both shoulders as if expecting to see people jotting down my easily verifiable birth year.

"*And* I have an accelerated metabolism."

"Believe me, dear, not a day goes by when I don't envy you for both those things," she says, dropping the glass—about a fiftieth of what it would take to give me a noticeable buzz—onto the empty tray of a passing waiter and then pulling me paradoxically toward the bar.

Leah's already there, nursing a cranberry vodka, and at the sight of my mom she instantly vanishes into the floor.

"Hmm, I didn't notice," muses my mother, looking me over.

"Notice what?"

"How revealing that dress would be on you."

She tries almost discreetly to hike the bodice up higher over my cleavage, making the spaghetti straps go slack and fall down my shoulders.

"A circus tent would be revealing on me," I say, wiggling it back into place.

She reaches for the straps. "Maybe if we—"

"Mom." I catch her wrist carefully on its way and deflect it with the bottom edge of my strength. "My boobs are fine. My dress is fine. You would know, you picked them out. Can you please, just, relax?"

This was the subject of a three-month argument between Mom and Uncle Ethan, after all the lab visits to test my limitations revealed my sensitivity to Jovium, a synthetic version of Jupiter core matter. It's the one known substance in the solar system that can knock me unconscious or cut my skin in a controlled, non-nuclear-concussion kind of way.

On the one hand, the discovery meant that I wasn't perfectly invulnerable, and my family had to rush to patent the substance to make sure it couldn't be manufactured and sold to supervillains to use against me.

On the other hand, the existence of something that could both cut and anesthetize me also meant I was suddenly possible to operate on, opening the door for a more in-depth wave of image consultations.

Mom and Uncle Ethan couldn't agree on an ideal bust size for me, between wanting to give me the maximum long-term career advantage without prematurely aging me out of the Justice Juniors image, which at the time referred to the team being in our junior year of high school.

Mom's D-cup insistence ultimately won out.

She backs away now and shakes off all the little worries, the way she always does.

"You're right. I suppose it won't matter so much soon anyway. I just wanted this evening to be perfect for you."

"Seriously? It is perfect. It's almost Christmas. There's a fondue fountain!"

"It wasn't supposed to go this way."

"Mom, a fondue fountain! It has macaroons in it!"

"You make it really hard to throw you a surprise party, you know."

I open my purse and pull out the stiff, oversized envelope that barely fits inside. "Um, actually, I think sending me an embossed invitation is what makes it difficult to throw me a surprise party."

"Well, all right, the party *itself* wasn't supposed to be a surprise," she says, "But we wanted to have the guests break the news to you. We were supposed to have a chance to address them before bringing you in, so we could catch your reaction onstage, but since you're here . . ."

She pauses interminably, and my impatience after Quentin's hint flares back up.

"Mom, *what?*"

She summons the bartender and orders two Wonder Whiskey and Cokes. The real stuff, designed for people with enhanced constitutions like myself.

"I think you've officially graduated from champagne for the night."

I like champagne, but I'm too curious to argue.

The glasses are set before us, and Mom raises hers to me, a suppressed smile bursting free.

"You made it, honey. You're in."

I know exactly what I *hope* she means, but I'm terrified I might be wrong.

"I'm in . . ?"

"The Pinnacle City Guardians," she confirms. "You made the winter draft. Congratulations, sweetie."

I can't keep my feet on the ground, and neither can she when I fly at her for a hug, the bartender and all the guests within about three yards of us turning to stare after the volume of my squeal.

"Ohmygod, ohmygod, ohmygod! You're joking! You're *not* joking! I love you! You're really not joking, right? Have I mentioned that I love you?"

Mom pats me on the back, and I set her down.

"The Pinnacle City Guardians. Like the real, grown-up, city-saving Pinnacle City Guardians? Does this mean I finally get to call myself Glitter Woman? Wait, that sounds kinda weird. I've never said it out loud before. Maybe just Glitter? Is that better? Captain Glitter? Madam Glitter?"

"Oh, it's better than that. Your uncle's made arrangements for an official passing of the mantle, his gift to you."

"You mean—"

My mom puts a finger to her lips, and I lower my voice.

"You mean I'm joining the Pinnacle City Guardians, *as the new Solar Flare*?"

She raises her Wonder Whiskey again and holds it up until I finally mirror her.

"To Solar Flare the sixth."

"And to making history," I answer and drink shakily, glad for the sheen of calm the WW gives me.

Solar Flare is one of the longest, most famous legacy superhero titles on the West Coast, and I'm about to become the first woman ever to carry it.

A mic taps and squeaks with feedback, heralding Uncle Ethan's voice.

"Thank you all for coming. Yes. Thank you," he waves politely from his floating leather chair, presently hovering over the room's main platform. His suit is unwrinkled by sitting, and he looks as comfortably at home as when the chair is parked in his study.

The guests gather closer, and several journalists click pens and focus cameras. I can even see the *Pinnacle Looking Glass* evening show's award-winning field reporter, Fadia Bakkour, up near the front. If I'm going to be giving interviews on what it's like to be the first female Solar Flare, I'd like her to be the first. She's always been my favorite, partly because she's the only reporter I know who never spends most of an interview asking about what I'm wearing or my love life.

Her eyes briefly meet mine, and we exchange polite smiles.

"I could say a few words about why we're here tonight, but I'm sure you'd rather hear it from the admirable young people of the hour. Please give a warm welcome to the Justice Juniors!"

I down the rest of my drink, lift off spinning into the air, and send out a few of my famous, sparkling energy blasts from my fingers. I don't charge them enough to damage anything, just enough to hide me in a cloud of lavender fireworks while I strip down to my pleated Glitter Girl minidress with the GG emblem on the chest, maybe for the last time.

When the smoke clears, I fly to join my gathering friends on the platform, and the room explodes with applause.

CHAPTER 3: THE DETECTIVE

It's a fitful, hot nightmare with flashes of madness and violence.

A war.

A war in the streets. A war overseas.

They're not that different anymore. Both of them senseless and full of fire and blood and broken promises.

A man in a chair who can't move or see me.

"We just need you to find where this asshole was; find out who he's been talking to."

"Come on, use what god gave ya."

"It'll be a whole lot worse if you don't. You don't want him to suffer, do ya?"

Friends aren't friends.

Enemies are still enemies but maybe not that bad.

Your heroes will betray you.

Fire from above, tearing through flesh.

You always remember your friends' dying screams.

✸

By the time I come to, the dream's already gone, almost forgotten, but never completely. It'll come back as it always does when I'm in a particularly sour mood, waiting to pounce like a starving scavenger watching a man crawl toward water in a desert.

I'm not dead yet, though.

What I am is face down on a wooden table in a slowly growing puddle of my own drool.

There's noise coming into focus: voices, chairs being pushed around. Familiar smells: smoke, stale beer, sawdust, weeks old vomit. The lighting's dim, though what passes for my internal clock tells me it's morning.

There's a pale blue koala sitting on the table, staring at me quizzically.

I'm home.

"Mornin', Petting Zoo," I say.

"Aw, nuts, how'd you know it was me?" she responds, jumping off the table and transforming into a short, scantily-clad Korean woman, still with pale-blue skin.

"Lucky guess," I say, sitting up and more or less instantly regretting it. Call it sleeping in a shit position combined with a hangover, but it feels like I spent the night getting repeatedly folded and unfolded. My left arm is on fire, the pain so intense it's curled up into a claw. I pull the pill bottle from my pocket, fumbling it through shaking fingers onto the floor with a clatter.

"Here," Petting Zoo offers.

"No, *I* got it!"

I bend over and pick it up with my good hand, reflexively popping the cap and chewing a couple pills.

"You good?" she asks.

"Will be."

"Cool, 'cause I gotta make sure the others are still alive before I head out," she says, going a couple tables over to wake Louie.

As the pills do their work, my eyes clear and the Lineup comes into focus around me.

While it won't be winning any awards with the Zagat's people, it's got its charms. Located inside the giant, severed foot of one of Killtron 8000's robots, its ceiling is low and lit with an improvised set of bare bulbs and extension cords, none of the police auction bought tables and chairs match, and every so often the power will cut out when one of Tragedii's improvised hacks inevitably fails.

However, the liquor's good and cheap, the company's usually good for a laugh, and it's one of the few places in town you don't have to fear the pro-heroes.

But that's not why it's home.

No, for that you gotta look to the people still coming to around me. Like Louie, the Gray alien left behind by his invasion fleet back in the seventies. Or Lucero, the sorcerer and healer who looks more burnout hippie than wizard and still won't say which side of the War on Villainy he fought on. Or Bosrallt, the Atlantean berserker who's more shark than woman. Even Petting Zoo's got enough history to match nearly everyone in this room, making sure we all got one thing in common.

We're all criminals.

Ex-villains, antiheroes, and vigilantes mostly, none of us really evil, but none of us saints either. Most of us regulars have our mugshots framed on the wall beside the bar (I'm in the third row, fifth from the left). The Lineup is the one place in Pinnacle City, even within the Crescent, where we can just be who we want to be without being judged, and twice a week we hold impromptu group therapy sessions for those who want to talk about trying to live life on the outside.

Sometimes they go later and have more alcohol involved than others.

I guess last night was one of those times.

I stumble over to the bar. Tragedii's wiping it down, her mechanical right arm split into several instruments, each with a different rag, while the laser implant in her left eye burns a piece of garbage on the floor to cinders.

A time traveler from a terrible future that no longer exists thanks to an assassination she pulled off sometime in the eighties, she specifically designed the Lineup to be a safe haven for us ex-villains, and because of that I think we've all got a soft spot for her.

"That coffee I smell?"

"Nothing but the finest for my favorite customers," she says, her voice gruff and calm. She's easily the biggest woman I've ever seen, a wall of pure muscle covered with scars and tattoos where she isn't mechanized.

She passes me a mug. "It's goin' on your tab, you know."

"I know," I say, sipping it down. The TV over the bar is muted, but filled by the fat, angry, yelling face of Pinnacle City's greatest (his words, not mine) ever mayor, William "The Conqueror" Card.

"What's he goin' on about today?" I ask, even though I don't really want an answer.

"Wall off the west half of Pinnacle City so the rest of it can reclaim its former greatness. More yelling to boost his senatorial campaign. Watch his family's reality show, every Wednesday at eight," she says, running her human hand through her silver Mohawk.

"So, same as always?"

"Pretty much."

"You're sure he wasn't the guy you were supposed to travel back in time to kill?"

"Pretty sure."

"But you never, hypothetically—"

"No."

"But—"

"I'm not gonna kill the mayor. Much as I'd like to introduce him to my Flesheater, doing so could fuck up the future in ways you can't even imagine. So, I'd advise you to either vote against him in November—"

"Non-voting felon," I say, pointing to the hair covering the back of my neck.

"—or pray that someone finally catches him in the act doing something illegal."

"Fat chance. Even so, nobody'd care. Maybe I'll just pray he gets the senator gig; he'll have a harder time fucking up the city direct that way."

Tragedii shakes her head, laughing, "And I thought education standards were horrible in my time."

"Hey, it's not my fault prison GEDs don't put that much of an emphasis on civics."

"But it is your fault you were in prison."

"Point."

I polish off the rest of my coffee and slide the mug back at her.

"Thanks for the coffee. And the table," I say, trying to straighten myself out. My left hand has started to uncurl, some, and almost feels like it'll be useful in a few minutes.

It's a good day.

"See you tonight?"

"Most likely," I say, walking to the exit.

"Hey, man, wanna play some dominoes?" Lucero calls from the table where he, Bosrallt, and Louie are slowly coming to.

Considering that the game's likely to come down to a shouting match between Bosrallt and Louie as to whose people really got screwed out of conquering humanity the most, and that Lucero tends to use magic to cheat at board games, I pass. "Tempting, but I gotta check messages."

I'm out the door before they can put up a good defense.

It's a clear day, for the moment, blue skies and a bright sun that wants to tear my hangover in two. One of the things you learn to appreciate about winters in Southern California is how quickly they can turn.

The Crescent comes to life around me.

People driving and walking to work, hailing buses, the air a fragrant mix of exhaust and food trucks and post-rain dampness. There are horns honking and music in at least a half-dozen languages I can identify. The businesses are as grimy as ever, with walls either covered in graffiti or peeling posters (or both), their front windows all covered in retractable gates and blast shields that a few proprietors are already raising, ready for the day.

The clouds have cleared enough to give a good view of the towers downtown, glittering and gleaming and stretching so high you can't see the tops of them for the clouds.

If there's one comfort in that, it's that they can't look down on us any easier.

I've seen enough old movies to know that there was, once upon a time at least, only one Pinnacle City. It had its divisions, for sure; the west half of the city was predominantly industrial and shipping while the east was where all the commercial, financial, technological, and entertainment business went down. It was hardly one big happy family, but with the protection of the Pinnacle City Guardians, the city got to avoid a lot of the worse parts of the War on Villainy.

For a while, anyway.

It was Killtron 8000's attack, and the Guardians' response, that made the Pinnacle City we have today. Swooping down on the city with his army of giant Killtron robots, he laid waste to WPC, killing hundreds of thousands. The Guardians fought a bloody battle to repel his forces, and though they died to nearly the last man, one final attack from their crippled sole survivor, Solar Flare, disabled the army once and for all.

His final blast of energy permanently disabled Killtron, and killed more than 12,000 innocent bystanders the villain had gathered as a human shield.

For this, Solar Flare got himself a statue.

EPC recouped its losses in a hurry, but hasn't been in much of a rush to rebuild the western end of the city, even thirty years on. After all, who lives in WPC but the working class, the immigrants, the unlicensed supers and outcasts and criminals and those who can't afford to go anywhere else?

Oh sure, they've rebuilt some of the ruined city; a narrow, curving sliver of civilization that separates the east and west halves. Us locals call it the Crescent, and though everybody knows it's an insult being handed down to us by the city's elite, we've made the most of it. It's the cultural melting pot that EPC does everything it can to avoid being, and though its crime rate can be pretty insane, it's still an easy place to call home.

WPC itself, though . . . calling it a wasteland would be charitable.

Painkillers kicking in some more, I'm sturdier on my feet. My office, thankfully, is in the strip mall right across the street, between the Chinese donut and VHS place, as well as a pretty passable Lemurian restaurant.

Traffic's bad enough this time of day that I seriously consider using the crosswalk, when I'm temporarily pulled from my path.

Petting Zoo stands at a nearby bus stop, frustratedly trying to adjust a long black wig with one hand while balancing her hefty purse and a couple shopping bags in her other.

I stumble over to her.

"Need a hand?" I offer.

"Thanks," she says. I reach for her scalp, edging the wig around into a snug fit, pulling the hair into place to cover the bar code tattoo on the back of her neck.

"I keep tellin' ya, grow your hair out and this won't be a problem. Works for the rest of us longhairs," I say, motioning to the shoulder-length hair that covers the bar code on the back of mine.

"If it weren't summer here nine months of the year, I'd agree with you, but it is, and short hair's a lot cooler and cheaper to maintain than long," she says, offering me a cigarette.

I take it, light it and the one she pulls for herself.

Petting Zoo's good people. Though I didn't know her when I was in juvenile superhuman detention, being that she was a girl and all, we both got freed in the same amnesty program when we hit eighteen and both hit the army. Though I got my discharge papers after being wounded, she served her term, and we reconnected when she came back to the city. She let me crash on her couch for a while when I was still sorting my life out, and I helped her get the job waitressing for Tragedii so she wouldn't have to dance so much.

"So how's things at the club?"

"The usual. Take my clothes off, grind some, run over test notes and construct essays in my head. Captain Pervo hasn't been back for a while, and I've been able to hold a 3.9 GPA, so, thanks for that."

"Hey, you just made the introductions. Harriet did all the heavy lifting."

"No, seriously, thank you. I'd have gone all cape buffalo on his ass if I could get away with it, but I really need the tips and can't afford to flip out on the job, and the other girls were scared, and, well . . . just thanks for making it easy for us."

"Don't worry about it. Captain Pervo shouldn't be a problem anymore."

She looks down at her feet, shyly for a moment. "Has Dissident mentioned me recently?"

"Not that I remember, but me and memory ain't so great. . . ."

It's only part lie.

"Well, if you see her again, don't let on that I've been asking about her, alright? And if you could, you know, drop some hints, like I've been maybe seeing some hot cheerleader or something, make her a little jealous, I'd really appreciate that."

"Will do."

This one's another lie. Unless someone's in serious need of a beatdown, I'm not getting in the middle of any lover's spat.

Double that when Dissident's involved.

Her bus is coming. I drop my cigarette on the ground, crush it out.

"Hey, Eddie. You be careful out there, alright? You keep doin' stuff like the other night, get your face all smashed up and . . . well, Tragedii would be real sore if you weren't able to pay off your tab."

"You too," I say, even though I don't have to. Captain Pervos aside, she's always been able to take care of herself.

As she boards the bus, I head across the street.

My office is essentially an office in name only. I could almost do my job out of my apartment if I wanted, but since I occasionally need to meet with clients (mostly insurance reps and spouses worried their other half is cheating), I need to keep up some semblance of a professional appearance.

Lost & Found Investigations is my compromise on that.

It's a hole in the wall even by strip mall standards; just a narrow box with a big, dirty front window, a backroom for storage, and a bathroom that sometimes works but is usually just a nesting ground for ants. I got a desk up front with an old computer, an even older phone system, and a non-working panel for a security system propped right by the window to try and convince people that stealing my stuff ain't worth it (and it isn't).

In between a few exposed pipes, the wall by my desk has framed copies of all my certifications, as well as a few testimonials from happy clients to make me look more impressive.

Hidden in the mix are my only two personal pictures.

One of me, Petting Zoo, and the rest of our superhuman unit back in the army. The other of three smiling teenagers with arms locked around each other's shoulders. On the left, a fifteen year old me, a hopeful smile on his face and a helluva lot less hair on his head. On the right, a burly boy with glowing green eyes. My best friend from the henchman years, Marco, though we all called him Blast Eyes (we weren't very creative). The slender girl in the middle . . . she may have looked strange, with no hair, muted facial features including nearly non-existent nose and ears, solid black eyes and scaled, pale violet skin, but Marco and me were both in love with her as only a couple teenage boys who'd never really been in love with anyone before could be.

Anya, or Bystander as she preferred to be called, could transform into anyone with only a thought. On her own she may have looked a monster, but Marco and me loved her just the way she was. Both of us were too stupid to do anything, and by the time either of us would've thought to do anything, Marco . . .

(*fire from above, tearing through flesh*)

After that, after the heroes captured the villain we worked for and broke the gang up, Bystander and I went into juvenile detention. Every once in a while since getting out, I've tried looking her up, but if I've got a talent for finding people, she's got a talent for staying the one that got away.

I try not to dwell on the past, but it's hard when the past won't leave you alone.

I get a pot of coffee started and check mail and voicemail while waiting for my ancient desktop to boot up. Not looking forward to the messages about last week's run in with Mr. Berryman; no charges filed against me and he's got a court date, but clients generally don't like it when you start beating on the guy you're supposed to be tailing.

Before I can rest my feet on my desk, the front door opens, the attached sensor letting off a digitized *ding*.

I can immediately tell that the woman doesn't belong in the Crescent. Dressed like she's headed to a country club in a tight, professional, and expensive-looking dress that shows off her not unimpressive physique, her face is nearly hidden by a wide black hat and designer sunglasses.

She's gorgeous, but definitely out of place, and people out of place around here tend to either be interesting or trouble . . . and I usually bet on the latter.

"Edgar Enriquez?" she says, her voice husky and enticing.

"Who wants to know?"

She takes off her sunglasses, revealing a pair of deep blue eyes. "My name is Ruby Herron. I need someone to look into a murder."

Trouble, I knew it.

✷

Ruby doesn't sit when I offer her a chair, and flatly declines a cup of coffee. She just stands before me, nervously running a hand through her bottle-blonde hair.

"I'm not what you think I am," she says.

"What do I think you are?"

"A lunatic. A madwoman. Take your pick. I've been called every name in the book by everyone I've tried to talk to about this. Nothing you'd say could surprise me."

I highly doubt that, but I choose not to test her. "So who died?"

"My . . . boss. His name is . . . was, Quentin Julian. Have you heard of him?"

"Of him," I confirm.

Quentin Julian's one of those rare bluebloods whose name gets passed around the Crescent without it sounding like a curse. A civil rights lawyer, he did a lot of work making sure the non-human community, especially the homeless gene-jobs that make up most of the wasteland's population, were given adequate legal counsel.

Losing him'll only hurt the Crescent.

"Hadn't heard he'd died, though."

"Few have. While it's technically made the news, it's not something they're giving a lot of attention. The gene-job lawyer for gene-jobs, beaten to death beneath a bridge in the Crescent . . . who'd want to make a story out of that? I mean, he got what was coming to him, didn't he? Helping *those people* only courts death, doesn't it?"

"So, the police are on it? The Guardians?"

"Guardians, no. Police, yes, but they're not making this a high priority. His distaste for the police is well-documented, and if I'm being honest, even if they didn't have a hand in doing this themselves, I doubt they'll ever solve it."

I sigh, running a hand through my hair.

"Miss Herron—"

"Ruby," she interjects.

"Okay, Ruby. While I love a mystery as much as the next Joe, I have to tell ya that you've got the wrong guy. If you're looking for someone to take pictures of your two-timing ex, I can do that no problem, but no matter what all the old black and white movies tell you, solving murders ain't exactly covered by my license. If you're really desperate for information, I've got names of people who got no problem working slightly outside the law to get things done."

"So you won't help?"

"As I said, it's not my thing."

Crossing her arms under her impressive breasts, she turns from me, walks to the front office window and slams her hand on the wall, dust flying outward."

"Miss Herron . . ."

I get up and walk beside her as she turns back toward me, tears begging to streak her makeup. "I have been fighting for three days, trying to find someone, *anyone*, to give a damn, even if I have to pay them to, and when I finally find someone I can pay to give a damn he says *no*? How am I supposed to respond to that?"

I get a box of tissues from my desk drawer and offer her one, though she declines.

"I thought you, of all people, would care about this."

"*I* of all people?"

"Quentin Julian was a remarkable man, and all he ever wanted to do was make Pinnacle City a better place, for *everyone*, especially those who've had it as rough as those from out past the Crescent. *Even* the longhairs."

The bar code on the back of my neck tingles at the thought.

"You've done your research, I can see that."

"I've asked around, trying to find someone to dig up proof about what happened to Mr. Julian. I know you've got the superpower to know with absolute certainty who killed him, and that you can generate evidence that even the police can't ignore. I know that you've done bad things, but that despite the image you've cultivated, you're making a serious effort to be a law-abiding citizen, and are prone to doing the right thing just because it's right."

I consider what she's saying. A job like this is a dead end if the cops are already on it. But if they're not, if she's right about them wanting to bury it . . .

No, I can't get into shit like this. Even considering this case is asking for trouble. And while I don't mind the occasional bat fight, getting caught in the crossfire of dirty cops . . . hell, it's not juvenile detention anymore; I'd go to a real super prison and never see the light of day again.

But she's right about one thing: you do have a bad habit of doing the right thing.

"You know I can't make you any promises, right?"

"I understand."

"And that this work won't come cheap?"

"Money is not an object."

Now there's a tune I can appreciate.

"All right," I say, trying to goad my computer to life. "Let's print you up a contract."

CHAPTER 4: THE SUPERHERO

The sky is clear for the first time since October, and bluer than a vacation postcard.

I couldn't have painted a better morning for my official induction onto the Pinnacle City Guardians, even if I could paint.

Mom called last night and offered to send a car to Juniors Ranch for me, but I told her I wanted one more flight through the city as Glitter Girl before I officially become one of its Guardians as Solar Flare.

She laughed at me, saying it was the same city I'd been protecting since I was eight and that it'd be the same city tomorrow, but didn't try to talk me out of it.

I soar over the Seaside Shopping District, the one beautiful stretch of beach south of all the old abandoned port facilities with its quaint, pastel-painted shops, returning the waves and greetings of the shopkeepers hanging up their Christmas decorations. I swoop down close to the pier until the spray from the ocean tingles on my excitement-heated skin, and then rocket through the sound barrier over to the hills, over all the cute houses balanced along the ledges like ornaments on a tree.

Barrel rolling between the skyscrapers of downtown, I spread my arms to catch the breeze, watching the blue above switch places with the post-rainstorm sparkle of wet glass and concrete below, then slow down to smile and flash a peace sign for a group of office-dressed women about my age trying to catch me on their phone cameras.

When I draw level with the tops of the buildings again, I check my own phone.

Text from Leah.

> *Sneaking out early? Don't worry, I didn't eat TOO*
> *much of your surprise going away cake :p*

Text from Cory two minutes later.

> *Don't think you're gonna ditch us that fast. Silver*
> *Cowl tonight, 9:00, the Justice Juniors PARTY!*

I start a group text back, add Derek, and then, mostly because it'd be way too obvious if I didn't, Mason too.

> *I'm there. Silver Cowl at 9. Love you guys, always.*

Checking the time, I turn to take another joy lap of the city center, to burn off some nerves, and instead catch sight of the outlines of the old Killtron battle wreckage in the distance.

I see it every day, but something makes me stop in midair to look.

Uncle Ethan's accident happen during that battle. He can still fly, even now, but he retired from active duty as Solar Flare when it became clear he'd never walk again.

That was before I was born. I've only ever seen pictures of him out of his floating leather chair, let alone in the Solar Flare suit. I wasn't around to remember the days he talks about, when the famous Pinnacle City skyline stretched all the way down to the river and back, when the Pearl Theater stood where the burnt-out shell of a giant Killtron bot's torso compartment does now, so I usually don't think much of seeing it sticking out of the horizon like that, the way it has all my life.

Today, it reminds me of Quentin.

His shelters are out there somewhere, on the far side of the city, and he still hasn't contacted me about whatever project was so urgent and dangerous at the gala. All I have is his company email, which he hasn't been answering. If I don't hear from him soon, I might fly out there and see if I can find what he's working on.

But I've stalled long enough.

I turn back toward Guardian Tower, its spire stretching ten stories higher than any other structure in the city, and zoom toward it.

✳

At the front desk, I receive a temporary access card, along with about ten pounds of questionnaires and contracts regarding my specific weaknesses (which I decline to state), my powers (which I include), my Tax-ID, R-SAL information, and the legal ownership of my image and likeness.

It's all so official. So real.

It's far from my first legal agreement, but it's my first one with the Pinnacle City Guardians, and my pulse thrums stupidly fast in the fingers I hold the pen with.

Twenty minutes past the start of my appointment, I'm finally ushered to the elevator to go up for my orientation.

I calm my nerves by playing the elevator game I made up with Dad as a kid. He wasn't a super, just a new money technology upstart my mom loved enough to take his weightless name, always a favorite romantic scandal story just mild enough to be shared around family dinners. I was only six when he was murdered by some third-string villain looking for a quick buck, but I remember scraps here and there, mostly the way I could make him smile by showing off my flying tricks. He worked at the top of an office building nearly as high as Guardian Tower, and every time I got to ride up and down the elevator with him, I'd hover a couple inches off the floor and try to fly at exactly the same speed as the car, then stop fast enough to avoid hitting my head at the top.

Ready, steady . . .

Nailed it.

"Engage stabilizing thrusters!" Dad would've said.

"HUMAN! DESTROY!" says the gray, windowless, basketball-court-sized room, right as the elevator closes behind me.

And then the robotic spiders start crawling out of the walls.

Each one is about the size of a Saint Bernard, and at least twenty of them emerge from the panels sliding open on all sides, hissing up a storm on their pneumatic pistons and scuttling toward me on serrated metal legs.

I lift off, hovering out of their reach.

"Hello?" I call out. "Guardians? Did I catch you in the middle of a thing here?"

No answer.

When the spiderbots find me beyond the range of their clacking steel pincers, they all turn, lift their abdomens, and fire their spinnerets at me.

I dodge most of the sticky jets of fiber, but one catches me around the ankle with an acidic sizzle.

It can't damage my skin, but it itches like crazy to let me know it's trying, and clings when I try to kick it off.

After my own startled yelp, I hear what I'm certain is a stifled chuckle coming from the room itself, the way the voice did before.

I'm being observed.

The certainty puts me at ease.

"Okay, I'm going to take care of this, is that cool?" I call.

I take the second shower of webbing as a yes.

The strand around my ankle tethers me to the floor, giving me a flying range about seven feet in diameter, but that's enough to let me evade further entanglement while I shoot a few energy blasts at the nearest spiderbots.

I put a little more bite into it here than I did at the gala, and the metal spider shells crack open, spilling out computer guts. The legs of a few of them shut down and curl inward, rolling harmlessly onto their backs.

A double charge of energy through my leg not only disintegrates the tether but is conducted along it to char and warp the floor panel it's anchored to.

From there I decide to put on a bit of a show. *If they're watching me, I might as well give them something to enjoy.* I take an arcing dive around the room, punching through giant spider motherboards before they can turn to get their pincers around me.

For my big finish, I grab one by its sharp little feet and spin around in the air until I feel the centrifugal tug, then add a particularly shiny energy blast like a bottle rocket behind it when I let it go, sending it boomeranging through the few spiderbots left intact on the floor.

When it comes to rest, there's nothing left but parts.

I land gracefully in the middle.

"Hello?" I call out again. "Anybody?"

"Shit, shit, I *told* you!" says a voice from everywhere.

"Don't you put this on me; you were laughing your ass off!" another argues back.

"What's going on in here?" a female voice joins two male ones.

"Nothing!"

"END SCENARIO," the room announces mechanically, straining to close its metal doors over the spiderbot debris in the way.

Finally, a panel slides open in the ceiling, and three faces peer down at me from a control room. *Oh my god, oh my god, it's Demigod and Bear Man and Strongwoman.* I don't know who else I expected it to be in Guardian Tower, but I can't get over the fact that it's really them.

The three of them drop into the room, and I'm wiping my hands sweatless on my skirt to shake theirs, but Bear Man crouches down by one of the gutted spiderbots instead.

"Yeah, dude, I don't think we can salvage any of this," he says to Demigod.

"No shit," says Demigod, nudging the broken floor tile with his lightning-patterned boot and quirking his lip at me. "You're more powerful than they warned us."

"Um, thanks?" I say, not sure it's a compliment, and more than a little disoriented by the fact that Demigod just spoke to me, and cursed in front of me, all in the same breath.

There's no reason he shouldn't, I guess, it's just that the Guardians all come off so . . . dignified, when they talk in public.

"For the record," says Strongwoman, "the bot shutdown is over there."

She points, and the little red button with the word SHUTDOWN written under it, half-hidden between the shadows of two gray wall tiles, suddenly looks perfectly obvious.

"The objective of that scenario was only supposed to be to get past them," she says.

"Oh. Oh god, I'm so sorry." Panic fills my chest as I begin to tally up an invoice in my head and imagine going back to Mom and Uncle Ethan and the Justice Juniors to explain that I didn't end up being a good fit for the PCG after all, on account of my thoroughly trashing their state-of-the-art training room on my very first day. "I'll cover the replacements. I didn't know—"

"No," says Strongwoman. "It's fine. No one bothered to tell you."

She directs this more at the other two than me.

I try not to accept the relief too readily, which isn't too hard when Pinnacle himself levitates down through the hole in the ceiling, his cape of the city's flag billowing behind him in the still air.

"This is the Erickson girl?" he asks, arms folded as he silently assesses the damage.

"These two knuckleheads thought it'd be funny to intercept her elevator on the training floor and toss her into scenario twelve without a tutorial," says Strongwoman.

"Is she mute?" asks Pinnacle, and it takes me an embarrassing number of seconds to realize that he means for me to answer for myself.

"Uh, quite garrulous, actually!" I assure him, reaching out my hand, which is sweat-slicked all over again. "And it's Kline, Kimberly Kline, but I'm an Erickson on my mother's side. Ethan Erickson was my uncle. Is my uncle. It's a real honor to be here."

Pinnacle takes my hand in a grip I doubt even I could break, sweat-aided or not.

"It's an honor to have you here. I had the pleasure of working alongside your uncle for a few years. It was after the accident, but he was a credit to the name Solar Flare," he says in the way people say nice things to distant acquaintances at funerals.

"Whoa, I would never have guessed," I say.

He gives me an odd look, and I clarify.

"Not the part about him being credit to the name. I mean, just that you two were on the team at the same time."

It's supposed to be a compliment, about how even though he's visibly the oldest person in the room, he doesn't look a fraction of his fifty-odd years. It's the kind of thing my mom would say, or want someone to say about her.

He looks like he's trying to decide whether I'm deficient at history, math, or both.

"Not that I'm doubting your experience or anything."

His face says that now would be a good time to become dramatically less garrulous.

"We're running behind schedule," he says. "The ceremony starts in an hour, but we can fit in the nickel tour first."

"Yes, please."

He's already levitating back out of the hole, and I hurry to follow.

Strongwoman catches my wrist on the way.

"Grow a skin," she mutters into my ear, neither kindly nor unkindly, only urgently. "Grow it fast, grow it thick."

I nod my thanks and fly after Pinnacle.

I have a skin. After all, I've been in the public eye my entire life. I learned how to ignore pornographic fan art of myself when I was ten. A skin I can provide. I just have to do a better job of showing the Guardians that.

The room above the one I wrecked is full of control panels and monitors showing the remains of the spiderbots.

"You've already made the acquaintance of our training floor," Pinnacle says, moving on and taking a right down a short corridor of closed doors. "This is your room," as he demonstrates the code on the number pad next to the door.

The door slides open to reveal what looks like a small but comfortable hotel room, decked out in blue and brown.

Perched at the end of the queen-sized bed, someone's left a box of tampons ("super" absorbency, naturally) and an official Glitter Girl toiletry kit wrapped in a big, pink bow.

I don't actually like the acrid cherry fragrance they insist on using for everything in those kits, but it's the thought that counts . . . I think.

Pinnacle takes note of the welcome package but doesn't comment.

"You're welcome to stay here as much or as little as you like, but when we hit crisis mode, I don't care how fast you are, you're going to want to be able to sleep in the tower."

That works out nicely. It was going to be awkward still living on Juniors Ranch without being on the team anymore, and I've been praying I wouldn't have to crash back with Mom while figuring out the transition.

"I'll be moved in by the end of the week," I promise.

Pinnacle pushes the tour along.

"This is the commissary," he continues, turning into a dining room built to accommodate a busload of visitors on top of the six PCG members (seven now, including me!). The last two of said members, Hedgehog and Mental Man, are currently playing an intense-looking card game over their bowls of Jell-O, rocking their shiny, circular steel table whenever they slam their cards down.

"Hot meals are served from six to eight, twelve to two, and five to seven daily, with snacks and beverages available around the clock, all free perks to members and up to three registered guests at a time," Pinnacle rattles off. "Downtime bonding among members is highly encouraged. Gentlemen," he prompts Hedgehog and Mental Man, "do you want to say hello to our new teammate?"

"Hello, new teammate," says Hedgehog.

"Hi, Solar Flare." Mental Man waves to me over his shoulder.

Mental Man just called me Solar Flare!

Pinnacle is already hovering purposefully through the door on the commissary's other side.

"Conference room." He breezes past an open door. "Salon. Briefing room."

We pause in a small, tiered auditorium with a podium and a screen taking up the front wall, like the lecture halls back in college.

"This is where you'll check in for mission assignments at eight every morning, suited up and ready to go, unless a previous assignment requires your presence."

I don't blink at the ready-to-go-by-eight-every-morning part, but Pinnacle isn't looking at me to catch this special bit of toughness.

We keep going, and I get the feeling we're running even later that he expected, though I'm afraid to stop and check.

"Armory," he says, with a touch of finality, coming to a stop in front of the last door at the end of another hall and waving his ID card in front of a sensor. "This is where you'll go for outfitting and replacements or repairs for any and all gear you might need."

We float along down dark rows of batons, color-coded grenades, caltrops, ray guns, and weapons I can't even make up names for, and I want to slow down to look at absolutely everything but I know there'll be time for that later.

The aisles through the racks all funnel toward a more brightly lit central space and a single desk with a portly man eating from a plate of pizza bagels.

"Any special requests, Rob here is your man."

Rob licks the red sauce off his fingers and hurriedly wipes them on the bottom of his chair as he stands to shake my hand, which probably makes us about even, since it takes me about that long to pry my eyes away from a display case of vintage PCG costumes to look at him.

He's in his late thirties, but grins like a kid on a sugar rush.

"Glitter Girl, I'm a big fan."

I spot a sketch on his desk of Mental Man's latest costume update, with the trench coat and asymmetric mask.

"You designed that?" I ask.

"Wha? Oh, yeah, that's one of mine."

"Then I'm a big fan, too," which makes him blush.

"I trust you're in good hands," says Pinnacle, hovering back toward the door. "I'll see you in thirty at the amphitheater, camera-ready."

Just thirty minutes until the ceremony!

"I'll be there," I promise Pinnacle's departing back.

Rob pays no notice to his exit, and I try not to be bothered by the abruptness of it either.

Thick skin.

Who cares? My Solar Flare outfit's been designed by the same guy who did Mental Man's!

"I can't tell you how excited I was to do your suit," Rob tells me. "It was like . . . like watching you emerge from Glitter Girl into Solar Flare right under my mouse, like getting to see that before anyone else in the world. I've been literally counting the days waiting to see you in it."

I'm bobbing up and down in the air with matching impatience.

"Then what are we waiting for?"

Rob takes the hint and runs his hand along a catch in the wall behind his desk.

"Ta-da!"

A dressing room opens and lights up automatically around the dummy inside, at last revealing my brand new Solar Flare costume.

The colors radiate out from the chest in shades of red and gold, a brilliant contrast against the constellation-speckled black cape, and . . .

"Well?" Rob prompts, both proud and a little nervous.

"It's . . ."

How on earth do I politely point out that it appears to be missing pants?

Strictly speaking, the costume I'm wearing now doesn't have pants, either, but the one on the dummy also doesn't have a skirt.

Or leggings, or shorts.

The leotard cuts away at the sides around waist height, leaving the hips bare, and tapers down to a strip maybe an inch and a half wide at the crotch.

Even that lush, iridescent cape isn't going to be able to offer any privacy for the wedgies I'm going to get.

Somehow I don't think this is the kind of skin-having that Strongwoman was advising me to demonstrate.

I don't have a problem with my legs—one of the many benefits of superhuman metabolism—but the sheer amount of shaving I'm going to have to do every day to wear this thing is already making my head spin. I'm legitimately doubtful it'll cover so much as the strings of those tampons in my welcome kit on such occasions when I'll need them, and now that I think about it, is that a really weird thing to get as a welcome present?

"Sorry," I say, shaking myself off in a way that makes me feel like a clone of my mom. "I think I just spent a little too much time staring at my uncle's old costume. Give me a sec to adjust."

"Oh yeah, he had a great one," Rob agrees. "The custom-molded body armor and all. It gave me a great jumping-off place. Had to update it a bit with the times, of course. Some deeper, crisper colors to go with the rest of the team's new palette."

He points out the color gradations radiating down the sleeves—it has full sleeves, which somehow make the bottom half feel even more incomplete—and I wonder if I'm fixating on nothing. Maybe it'll suddenly look normal once I'm in it.

"And we want to remind people that you're not just Solar Flare; you're the *new* Solar Flare. You're honoring your uncle, but you're not your uncle. Not that anyone could make that mistake with you."

He smiles, and I smile back.

Is the tailoring so standard that it's not even worth mentioning?

"So, and I know this is weird to talk about with someone you've just met, but since it's kinda my job to notice and accentuate everyone's assets, I'll just tell you . . . you have really terrific thighs."

Okay. We *are* going to talk about this.

"Thanks."

"So, since you've got a way higher invulnerability rating than Mr. Erickson did—I *love* designing for invulnerables, by the way—I figured, to make things a little more personal, now you're not stuck only representing tweens, it'd make a nice statement for you to get to stretch your legs a little, so to speak. Show people you don't have to hide anymore."

"I'm not hiding now," I say, folding my fingertips around the short hem of my Glitter Girl dress.

"Good!" says Rob. "Seriously, good. Nobody normally believes anything nice about their own bodies, which makes my job a whole lot harder, but yours, I mean, it speaks for itself. So, give it a try!"

He steps back from the dressing room.

"See how it feels. If anything doesn't fit right, we can make adjustments."

It's not going to fit right.

But he's all Christmas morning levels of excited about this, and he's so talented and did such a gorgeous job on the colors and I've got about sixteen minutes left to get changed, deal with the body hair issue, and zoom over to the amphitheater to take the Pinnacle City Guardians oath on live TV, and heck if I'm going to be that diva who's so insecure and picky about the wardrobe that she misses her own initiation ceremony because she was too busy making the nice armory specialist cry.

✳

Any lingering doubts or disappointments feel a million star systems away when I stand on the stage in Pinnacle Park, in my new Solar Flare regalia, with my hand over my heart.

The grass and the bleachers are packed shoulder-to-shoulder, all the way out to the sidewalks on the far sides of the street. Thousands of people are here in the early December chill to witness the ceremony in person. There's a thicket of camera crews in a semicircle around the stage, and drone cameras circling our heads for the best angles, and through all of them I can see Mom and the Justice Juniors holding up a banner with the words "Kongratulations, Kimberly!" stitched on it, screaming their encouragement.

Well, Mason is more telegraphing his encouragement through intense attempted eye contact, and Leah's image prevents her from screaming, but I'm sure she's deadpanning some affectionate snarkery I can't hear, and they're both holding corners of the banner over their heads.

The Guardians stand in a solemn line behind me onstage, ready to welcome me into their family, and Uncle Ethan sits in his floating chair, dressed in his own Solar Flare suit for the first time that I can remember, smiling down on me proudly with a ceremonial tome on his lap, ready to administer the oath.

It's not necessary.

I've known the words since I was five.

"On this day, I pledge the power of my body, mind, and soul to the protection of Pinnacle City and the good people who dwell within her. I swear to uphold the values of loyalty, family, community, and heroism, set forth by the noble men who came before me."

When Uncle Ethan reaches up to dab his eye, I wonder if he remembers me practicing this on top of the dining room table with a towel tucked into the back of my swimsuit, and I start to lose it a little. There's no avoiding it, some sniffling's gonna happen.

"I am the tooth of the guard dog," I croak out. "I am the edge of the ax. I am the fulcrum of Justice. I am the strong arm of the people."

I hold the moment and swallow, while the audience holds its breath.

"I am a Pinnacle City Guardian."

I can't hear what Uncle Ethan says over the crowd as he presses the Solar Flare emblem from his suit into my hand.

CHAPTER 5: THE DETECTIVE

There's a lot of different places you can find information if you want to put in the effort, but I always Google first. There's a lot of cranks and crazies out there when it comes to walk-in clients, and if you want to vet them before going further, the Internet's one hell of an ally.

I don't know what I hoped to find when I started looking into Ruby's case, but part of me was disappointed when she turned out legit.

Ruby Marie Herron, age twenty-eight, legal assistant to Quentin Julian, deceased.

No red flags about her on social media. She liked to party some, but mostly vanilla stuff. A fair handful of condolences on her pages after Julian died.

His death, too, is verifiable, though not as easy as usual. There's only a few perfunctory news stories posted about his passing, only one of which alludes to possible foul play. The coroner still has his body for "ongoing investigation," but no listed information on cause or, for that matter, location of death.

Breaking into the coroner's office and trying to get a read off his body is always an option, but considering the kind of security they have around there, I rule that option out.

I could snoop around his office and home, try and get a read that way, which is somewhat more reliable, but if they're considered crime scenes too, well, I'll have the same problem.

And so, my best shot at knowing what happened is reading the murder scene itself.

There's one way I can find out where that is, though it's not my first choice.

✳

I can't believe I'm about to say this.

"My name's Eddie Enriquez. I'm on the list."

The bouncer, an eight-foot tall behemoth with skin of cracked stone, checks his tablet and nods. The people waiting behind the velvet line, many dressed in their finest "superhero couture," look on disgruntled as a guy from the Crescent in a T-shirt, jeans, and black trench coat cuts past them.

If there's one upside to this, it's their faces . . . unfortunately it's likely the only upside.

I despise nightclubs. I hate the noise, the activity, how most of them are shrines to superhero celebrity. If people want to get wasted and do stupid shit, there's cheaper places you can do it.

Better booze, too.

A couple women pass me by, hot little numbers in skimpy dresses and short capes. They eye me appreciatively. I return the favor.

All right, there are a *few* benefits to EPC clubs.

The Silver Cowl is one of the newest and trendiest clubs in town. An old bank that was one of the first documented locations of supervillainous crime in the United States (yet still not a national landmark, go figure) was in danger of being torn down until Mayor Card's son bought the place up and turned it into this trendy spot. It's now a monument to garish superhero luxury, with scantily clad, masked girls dancing in go-go cages, while beefy (and also scantily clad) "henchmen" fly around them in coordinated dances. Heavy glass cases line the walls with superhero costumes and artifacts that'd be better off in museums, the bartenders and servers are all dressed in pinup-style costumes, and, of course, everyone on the dance floor, at the bars, at the tables, is dressed in cheap approximation of superhero chic.

It's my version of hell, which I'm sure is part of the joke.

"Hey, Eddie!"

I see her waving for me from one of the second floor tables, and I make my way up through the crowd.

By the time I'm there, she's finally shooed away the last couple of autograph seekers.

Fadia Bakkour.

Known as one of the most trusted television anchors in Pinnacle City, she's as beautiful and modest as ever in one of her more stylish hijabs.

Before I knew her, she was just another media personality I wouldn't have given two thoughts because I've always avoided news like the plague (don't want to hear about the fucking heroes any more than I gotta), but she spent a long time doing a series on life for the rehabilitated villain community in the Crescent a few years back. She really got to know a number of us longhairs, spent a lot of time at the Lineup, and I was able to find out that she's not only intelligent, but a genuine believer in truth and justice.

While I won't call us *friends*, she's on my shortlist of people I'd choose to spend time with.

"Took you long enough to get here," she says as I take a seat opposite her.

"Traffic. Parking. You know the excuses."

"Too true," she says, summoning a waitress.

"You buying?"

"For my very dear friend? Of course."

"Whiskey—and not your well stuff."

Fadia orders another cranberry juice and sends the waitress away.

"This doesn't interfere with your night job?"

She surveys the crowd beneath us. "Oh, come now, Eddie. We must always make time for leisure, otherwise what's the purpose in living? Besides, if I'm gone all night, every night, people might start wondering if I'm leading a secret life."

"But you *are* leading a secret life."

"Precisely why I must be seen in public from time to time."

I didn't find out that Fadia was Dissident until about a month after her series on the Crescent. Dissident was already active for almost two years by that point, and she rescued me from a pretty bad fight with a couple of Milgram's henchmen. Enough contact with her armor gave me an easy read of who was hiding behind it.

Given Dissident's rep, I thought she'd kill me for discovering her secret identity.

Instead, she asked me if I could keep a secret. Now we pass each other info from time to time. Seems to me like I got the better end of this arrangement.

"So, what do you want from my secret life today?"

"Actually, it's your public life I need help from."

"Really? Now you've got me positively intrigued."

"Quentin Julian."

Her smile disappears.

"What do you want with Quentin Julian?"

"His assistant contracted me to look into his murder, which she thinks looks suspicious as hell."

"Probably because it *is* suspicious as hell."

"Why?"

"Because we're not *not* allowed to talk about it."

"I'm not following."

"If you want to black out a story, you don't completely cut off information about it. A hole like that, that'd make people suspicious. So you just control the *flow* of the news. Let a little of it get out, but limit its spread and detail so it falls into the background of flashier news. Why follow a small story about a dead nice guy lawyer when Mayor Card saying something racist or a new Solar Flare being christened trends much better? That's how it's been trying to report on his death."

"I thought Julian traveled in your circles? Rich guy killed in the Crescent, you'd think someone would want to make a big deal about it."

"True, and for any other blueblood they would."

"But not Julian?"

"Not Julian."

Our waitress comes with our drinks, and I take my whiskey gratefully. Fadia and I both check her out as she sashays away.

"Has Petting Zoo mentioned me, recently?" Fadia asks, a little dreamily.

"Julian?" I say, trying to bring her back on topic.

"Fine, spoil my fun. The Julian family is one of the oldest big-money families in Pinnacle City, going back almost as far as the Ericksons and Cards, and were every bit as ruthless. However, that all went down the tubes when Richard Julian, Quentin's father, married a gene-job from the Crescent, and they had a son. They were still part of the upper-crust by name and blood, but not much else. Quentin was never fully welcomed in, which is probably why he started to forge his own path. While the other great families saw to pillaging Pinnacle City, he fought for people's rights and for feeding, housing, and employing as many people as his trust fund would allow. He was, for lack of a better word, a hero."

"Then why hasn't Dissident been on this?"

"Because she's been busy preventing Milgram from burning the Crescent to the ground."

"Fair enough. Julian have any enemies?"

"Too many to list."

"Do you at least know *where* he was killed, so I can get a read?"

Fadia raises an eyebrow. "I might."

"Where?"

She laughs. "Oh, no, you're not getting it that easily."

This is the part I dread.

Fadia never gives anything up for free.

"What do you want?"

"I want you . . . to have fun."

"I have fun," I say, defensive.

"Passing out drunk on your couch alone every night isn't fun. No, I brought you here, even though I know you hate it, because I want you to have fun. Give me that, and I'll give you everything you need."

I grumble. "I'm gonna need a bigger drink."

"That can be arranged," she says, waving for a waitress.

This is gonna be a long night.

✴

THE SUPERHERO

"I need another of these," I say, sucking on the ice of my last drink, the name of which I can't remember. I think it had coconut shavings in it.

"Check your blind spot," Cory snickers, and I turn to find a fresh round on the table next to me.

Cosmic Rays. That's what they're called.

I must have blinked when he went to pick them up.

It seems Derek's already been enjoying them, because he's curled up sideways on the couch across from me, another empty glass added to his collection.

We're squeezed together in one of the first floor lounge alcoves of the Silver Cowl, just off the dance floor. All the VIP lounges were already booked. We probably could have gotten somebody bumped if we'd tried, but this is fine. Better, in fact, closer to the action, and I'm less likely to run into someone who knows me, other than my teammates, if I don't go upstairs.

Yesterday, I took my final patrol with the Justice Juniors, and tomorrow I receive my first official assignment as a Pinnacle City Guardian. But tonight? Tonight is just tonight, and I want to keep it that way . . . for as long as I can.

A pair of useless (but undeniably stylish) glasses and a black dress instead of purple have successfully camouflaged me into the crowd. All the capes, masks, and tight leggings on the staff and half the people on the dance floor don't hurt, either. There are at least half a dozen people within ten yards of us who look more like Glitter Girl right now than I do.

I push the leftover ice aside and take a sip through the whipped cream on top of the new glass.

"Don't you have to be up early?" Leah reminds me.

This clashes with my ideal of tonight staying tonight, so I shrug.

"Have you ever seen me hungover?"

"Never seen you trip in heels either, but there's a first time for everything."

In my defense, someone had spilled a drink on the floor when that happened. I might also have had a shot or two of that Wonder Whiskey stuff by that point in the evening, but I think I'm getting the hang of compensating for its effects.

"Hey, let her enjoy it while she can," Cory chimes in.

"Thank you." I take a sip. "What do you mean, '*while I can*'?"

"Didn't we tell you?" says Leah. "This whole going away party was just a ruse to kidnap you and tie you up in the Juniors Ranch cellar so you can't ever leave us."

Her expression doesn't budge under the curtains of dark hair she's brushed forward over her face in lieu of her Gothique hood, but I can't hold back so easily.

"Aw, guys," I hold the glass close to my heart for the sake of holding something to that aching spot. "It's not like I'm moving *away* away. We're still gonna hang out. Every weekend. Or, whenever they give me time off, but every week. Promise. And we'll do team ups! Loads of all-star team ups."

"We might let you out every month or so," says Cory. His poker face isn't anywhere near Leah's league, but he gives it his best. "Public appearances, just so people don't think you're dead."

"And once you're properly Stockholmed," Leah jumps in, "Sunday walks in the park might be permitted. We'll have to review your behavior when the time comes."

I don't want to cry right now. Tonight is just tonight.

"Okay, refreshment break accomplished, dance time!" I finish my drink and fly over the couch between me and the dance floor, bracing my hand on the back of it in vaulting posture as I pass, to make it look like I'm just reasonably athletic rather than super.

"I'm in!" declares Cory, already on my other side.

"Have to keep an eye on the hostage, don't I?" asks Leah.

"You're a freakin' machine, Kimmy," Derek moans, nestling further into the threadbare couch cushions.

Mason puts his feet up wordlessly.

I shrug, and the shrug becomes a shimmy, and in three steps I'm rocking to the rib-strumming bass, watching the lasers change color under my feet, and this song is just this song, and tonight is just tonight.

No matter the beat, Leah dances slow and Cory dances fast. So it's not long before our perfect little triad of discord begins to bleed in and out of the undulating crowd around us.

A man with about a million piercings is eyeing Leah, and she's eyeing him back, and Cory's dancing with two different women who haven't noticed how blurry he gets when he's doing the two-places-at-once thing because of the low, pulsating light, so I'm wide open when a guy in a neatly pressed pinstriped shirt moves in.

"You're pretty good at this, huh?" he shouts over the music, showing off nicely clean, even teeth.

"Yeah!" I shout back. "Need some pointers?"

He laughs. "So, fuck modesty is what you're saying, right?"

"You asked the question."

"True, true."

He comes a little closer, syncing almost to my rhythm.

"Chad," he introduces himself. "I can take pointers."

Meh, why not?

"You're thinking too much, Chad," I tell him, taking one of his hands, which is pleasantly soft. "If you have to think about when the next beat is coming, you've already missed it."

He takes the invitation to put his other hand on my waist, and we follow the song together, him without much improvement but with plenty of enthusiasm. He pulls me in close, and pretty soon he's rubbing up against me in a rhythm that still has little to do with the music, and maybe it's the cheesy would-be sexy song lyrics or the long day or Chad's friends watching us from the bar like a panel of Olympic judges, but I'm just not feeling this at all.

I gently peel his hands away, clasp them together between us, and give them a squeeze.

"Yeah no, that might be a lesson three move," I say. "But keep on practicing those fundament—"

KLUDD!

I don't even see the fist coming until it clocks Chad in the side of the head, and Mason steps in front of me to tower over him the only way Mason *can* tower over someone—when they're sprawled on the floor.

"The lady said no."

"Oh, for the love of crullers," I bury my reddening face in my hand for a moment.

"Dude, the *fuck*?" yells Chad from the floor, clutching his ear on the side Mason hit.

"I am so sorry." I push my way back in front of Mason and hold out my hand to Chad. "And also no. But also sorry!"

He gets to his feet without my help and makes for the far row of tables with only the briefest glance back to confirm his conviction that we're both completely insane.

I don't know if Mason would have graced me with a spontaneous whole sentence in honor of the occasion, but I don't give him the chance.

"You. Me. Conference. Now."

I shove him off the dance floor. He acquiesces, and I don't stop prodding him forward until we reach the closest thing in the building to a pocket of quiet, which happens to be the corridor leading to the restrooms. There are queues of people spilling out of both doors, but I don't care. It'll have to do.

"Christ, Kim, I'm sorry for trying to help, okay?"

I ignore his pathetic plea. "Do you want to be with me?" I demand.

"What?" Mason sputters out, as if the question is absurd.

"Do you want to be with me? Really with me?"

The people in line avert their eyes, and a few begin to chuckle, but I ignore them and keep going.

"Because you've made it pretty clear that you don't," I go on. "Y'know, between all those other times when you've made it totally *unclear*, like all the times we were naked, but it still averages out to a positive net total of clarity."

He might be about to say something, but I'm on a roll.

"And that's fine! If you don't want to, you don't have to, just spare me the jealousy fits then, okay?"

"I wasn't jealous," says Mason, and I feel a little bad that I'm not the only person in this corridor laughing at him, but not bad enough to stop me from laughing a little inside. "I was concerned. Don't worry, it won't happen again."

"Oh, you were *concerned*. Leah's out on the smoking terrace with some guy who looks like Marilyn Manson's creepier little brother and Derek's practically passed out drunk with no physical enhancements and no one watching him but *you*, yet you decide you'd better take care of the problem of someone else asking me to dance, because you're *concerned*?"

"I care about you, okay? Is that what you want me to say?"

I catch one of the hands he flails irritably in the air, push it to the side, and hold it there. He pushes back, like arm wrestling without a table, and makes no progress. I can feel the fragility of the bones inside his hand, in spite of its roughness and size.

I don't want to hurt him, just remind him that on the off chance I ever find myself on a bad date with someone stronger than I am, there's zero chance he'd be able to do anything about it.

"Actually, I'd rather you go back to '*it won't happen again*.'"

He pulls away from my grip and I let go, turn, and almost walk headlong into a bouncer. His badge reads S. WINTERS.

Chad is standing at the end of the hallway in a huddle with his friends and gives S. Winters a nod from a distance.

"Sorry, ma'am, but is this guy bothering you?" Winters asks.

"No!" I snap, take a breath, and remind myself he's just doing his job. "No, sir. Thank you, but no, no one's bothering me. Everyone's fine."

Chad looks like he wants Winters to do something more.

Mason breezes past them both.

"Don't worry," he mutters. "I was just leaving."

"Hey, are you Glitter Girl?" someone in line for the bathroom calls out as I hurry out of the hallway.

"Nope, sorry."

By the time I find our table to check on Derek, Leah and Cory have already beaten me to it.

Derek's out cold.

"Where's Mason?" asks Cory.

"Finding his own way home," I say. "The usual."

This doesn't warrant any follow-up questions.

"We gotta get Derek to bed," says Leah "You riding with, or flying?"

"You mind if I stay for a bit?"

I know Cory can carry Derek without breaking a sweat, but it seems only right to ask.

"Well, I guess we can postpone your kidnapping for a week or two," says Leah. Then, with the tiniest transition from straight-faced to actually serious, she asks, "You sure?"

"Very."

Usually, I feel awful being angry with anyone, but finally telling Mason off has left me strangely energized. It was all stuff I should have probably said years ago if I didn't have to worry about coordinating a villain smackdown with him the next day, but now I don't. That and the WW have made me invincible, more so than usual, and I don't want to waste it.

Tonight is just tonight, and I want it to last.

When the others head out, I head for the bar.

✳

THE DETECTIVE

For someone who doesn't drink, Fadia still knows how to party. It's probably all the vigilante training, but start her dancing and she just won't stop. I don't think I've moved this much all at once since boot camp, but she's not even breaking a sweat. It's a shame that she's not out, because there's a lot of pretty ladies here and she'd have her pick easy.

Easier than me, at least. I cleaned up as much as I could, but a lot of the girls here take one look and it's like they can just smell the Crescent on me. Since I don't really give two shits what EPC girls think of me (and have three double shots of whiskey in me right now), I don't mind.

Fadia, unfortunately, does.

We're back on the second floor by her table, leaning over the dance floor.

"We need to find you a girl."

"I do fine on my own."

"Prostitutes don't count."

She's probably right about that. While I don't do it *that* often, acquiring the services of a lady of the night every so often (always gotta make sure they're free agents and not one of Milgram's girls first; I'm no monster) is easily my third or fourth worst habit, so I don't argue with her.

"This ain't exactly the best place for me to pick up girls."

"Not the kind you usually go for. See, the girls who look trashy here aren't really trashy, they just put on the trashy look because they think it makes them look edgy. No, what we need for you is . . . a good girl. One who might be interested in taking a walk on the wild side."

"I'm wild?"

"As wild as most of them will ever see," she says, scanning the crowd. Her eyes stop, and she stifles a giggle of what looks like a bad, private joke.

"Her," she says, pointing to a girl at the bar.

Fadia has good taste. The girl at the bar is tall and pale, with straight red hair down to her waist. Her little black dress shows an impressive and no doubt very expensive bust, while her glasses, which probably cost more than my car, give her that naughty librarian look. It's a crime she doesn't have a line around the block, though how modestly dressed she is compared to the rest of this crowd might explain why.

"Introduce yourself. Make small talk. Offer to buy her a drink. Do all that, and I'll give you what you want."

"I can do that with my eyes closed."

"*And*, no powers. You don't get to cheat by reading her, not even if she says you can. You go in there like anybody else who can't read people at a touch."

My head is swimming, but the alcohol's given me that sweet swelling of false confidence. "Fine. I'll play your game, vigilante, but let it be known you can be one sadistic bitch."

"Thanks. And enjoy!"

There's another shoe about to drop, but what it is, I can't guess. Fine.

She wants to play games, she can play games. This one at least looks more fun than her usual picks for me.

I make my way across the dance floor, glad for the pick-up the whiskey's giving.

Finally, I make the bar, and luckily get a spot next to her.

She notices and offers a polite smile.

Here goes nothing.

"So, I was debating between three different lines to break the ice. Would you be up for hearing them and telling me which'd work best?"

"Sure. Why not?" she says, amused.

"Alright. Now, the first one's a classic."

"I like classics."

"Good. So, you come here often?"

She's still smiling politely, but no more than that. "What's the second one?"

"What's your major?"

"Sorry, not in college anymore. Next?"

"You gonna make me bust out the big guns?"

"After this much buildup, how can I not?"

"Then here goes nothing: What's a nice girl like you doing in a place like this?"

This one gets a short bark of a laugh.

"So, any winners?" I ask.

"Sorry, but thanks for trying."

"Wait!"

"What?"

"I've got one more. Just came up with it. Might be brilliant, might not be. Since you've been so honest with me, let me try it on for size?"

"Well, I don't have anything better to do, so go for it."

"Now you sure you want to hear this? It's something you probably don't hear very often around here; I think it might be too powerful for an average night out at the club."

She's laughing now, whether at me or with me, I can't say.

"Go for it."

"Hi," I say, holding out my hand. "Would you prefer it if I left you alone?"

She considers my question and my hand for a long moment.

Then, still smirking, she reaches out and takes it in hers. "You're right. That isn't something I hear very often."

"Strong handshake," I say, withdrawing my somewhat aching hand from her grip.

She eyes me, curiously. "You really don't—you know what, scratch that. I'm super."

"Nice, me too."

"Really?" she perks up. "What can you do?"

I refrain from telling her *I'll show you mine if you show me yours*, because I'm not fucking twelve, but it's really hard—er, difficult.

"I need to be a little drunker before I start showing that off in public. But it's impressive."

Bet she's never heard that one before.

"I'm pretty sure mine's cooler."

"No doubt, no doubt," I say, scanning the bar area. "So, you here with friends?"

"Was."

"You and me both."

"Really? What happened to yours?"

"I'm hoping they'll take a hint and not interrupt me while I'm trying to have a conversation with the most beautiful woman in the bar."

A brief silence passes between us as she looks down at her drink, then up to me. "Smooth. How long were you hoping to work that into the conversation?"

"Since the beginning. What do you think?"

"Not bad. A little forced, but it came off pretty natural considering how many it looks like you've had."

"So, yay?"

"I'm not sure if I'd go full yay with an exclamation point, but I'd say you've earned yourself a drink," she says, calling the bartender over.

She's buying?

She's kind of funny?

She's got a killer body?

She's buying?

I might be in love.

＊

THE SUPERHERO

He's got one of those faces that was probably a little *too* pretty, too bland, before taking a few heavy blunt impacts. I'm betting on a full-contact college sport or maybe even low profile crime fighting. The little scar cutting through the stubble at the left of his chin supports the latter theory.

His long, dark hair is neglected but suits him, and with his trench coat off and draped across his lap, I notice part of a geometric tattoo climbing his nicely defined right bicep into the sleeve of his T-shirt, and I'm interested in seeing the rest.

I totally have a type, don't I? This is what having a type looks like.

All mysterious and unkempt, with those compact muscles and that look that says he knows things other people don't.

But my insides are warm from the WW, and the effort of balancing on a barstool is a crazy carnival game right now . . . and I don't care.

Besides, I'm not into the similarities half so much as the differences. He's shameless without being too pushy, the smart-aleck banter is a nice change from sullen silences, and he even lets me coax out his smile once or twice.

It's a cute smile.

The barstool difficulty level is ramping up exponentially, and it's definitely time to say the magic words.

"Wanna get out of here?"

I get another smile in return. He gulps the last of his drink and stands to offer me assistance balancing back on my heels, which I gladly accept. He's not too steady either, but together there's a kind of mutual leaning post effect.

Out on the sidewalk, in the sudden, breezy silence away from the music and the heat of bodies, the sky is still as clear as it has been all day, glittering now with all the stars the city will allow, and it gives me an idea.

"You scared of heights?" I ask.

"No, you?"

"I'd have a serious problem if I was," I say, levitating off the ground with a grin. It's so much easier to stay upright this way.

I slide under his arms, facing away from him, wrapping them tight around my shoulders.

"Don't let go," I advise. He squeezes in acknowledgement, and I take off, leaving the ground far behind.

He squeezes quite a bit harder after that, and flight and the firmness of his body tight against my back might be the greatest combination ever.

I already know where I'm going. It's a bank office high rise, vacant at this time of night, with no guardrails and a perfect view of the city and the valley beyond, one of my favorite spots to catch the breeze and watch the stadium fireworks, or just the hypnotic, fluid collage of the city lights.

He doesn't jump on the chance to take his hands off me when I set us down, just loosens his grip enough that I can turn around, and that's how the make-out phase of the evening begins, all at once, leaning into each other with too little balance to support any kind of reserve. His lips are soft and his hands are careful but sure, and I'm feeling it, thoroughly feeling it this time, so I'm just gonna say it:

"Ever done it on a rooftop before?"

He looks around and genuinely appears to rack his brain. "Probably."

"Well, you haven't with me."

I take both our coats and toss them in a heap together, then give a tug at his T-shirt, which he surrenders readily.

I try to mirror him, then remember how long it took to get this dress on in the first place, and just point him to the back of it.

"Um, would you?"

He wrestles with the tiny zipper for a moment but finally gets it to move without breaking it, and then takes a moment to absorb the full reality of my distinctly unnatural proportions.

This is a disclaimer I've had to give before.

"They're not real, but they're durable. Go nuts."

He doesn't wait to be told twice, diving in face first and with both hands.

His lips are still soft, if a little cold, and they begin to explore upward and downward, a little farther each time, always finding their way back to the base camp of my breasts.

His shirtlessness reveals a few details he wasn't born with either: more ink and healed injuries.

I run a finger from the army tattoo on his left shoulder to the scar next to it, the thickest one of the collection nearly separating his arm from his chest, and then up to the nick on his chin, a segment of the same line.

He catches my tracing finger carefully between his teeth.

"What are you doing?" he says through it.

"Connecting the dots."

"Could you not?"

"Sure. Give me something else to connect."

Fumbling his jeans open, he does so.

"Nice. Hold a sec," I say. He graciously returns my finger so I can do the accompanying *hold a sec* gesture with it, while I pick up my fallen purse and dig through it with the other hand.

This isn't something I do a lot, but I never gave up the high school preparedness habit.

How on earth can eight square inches of chiffon so completely swallow whatever I happen to need in a hurry?

Hurrah! A condom!

I reach down to feel him, as ready as I am, roll the condom into place, and hold him steady while I lift off and slide myself onto him, locking my legs and then arms securely around.

He grabs my hips and pushes in deeper, then tries a few experimental thrusts, grinning at the novelty of our unsupported verticality.

Ha, I *can* do something he hasn't tried before!

With his feet still planted on the solid rooftop, my flight gives the cool illusion that he's stronger and I'm lighter than we really are. But where's the fun in stopping there? Holding on tighter, I inch upward until we're both hanging in the air. He's prepared, smoothly shifting his weight to his arms, locked around my shoulders for leverage.

In better light and from a spectator's angle, I'd love to watch how long he could keep this going, but it's not the most practical trick, and after the first minute or two he's favoring his left arm, so I pull close to his ear.

"Ready?" I ask.

"For . . . ?"

I swing myself over onto my back, taking him with me, holding him firmly close so that I cushion his fall and don't bend him the wrong way.

I land on the ledge, my upper torso hanging naked and upside-down over the city, held securely to the roof from the inside by his weight.

The street is too far away, and beneath too many downward-facing streetlights for anyone to see us, but I can see the city, miles and miles of its nighttime face, and the stars above it, and tonight is finally just tonight.

"Whoa, right?" I say, looking up at him and nodding out at this lightshow more brilliant than anything at the Silver Cowl.

"Yeah, whoa," he agrees, holding the edge with both hands, going at me a little more cautiously to avoid nudging us farther over, and my whole body opens up, nerve by nerve, to catch every beat of the more measured rhythm. "There's, uh, there's no chance you're going to drop me, is there?"

"Only if you stop what you're doing."

This doesn't reassure him as much as I intended it to.

"Kidding!" I say. "Sorry, totally kidding! But seriously though, please don't stop."

CHAPTER 6: THE SUPERHERO

S
o this is what a hangover feels like. No wonder people complain about them so much.

The sun is too bright, the floor is too hard, and even from inside my purse ten feet away, my phone alarm is way too loud.

If I feel like this, the guy I'm spooning from last night must be in agony.

Or maybe not; he never did get around to telling me his superpower.

I flex circulation back into one of my arms and clumsily stroke a tangle of hair behind his ear to wake him. He doesn't budge, but his loose, sleep-mussed ponytail falls to the side, baring another tattoo at the back of his neck, and in an instant I'm wide awake, scrambling over to quiet my phone, panic equivalent to about a dozen espressos fresh in my blood.

Oh sweet fudge, he's a supervillain.

I'm due for my first ever PCG mission briefing in an hour, my head feels like it's sealed full of Diet Coke and Mentos, and I just woke up next to a *fracking Glamper's Island inmate.*

Cripes, this is bad.

But he hasn't woken up next to *me* yet. That's good. I can fly away any time I want, just disappear. I've got time to think this through.

First thing's first, find my bra.

Check.

Zip up the dress I'm half wrapped in.

Mostly check.

Then I close the alarm message on my phone and swipe through the menu. What does that icon look like again? Did it change in the last update? How did I end up with this many apps I don't recognize? But I know it's here, and finally I find it: VillScan.

Basic tool in every hero's arsenal, but this is thankfully the first time I've had to use it on a naked guy sleeping under my favorite coat.

I lean over the back of his neck with my phone's camera, then lift my feet off the ground to hover at a better angle until the barcode on his skin finally registers.

I back away to read the file that comes up.

Theft.

Assault.

Extortion.

Possession.

Vandalism.

Henchman-level accessory to criminal conspiracy.

There's a listed release date just shy of nine years ago. No name on the file, just a number. Juvenile privacy regulations. Which is good, I think, because if he'd added to his rap sheet recently, that courtesy would have been waived.

A name would be nice info to have, though. I could do some digging, but that'd take more time than I have. Why on earth didn't I ask him yesterday, when it would have felt natural? I *never* forget to ask.

Okay. I'm breathing.

This isn't . . . terrible. He's out legally, and he's just an ex-henchman.

But he's still sleeping under my favorite coat.

True, I don't need the coat for warmth, and he obviously does, particularly on this breath-revealing December morning, but it's a *really* cute coat that I'll never find in that last-season pinkish crimson color again, and his own trench coat is two feet away and much thicker.

I pick up his coat and spend about a minute trying to gauge whether I can get away with making the switch without waking him, before accepting how moot a point it is.

We're forty stories in the air, on top of a building with no roof access, and I brought him here. Villain or not, there's no chance I'm abandoning him in his sleep—and I know it.

I take a breath, then another, and another, and then give him a nudge with my foot.

Then another.

And another.

It's not easy, finding the narrow window of force adequate to get a response out of him, but inadequate to rupture his non-invulnerable internal organs, and when I do zero in on it, he curls up into a tighter ball with a moan.

No, definitely not a hangover-proof superpower.

"Hi," I say, nicely but not too loudly. My own voice hurts my head. "I'm Kimberly, by the way, nice to meet you." I offer him a hand.

A shred of last night's smile seeps through his grimace, but he makes no move to get up, with or without my help.

"Smooth move, not making me ask. I like it."

"You can steal it, if you like."

"Eddie," he says, reaching for his pants, probably for a phone. "'Time is it?"

"A little after seven. I have to go to work."

He gives a little snort, like he finds the phrase funny somehow, coming from me, and I try not to be too annoyed. Maybe it's just morning phlegm.

"Yeah, me too."

Whatever he's looking for isn't in his pants. He tugs the trench coat out of my grip, pulls a prescription bottle out of one of the inner pockets, and shakes three tablets into his hand.

"There's a coffee shop around the corner," I say. "If you need water. I can be there and back in thirty sec—"

He bites down on all three pills at once.

Ew.

They make a chalky, crunching sound as he chews.

I can ask, or I can hope for the best.

The coin flipping in my head comes up heads.

"Look, Eddie, this might sound kinda bad . . ."

He swallows and looks up at me, shielding his eyes against the sun, interest piqued, and I sort of have to finish.

"Would you . . . would you mind terribly . . . not mentioning me to anyone?"

"Like who?"

"Just anyone."

"Would I mind terribly not mentioning to anyone that I once met a girl named Kimberly in an EPC club?"

"Yes, please?" I emphasize this with a hopeful smile and imploringly clasped hands.

"I guess." He shrugs into his T-shirt.

Just when I'm starting to hold out hope that he'll never realize or care, he puts a hand on my coat to push it away, and I see it click.

"Kimberly," he repeats, and this time it means something to him. "Kimberly Kline. Fuck me, I thought those were dreams!" He shoves the coat off as if whatever dreams he's talking about are still wrapped in it. "You're a fucking *superhero!*"

He says it like an accusation, like something dirty.

"Uh, yeah. Yeah, I am."

"Oh, that bitch. That *bitch!* She set me up. I'm gonna *kill* her!" he spits, finally motivated to get up and stumble into his jeans. "I am. I'm going to kill the shit out of her."

"Who are you going to kill?" I start charging up an energy blast, just in case.

"Fadia fucking Bakkour!"

"You're going to kill the award-winning senior field reporter of the *Pinnacle Looking Glass*?"

He takes one look at my face.

"Oh, for fuck's sake, not *literally*."

I let the charge dissipate.

"Oh. Good. And . . ." I'd really like to feel sure, especially now that he's mentioning reporters. Fadia doesn't specialize in celebrity scandal, but still. "You won't tell? It's not you, exactly," I try to explain. "It's not personal. And it's not even that big a deal. It happens all the time. With guy heroes, at least. But even then, it's always this big dramatic incident, and I'd rather not have that be the *first* thing I do as a Guardian, you know?"

No smile from him now. "What happens all the time?"

"Um. Doing it with villains?"

His hand goes to the back of his neck, then pulls away and clenches deliberately at his side.

"First off, I'm not a villain anymore, I'm reformed, not that that makes a fucking difference to you people, and second, '*doing it with villains*'? What are you, ten?"

"Just because I know a few words with more than four letters," I mumble, unable to keep the irritation out of my voice any longer.

His language didn't bother me yesterday, maybe even excited me a little; made me feel far from home in a good way. But everything after "fucking superhero" has lost its charm. Now it just feels rude.

"Oh yeah, 'doing.' Five whole letters. You're a fuckin' thesaurus. I'm in awe."

He bundles up my coat and throws it at me like he can barely stand to touch it.

"You can keep your precious reputation," he says. "Believe it or not, not everyone from the Crescent lies awake at night dreaming of the day when they'll get to tell some sordid tale of that one time they fucked an airheaded EPC celebutante. And I wouldn't touch that lie factory you call the news with a hundred foot pole."

Airheaded?

Shake it off.

"Then . . . then what does Fadia have to do with it?"

"Just her fucking with my head. She knows what I think of pro-heroes, and still she talked me into talking to you. Her idea of a joke, I'd bet."

"You chatted me up on a *dare*, and I'm the ten-year-old?"

"Don't you have to be at 'work'?" I can hear the air quotes.

"I do, and I only woke you in the first place to ask if you need a ride somewhere first."

"Very heroic. I'll pass."

"Like, maybe to the *ground*?"

"*Pass*," he repeats, approaching the ledge where I cracked the paint slightly in my enthusiasm last night. "Also, where am I?"

"23rd Street," I point out. "Riverside Avenue," I point to the perpendicular thoroughfare.

"Deep in EPC? Fuckin' wonderful," he mutters.

"Are you sure I can't—"

"You still here?"

He's diving back into his pill bottle, and I try to rationalize whether dry-chewing unlabeled prescription medication on an exposed rooftop with no stairs qualifies as the immediate danger to self or others that could justify using my powers to move him without his permission, but I know it's a stretch.

I gather my things and fly away.

He doesn't call after me.

❋

Whatever.

Whatever.

I had a good time and probably didn't mess up my career, which is all I wanted anyway, and it's not the first time a guy's found different words to describe me in the morning than he did the night before. At least the feeling was mutual.

Whatever.

I do feel scummy asking him to hush up about it. It's a horrible thing to say to someone, but the potential fallout if people knew—if my *mom* knew—matters so much to me and so little to him. He seemed more ticked off about finding out who I was, and on that point, he has zero high ground.

Whatever, whatever, whatever.

Not going to spare him another thought, starting in three . . . two . . .

I don't stop at Juniors Ranch, not wanting to budget the time to explain to the others, especially Mason, where I ended up spending the night. After all, I've got my Solar Flare outfit and a room with a freshly stocked private bath waiting for me at Guardian Tower.

And that's how I end up zooming through the tower lobby, hair and teeth unbrushed, carrying my shoes, into an elevator being held open for me by Demigod.

He's carrying a coffee cup, already dressed in his modified toga supersuit, hair gelled perfectly into place under his laurel leaves.

"Morning," he says, a smirk crossing his very square jaw.

Nothing to do but own it.

"Morning." I smirk back, trying to look mysterious and devil-may-care, instead of unwashed and vaguely nauseous.

The elevator dings.

Demigod reaches behind me and jerks my half-zipped zipper the rest of the way up.

The door opens.

"See you in briefing," he says without a change on his face.

I just had my first coworker elevator ride with Demigod!

Now, which room is mine again?

Entry code, entry code . . . yes! Third try!

Superspeed shower, extra detangler, shaving touch-ups with my energy blasts, half a bottle of mouthwash, supersuit, in my seat twenty seconds before the bell.

Just like school.

Demigod pretends not to notice my arrival, and the others are already talking amongst themselves, except for Pinnacle, who clacks the file folder in his hands against the podium to call everyone to order.

"Hedgehog and Bear Man," Pinnacle reads off without preamble. "You're following up on that smuggling operation by the docks. Mental Man's found evidence they may be operating out of the I-6 weigh station. Make sure they're Tickler's people before engaging."

Wow. The Justice Juniors almost never handled anything as big as the cartels, and Pinnacle talks about them like it's a slow day.

In spite of the lingering pressure behind my eyes, I'm inching to the edge of my seat waiting to hear what mission he has for me.

"Strongwoman, there's a protest scheduled at the university today. I need you to represent the Guardians from the ground. Make our commitment to education clear and ensure the situation remains peaceful; nobody wants any more pictures of beat-up cops making the news. And if Dissident shows up again . . . you know what to do. Mental Man, stay on those transmissions from last week. Demigod, you're on emergency call. Solar Flare . . ."

That's me!

"You're on protection detail, open ended."

I excel at protecting people!

"You'll have a few days to look at the case file and put in your hours on the training floor before checking in with Mayor Card's chief of security. He'll get you up to speed on the recent threats against the family."

. . . Wait.

"Protection detail . . . for the Card family?"

I don't mean to question my first-ever mission assignment, certainly not in the tone that I do. It just . . . kind of slips out.

Pinnacle levels his gaze on me, and I get the sense that I'm precisely meeting his expectations—and not in a good way.

"Is there a problem?"

"No," I lie. "No problem."

"Spit it out now, kid. I'd rather hear it before you drop the ball than after."

I sit up straighter and search for a way to put it, other than, *maybe he kinda deserves a few death threats.*

"Frankly," I imitate Pinnacle's confident bluntness in a way I'm crossing my fingers he'll like, "Mayor Card is an embarrassment to this city, and any form of partnering with him would be a stain on the PCG's history of integrity."

"Is it 'partnering' to save a person's life?" asks Pinnacle. "Do you plan to audit the investment portfolio of every passenger on the next train you prevent from crashing?"

"Of course not, and if Mayor Card ever happens to be on a crashing train, I'm not saying we shouldn't stop it, but he's not. Politicians get death threats all the time—especially politicians who threaten their own constituents in every public address. The things he's said about gene-jobs, aliens . . ." I could babble on for hours trying to list the reasons Mayor Card is an unimaginable jerk, closing public hospitals, giving tax exempt status to the Human Supremacy League, trying to wall off half the city into some kind of unincorporated no man's land, but Pinnacle's running out of what little patience he started with, so I jump straight for what I think might possibly strike a chord for him. ". . . All those anti-*super* rants he does. If we offer him proactive protection, on top of his own security team—"

"We demonstrate that we're the bigger people, don't you agree?" proposes Pinnacle.

"Or that we endorse his position against anyone else we miss the chance to protect while a seventh of our efforts are focused on *him*," I counter-propose.

"Is that your whole objection? Your belief in our inability to adequately protect the city as a whole?"

"No!" I backtrack, take a breath, and do my best to convey the gravity with which I do not want this assignment. "If Mayor Card had his way, I wouldn't be allowed on this team. Or much of anywhere else." I've hardly been online since the ceremony, so I don't know if he's said anything about me personally, but I can guess based on precedent. "In his words, I'd be a distraction, a whiner, and an unacceptable insurance liability."

I glance at Strongwoman for support, but she doesn't glance back.

"Are you informing me that your personal politics might interfere with your ability to preserve the life of a man receiving terrorist threats against his safety and family?" asks Pinnacle.

"I only mean . . ." I scrounge for a professional-sounding reason. "If he holds true to form, I doubt he'll accept security advice from me."

Especially in this outfit.

"If he absolutely needs PCG protection," I say, "it might go smoother if—"

"Are you suggesting that just because a citizen in need has some kind of antiquated preference for a male hero, we should go out of our way to indulge his prejudices?"

. . . Drat.

I slump back into my chair.

"No, sir."

"Good." Pinnacle nods with finality. "Whatever false impression you imagine Mayor Card may have of you, or any of us, consider this your opportunity to prove him wrong."

CHAPTER 7: THE DETECTIVE

I'm never gonna live this down.

"So let me ask this question," Tragedii says, transforming the pinkie finger of her mechanical hand into a pair of bolt cutters that make short work of the gate's padlock. "When she came, and I'm assuming she did 'cause you're a nice guy and all, did she shout, 'GLITTER GIRL, *GO!*'?"

Petting Zoo's laughing like hell, the sound equal parts human and hyena.

I'm not.

"No, no wait," Petting Zoo gasps. "I've got one. Did she shout, 'GLITTER GIRL, *COME!*'?"

"I was drunk," I say, pushing my way through the gate and past the pair of them. The maintenance access ramp we're on leads down into the Pinnacle City River, which is just a massive concrete ditch that bisects the city most of the year, but a pretty impressive actual river when it does decide to rain around here. As it's been a few days since the heaviest rain, most of the river's drained, leaving dry sides for us to walk along. Lucky, since according to Dissident, the badly beaten body of Quentin Julian was discovered under the bridge at the end of this access ramp.

If only the cost hadn't been so damn high.

"You get drunk all the time, and you don't usually wind up screwing a superhero," Petting Zoo says, bouncing alongside me enthusiastically.

"Remind me why I invited you along again?"

"Because I had the day off?"

"Right. That."

"It's nothin' to be ashamed of," Tragedii says. "She didn't rob you, and she's a looker. Having a one night stand with a pro-hero, that's something you can boast to the grandkids."

"Unless she turns into one of those one-hit wonder heroes, saving the city once and then having to quit due to some drug scandal," Petting Zoo notes.

"Always possible," Tragedii admits.

"Well, I'm not gonna boast about it to anyone, let alone the grandkids I'm *not* gonna have."

"Why not?" Petting Zoo asks.

I fume. "Because pro-heroes stayed in their towers, putting our friends and families in jail while people like you and me fought overseas in wars they could've ended but wouldn't get anywhere close to touching. Because they pad their pockets with commercial endorsements and attend charity balls to benefit the less fortunate, all without taking their feet off the throats of those same poor. Because my best *fucking* friend when I was just a dumb fucking kid . . . Do you want any more becauses?"

"Eddie, be cool, this isn't group," Tragedii says.

"Jesus, Eddie, I was joking," Petting Zoo adds.

"I wasn't. I fucked a superhero. It was one of the worst mistakes I've made in a life full of mistakes, and I'd appreciate it if you'd just let me black this out and didn't joke about it, at least not to my face."

"So, you're saying we can joke behind your back?" Tragedii asks, hiking her duffel bag up her shoulder.

I flip her off for an answer, but at least it has some humor to it.

Little else does these days.

Dissident meant well. I know this because I know her. She's always been on me to get out more and have fun, and I'm sure she thought it'd be a great joke on both me and *Solar Flare* (since she has nearly as much contempt for the pro-heroes as I do), but she only got half the equation right.

Solar Flare.

If I hadn't fallen asleep touching her and that thin, useless coat of hers, if my powers hadn't slipped out in my dreams, I'd have thought she was just another girl at a bar. The night would've been just another night of drunken fun, and we could've let that be that.

But that couldn't just be that, could it?

Now I can't get rid of that night I'd normally forget without trying. I remember every false feeling she gave me, every taste, every curve of her body. Every sound she made. How good she smelled.

Memories that should be pleasant mixing with the worst memories.

Us on that roof flashes to me, Bystander and Marco pulling that robbery in EPC.

Burying my face in her breasts and hearing her moan makes me see those pro-heroes floating above us, and Marco yelling that we had to run.

Entering her, floating above the city, makes me see the glow of the hero's eyes before the lasers shot from them, connecting with Marco's body.

Her cries of pleasure become his screams.

Her smile becomes Marco's bleached skull, sitting on the street and looking up at me with hollow eyes.

If I could erase that night, I would. But I can't, and now I'll have to live with it.

A three-day bender of pills and whiskey helped with some of that, but after the third day, the pileup of messages from Ruby Herron and Dissident were enough to get me off my ass to attempt some semblance of an investigation.

Bringing Tragedii and Petting Zoo along for the ride, well, that just keeps me honest.

And safe.

Can't forget that.

When we reach the end of the ramp, I'm hit by a powerful wave of nausea, so strong I need to brace my hands against the wall of the river and vomit.

Petting Zoo pats me on the back. "Feeling better?"

"Actually, no. I think I need a drink."

"I think you need to sleep this off some more," Tragedii says. "Drink some water. Eat some real food. Or *any* food. Lay off the booze for a while. Which you know pains me to advise you on, as your favorite bartender, but I can't have my customers dying on me, can I?"

They're saying this because they want me to suffer. This is a fact my cloudy mind knows. Also, in my current, infinite wisdom, I know that I have to get away from these dangerous women as quickly as possible.

Guess I might as well do my job.

The bridge we're at matches the crime scene photographs Dissident sent to my phone. The winter rains have washed away any visible proof something happened here, but for me that doesn't matter. I walk to the stretch of wall with a very identifiable earthquake crack cutting in half about two decades worth of faded graffiti.

"We're here," I say, taking off my trench coat and tossing it to Tragedii. She and Petting Zoo take up casual defensive positions on either side of me.

"Got any good Twenty Questions?" Petting Zoo asks.

"I'll think of one," Tragedii replies.

"Nothing from any alternate futures! It's gotta be something I'll know!"

"Spoil my fun, why don'tcha."

I close my eyes, tune them out, get a feel for the place. Stretching my arms out, I fight back the pain in my left arm. Much as I'd like to be doped to the gills right now, I've found this next part often gets clearer results with the hurt.

If you go by my R-SAL card, my power is defined as "psychom-etry," though that's never sounded right by what I do. Psychometry sounds like something involving a leather couch and some sort of hypno-coin.

What I *can* do, I'm able to do anywhere, at any time, with any-thing. Give me a place, an object, a person (though they're always less reliable) and enough time, and I can tell you what happened. The longer I'm in contact, the further back I can look. It puts me in—I guess you'd call it a trance, taking me to another place. But while I'm there, my body's vulnerable.

That's why I'm glad for friends like Petting Zoo and Tragedii, keeping an eye on me (for a modest fee, of course).

"Petting Zoo, plug me in?" I ask.

"Sure, why not?" she says, pulling a memory stick from one of my coat pockets.

Call this the one decent thing the Army did for me, the one thing that makes me different from your average psychometrist. For some extra cash, I volunteered for a program where they inserted an implant in my left arm I can use to download any active vision I'm having. While the thing itches to high hell, it's made my job a lot easier—especially when I'm called into court.

Petting Zoo plugs the memory stick into my arm.

"Okay, here we go," I whisper, crouching down and placing a hand on the ground.

Time rewinds before me.

Seconds become minutes, minutes become hours, hours become days.

I watch as the water levels of the river rise and fall with the winter rains.

I watch as gene-jobs and the homeless climb the slanting concrete walls, trying to find cover and warmth as high up as they can go.

I watch a police investigation cleaning up, then fully active, then setting up as they go from taking a body out of the coroner's van, retrieving evidence, taking pictures of it, and finally (or originally) establishing the crime scene.

Then the police clear out, and I'm just staring at the body of Quentin Julian lying in the Pinnacle City River. A night and a day pass with the body undiscovered; it's too well concealed under the bridge to be seen from anywhere else, but I'm not being paid to figure out how he was found, just who killed him.

It's night again. His body's looking fresher, the blood around him pools back into him in reverse. He starts moving again, twitching, breathing heavily, trying to move.

Then things happen so fast, it's a blur.

And then he's on his feet again, looking around.

I slow things down, put time to rights.

Then I'm just a spectator.

***

Quentin Julian stands beneath a darkened bridge in the Crescent. Even with his light gene-job fur, he's cold, pulling a heavy coat around him. His phone vibrates, and he answers it.

"Hey, Ruby. Listen, I'm going to be in late tomorrow. I've got a meeting tonight. It's not in my book. I can't tell you, I'm sorry, but if it goes the way I'm hoping, it'll solve a lot of our prob—"

There are sounds nearby. Footsteps. A glass bottle rolling down a wall of the river.

"I have to go."

He hangs up. He smiles.

"Gentlemen. If you really wanted to meet, we surely could have found someplace a little warmer, couldn't we?"

His ears perk up. He looks around. He can sense he's surrounded by several figures coming out of the darkness.

"What's going on?"

One of them turns on a powerful flashlight in Julian's eyes, blinding him.

"Hey!" he exclaims.

Then they're on him. Punching and kicking and slashing at him with their claws.

Gene-jobs. Four of them. Not professional jobs like on Julian's side, these guys are lopsided messes, with features stretched and twisted and mixed with all sorts of different animals. Victims of gene bombs, or their kids, maybe.

The people Julian dedicated his life to protecting.

They attack with a ferocity you wouldn't expect men to be capable of. I see their faces clearly, get every detail I can so I'll earn my pay for this job.

I watch every impact. Hear every bone break. Every moan and protest from Julian. He doesn't fight back. Maybe once he tries to plead with them, but through bloody, broken teeth, his protests are just a whimpering gargle.

After only a few seconds of this he's on the ground, and still they don't let up on their attack.

Then, almost as if a switch is flipped, the four of them stop the assault.

"Did you record that?" the man with a muted beak asks.

"I thought you were supposed'ta!" the man with a single, curving ram's horn coming from the side of his face says.

"Let's get the hell out of here!" another yells.

At once, they flee.

Julian lies still for a while, but achingly, he coughs up blood and rolls onto his stomach. He crawls away a few feet, then collapses. He reaches for his cell phone, but its screen is shattered.

Then he's face down on the ground.

Then, well, you know the rest.

✳

When I come out of the trance, I'm breathing heavily, sweating even though it's cold.

No matter how many times I've seen it, I've never gotten used to watching a person die.

I don't think anyone does; not anyone who can still call themselves human at the end of the day, at least.

"Oh, good, you've rejoined the living," Petting Zoo says. She looks agitated, tosses me my trench coat and instantly transforms into a leopard.

"I miss something?" I ask, standing up slowly.

"Just some local color. Let us little ladies handle it," Tragedii says.

As my eyes clear and I get my bearings, I see a trio of well but darkly dressed people sauntering toward us; a large gene-job man with reptilian skin, sunglasses and a goatee, a woman with spiked hair and a scarf covering the lower half of her face, and a man made entirely out of running chainsaws.

"Be my guest," I say. Quickly, I pull the memory stick from my arm and pocket it, and pull my trench coat on. Petting Zoo pads up beside me, growling.

"Well, well, well, we've found us three billy goats beneath our bridge, haven't we?" the chainsaw man says in his southern accent.

"We don't want any trouble," Tragedii says, calmly unzipping her duffel.

"And neither do we," the chainsaw man says. "As a matter of fact, we're here as a public service on behalf of Mr. Milgram to keep people *out* of trouble. This river's a dangerous place. You'd be amazed at the accidents that can happen if you're not careful."

Milgram.

And I thought it wouldn't be worth it to bring Harriet today. Live and learn.

"Well, thank you for the thought. So, we'll just be on our way then," Tragedii says, stepping toward them.

The chainsaw man puts one of his chainsaw hands up, calmly blocking her path.

Petting Zoo snarls.

"Now if only it were that simple. Offering public services is costly and time consuming. While Mr. Milgram is indeed a conscientious fella, he's not running a charity, and would greatly appreciate a donation from you fine people," the chainsaw man says.

This is not a suggestion. The woman opens her jacket to reveal a row of glowing, magenta daggers, while the gene-job opens his mouth to reveal rattlesnake's fangs. Petting Zoo bares her own fangs and looks ready to pounce. Much as I'd rather avoid this fight the way I'm feeling, I'll throw myself in if I have to. Not gonna leave two friends in the dust.

Tragedii just raises her human hand to us.

"You want a donation?" she asks.

"If you'd be so kind," the chainsaw man responds.

"Fine, here's my donation," she says, reaching into her duffel and pulling out a massive gun that continually unfolds and extends into a seven-foot-long monstrosity of rotating barrels, glowing lights, and rockets.

The body language of Milgram's team drastically shifts to terror as Tragedii narrates, "Fresh from the year 2147, meet the Genentech Model 39-27b Flesheater, a phased temporal-plasma cannon capable of firing nearly a thousand rounds per minute, with a variable time-displacement range agony generator that'll give your ancestors third-degree burns the moment I blast your guts all over the river. While I'm rusty when it comes to murder, I'd be plenty happy to oblige you with a demonstration."

The chainsaw man keeps Milgram's other goons from running.

"Perhaps, this once, your donation can be excused. But don't think this disrespect will be forgotten. As far as he's concerned, a threat on Milgram's employees is a threat on Milgram himself, and he doesn't cotton to threats particularly well, especially from uppity cyborgs."

Now, if he wanted to piss off Tragedii, he did a damn good job, because she starts to charge up the cannon. Before she can get off a shot, though, the woman with the glowing daggers throws one at the ground before her, creating a vortex that Milgram's thugs disappear into.

"Pussies," Tragedii says, spitting on the ground they disappeared into.

"You sure you want to piss these guys off?" I ask.

"Someone's gotta stand up and shove some cannons up the right asses. Might as well be some high-powered, non-traceable, future cannons, right?" Tragedii says.

I smile. "I know. I just like hearing you talk shit."

"Did you get what you needed?" Petting Zoo asks me, human again.

"Yeah."

"Good," Tragedii says, retracting her cannon back into something that'll fit into a duffel bag. "Then let's head back to the Lineup. First drink's on me."

And this, ladies and gentlemen, is why it's not about *what* you know, but *who* you know.

✳

While I'm all set for a night at the Lineup trying to forget everything I saw today, and maybe even some group therapy if Tragedii gets insistent, it's not meant to be.

After a couple drinks, I text Ruby Herron that I got what she wants.

I probably shouldn't have done that.

She texts back and wants to meet right away.

I'm not ready for anything *right away*, but since she's still got me on contract, I tell her to meet me at the Lineup.

At least this way I don't have to unlock the office.

I'm not sure how many drinks in I am by the time she finally arrives, but it's not enough to make me forget how gorgeous she is.

Or how out of place she is in here.

Nervously, she meets me by the bar, her eyes darting to Tragedii and the various barflies as if worried each of them is going to attack her.

The way Ruby looks, I'm getting flashbacks to the other night, to the *hero*, but I fight them to the back of the mind.

"Evening, Miss Herron," I say, putting on my PI face, which seems like a brilliant idea with my head swimming the way it is.

"You know your office is just across the street, right?" she says, taking the stool next to me. Her coat opens slightly, revealing a dress that tightly hugs her frame.

"Look, I've had a long day, and I've seen some things I wish I could forget. Cut me some slack."

She readjusts her coat. "You . . . have it?"

I slide the memory stick across the bar toward her, and she picks up enthusiastically.

I explain, "The murder of Quentin Julian. I wouldn't recommend watching it if you want to sleep tonight, but if you take that to the cops they'll be hard-pressed to ignore it."

"Thank you," she says, looking at the stick in her hand thoughtfully. "Who killed him?"

"A few gene-jobs. Got good enough looks at their faces that they should be pretty easy to find."

"Good. I'll transfer the remainder of what you're owed immediately and deliver this to the proper people so justice can be served."

"Good."

I can end this right now. Just let it all go. But there's things I saw in my vision that just don't add up, and I'm liquored up enough to consider them worth asking about.

"Did you know why Julian was there? Who he was meeting?"

"No," Ruby says.

"And you were his assistant?"

"I didn't pry into his personal life," she says, though I don't buy that for a second.

"Even though you wanted to be a part of it?"

She doesn't meet my eyes.

"Did you know he was killed in Milgram territory?"

I notice a twitch at the word Milgram, but nothing more.

She stands up from her seat. "Unless there's anything else, Mr. Enriquez, I'll be going."

"Just one more thing," I say, the liquid adding a bit of boldness to my voice.

"What?"

"You have any plans this evening?"

She doesn't look too disgusted, but doesn't answer me either as she heads for the door.

"Can you at least give me a good Yelp review? I could really use some!" I call after her.

She doesn't respond as she leaves the bar, and my life.

Turning back to Tragedii, I order another drink and try to ignore whatever nonsense is blaring from the TV.

And now back to our regularly scheduled programming.

CHAPTER 8: THE SUPERHERO

I don't have to look up directions to the Card mansion. Everyone in the city knows it on sight.

It's the opening shot of that show, *In the Cards*, the one that follows the family around recording whatever they do, but it's also the most ostentatious building in the North Hills, overlooking the valley and the I-6, so even if you've managed to never stumble on it while channel surfing, everyone who commutes anywhere in the city sees it daily.

Mayor Card's installation of a defense force field over all ten acres of the property made news a couple years ago, so I land outside the ornamental front gates with the giant "WC" on them and push the button on the intercom.

It crackles.

"Estate of the beloved mayoral family," the answer comes in a habitual monotone. "State your business."

Beloved. Right.

"This is Solar Flare with the Pinnacle City Guardians," I say. "I believe I have an appointment."

Okay, even on a first assignment this crummy, announcing myself out loud sounds pretty cool.

"Thank you for coming, Solar Flare. Please approach through the staff entrance on your left to sign in."

The gate swings open, and I have to abandon the intercom promptly to dodge out of its path.

The main entrance up ahead is shaped like a diamond and flanked with marble pillars and topiary sculptures of Mayor Card, his current wife in her runway model strut, and three of his assorted known kids from the previous two marriages.

I don't mind turning left.

The staff entrance leads directly into a room full of lighting and sound equipment with several curtained off dressing room spaces. People in black button down shirts are buzzing frantically in and out of the space, the air is thick with aerosol, and no sooner do I shut the door behind me than I'm being yanked into a chair in front of one of the lighted mirrors by a woman in a black apron.

"Finally," she mutters, attacking my face with an alcohol wipe. "Who did your makeup this morning, a blind chimp?"

"No, that's just my face." I joke agreeably, dodging her hands.

I skipped the salon at Guardian Tower this morning and am rocking the barebones lip gloss and mascara look.

One of the men in dark shirts—this one with an earpiece—hurries over and holds out his hand.

I take it, a welcome rescue, but he only gives mine the briefest shake before nudging me back into the seat.

"Solar Flare, welcome." He talks faster than Cory, like he's challenging himself to fit twice as many words into half as many seconds. "I'm Jacob, producer of *In the Cards*. Sally, can you do something about her eyebrows before we go on?" he turns to the woman in the apron, who's already comparing different pairs of tweezers from her apron pockets.

"Oh, I'm not 'going on,'" I try to explain. "I'm just here to meet with Mayor Card or his chief of security about the family's safety."

"We know, hun," says Jacob. "But in this house, we're always rolling. No one goes beyond this point unless they're camera-ready."

Oh god, please no.

I'd rather star in a full season of Rickie Maroon's undercover celebrity journalist show than do a ten second cameo on *In the Cards*.

I'd rather appear during the commercial breaks, selling rash ointment and vibrating dumbbells, than do a ten second cameo on *In the Cards*.

Can't I go back to worrying about that henchman, Eddie, bragging to the paparazzi? Even that would be better.

"I haven't signed a release for that," I tell Jacob as casually as I can.

"Don't worry, the PCG have the rights to your image," Jacob speed talks, gesturing Sally and her tweezers to continue. "They took care of all the paperwork in advance."

Crud.

That's it. I'm trash. I shall forever be known as that superhero who appeared on *In the Cards*, chumming it up with bigots and narcissists, and thus will die the legacy of Solar Flare.

No. I think it over in a rush, while I let Sally yank fruitlessly at my eyebrows to her heart's content.

They can film me all they want. It doesn't change the vows I took or who I am or why I'm here. I'm Solar Flare, I'm a superhero, and I'm following up on some terrorist threats just like Pinnacle said, because killing the Mayor is illegal no matter what kind of a person he is, and superheroes uphold the law.

That's all this is, and as long as I'm careful, as long as I stick to what's right and don't say anything that could be taken out of context, that's all anyone will see.

I just have to be myself.

Sally finally gives up on prying my already sparse eyebrow hairs out of their invulnerable follicles—no way am I letting her know that I could remove them with my energy powers if I wanted—and settles for penciling over them.

It takes almost half an hour of brushes, sponges, and pens before she gives me the aesthetic all clear, and Jacob ushers me out of the dressing room at the same speed he uses for talking.

The farther we get from the staff entrance, the more mounted cameras there are in the ceiling and walls, and the shinier the house's décor becomes, until literally every surface is encrusted with gems in various playing card motifs. Real or glass, I can't tell, and I'm honestly not sure which answer would be better.

Not going to ask. Not going to say a word. I know it's not what's important. It's just interior design. But . . . holy *wow*, this place puts the *ack* in tacky.

Ack.

I mean, my family's never been exactly shy about our money, either, but somehow we've never felt the urge to bedazzle the tar out of everything we own.

"You like them?" Jacob wildly misinterprets my reaction to a set of velour couch cushions studded with bright red stones, veined with gold. Thankfully, his vocal schedule-keeping leaves no gaps for answers. "They're Wubblyan blood crystals."

"I thought trade with the Wubbly system was illegal," I say, even though I don't think so.

I know so.

"Yes, they're very rare. Mayor Card has some fortunate connections in the Roball Empire that excel at obtaining unnecessarily controversial off-world items. Get your fresh batteries ready!" he shouts abruptly down the hall in front of us. "First meeting of the kids and Solar Flare! Let's try to get this in one take, shall we?"

"Your security here *looks* more than adequate," I hint. "But if there are possible weaknesses, I should really talk to whoever knows them best right away."

The Guardians' case file was annoyingly sparse on this subject.

"Yes, yes, next stop, I promise," says Jacob. "We just have to get a quick initial reaction shot. The kids have been talking nonstop about you. We can't leave the thread hanging."

I don't want to be a thread, but before I can reiterate this, Jacob shouts, "Natural chatter in 3 . . . 2 . . . 1 . . ." and pushes me down the hall in the direction of the chatter of voices that rises in response.

In the room ahead, two teenage girls and a guy in his early twenties sit together on a jewel-encrusted sofa in a staged attitude of casualness, while three separate camera crews hover around them from different angles. A TV takes up most of the wall across from them, and the guy is flipping channels disinterestedly.

I could go on pretending that I don't know their names, but I don't live under a rock, so yeah, I do.

The guy with the gym muscle chest that makes him look too top-heavy to stand is Ace. The older girl in the too-red lipstick is Jackie, and the younger one dressed all in pink is Diamond.

"We can always order from the location in Amber City," Jackie's saying comfortingly, with her hand on Diamond's knee.

"But that's not *fair*," Diamond sniffles.

I hover for a moment, waiting for someone to do an introduction, then realize that the cameras are framed on me lurking behind them, and the whole crew's waiting for me to . . . I don't know, jump out and say, "surprise?"

Fine, let's get this over with.

"What's not fair?" I ask.

Three heads swivel toward me with artificial shock.

"Solar Flare!" Diamond leaps over the back of the sofa and jumps me with a hug. "We're so glad you're here! Everything's been so *scary* lately. People are talking about, like, killing us and stuff, and now they're breaking things and setting fires!"

"Yeah, don't worry," I say, because when someone threatens to kill a fifteen year old, you kind of have to say that. "No one's getting through me."

Then, because someone's finally giving me some actual details about the supposed danger they're in, I ask, "Who's lighting what on fire?"

"People, stuff," Jackie answers unhelpfully, pointing at the TV.

Ace changes channels past several breaking reports of violence and rioting spilling out of the Crescent, settling on one headline.

"Humanoid Rights Attorney and Philanthropist Murdered by Gene-Jobs."

Under a warning of disturbing imagery, a video plays, dimly lit but crystal clear, of four gene-jobs savagely beating a fifth.

The breath goes out of me when I recognize the unlucky fifth, long before the video ends and is helpfully replaced by a photo of him alive and well at a shelter fundraiser just weeks ago.

"*Quentin?*" I breathe, taking an uninvited seat on the armrest of the sofa, the jewels of which dig into my bare thighs.

"You knew him?" asks Jackie.

"Just a little," I mumble. "He was a good guy."

All three manned cameras in the room angle in on me, and I want to break each one of them into a million pieces. I want to ask Jacob what on earth he was thinking, springing this on me here.

But that's insane. He probably didn't even know that I knew Quentin, let alone that I'd show up today without having glanced at the news. That would be downright psychic.

"It's just so *mean* of them," Diamond laments.

"Yeah," I say softly. "Yeah, it is."

"I mean, I get that everyone's sad and angry about the murder and stuff, but what kind of monster wants to burn down Gidgette's?"

". . . What?" I try to recapture the train of the conversation.

Ace changes channels again, away from Quentin's face, across images of picket signs, gene-job rights slogans interspersed with slurs against not only gene-jobs but a dozen other groups, broken windows, looting, police shooting a fleeing suspect, and finally a Seaside boutique in flames. Gidgette's. I remember the place now.

They sell cheap purses for designer prices.

This is the image that refreshes Diamond's sniffles.

"What do you expect them to do, be reasonable?" says Ace. "They're barely better than animals."

"That's not true," I say. "There's no proof that gene bombs alter cognitive function." But the words come out flat as the clip plays again in the background, while one of the news anchors goes over some reports that the killers might have been regulars at the Julian Foundation shelters.

This is wrong. Quentin devoted his life to helping people. The exact people in that video. It doesn't make any sense.

Ace snorts and nods at the TV. "No proof, huh?"

I'm not having this conversation right now.

"If you want my help, I need to have a talk with your dad," I say firmly. "Now, please."

Apparently, all I had to do was ask on camera.

All three Card offspring point in the same direction.

"His office is seventh on the right," says Jackie.

If I stay another moment, I'll make a scene. I don't know what kind exactly, whether I'll pick an ill-planned fight with Ace or worse, accidentally agree with him, but either way it's sure to be immortalized.

Instead, I take the excuse to walk out of the shot. That is, I try to. The automated cameras watch me along the hallway.

"That was dead fish, kids," Jacob berates them behind me. "Ace, you'll fuck a hole in a durian fruit, would it kill you to give us a little heat? She's the first attractive girl you've been on camera within weeks who's not your sister. Just play it up, and we'll do a nice, steamy fight and make-up arc with you and Jessica when she gets back in town and finds out, 'kay?"

"I keep telling you, Jake, chicks who can fold me in half are never gonna be my thing."

I pause with my hand on the knob to Mayor Card's home office.

I can handle this.

I *can* handle this.

And whether I can or not, I have to handle this, right now, because the cameras are still rolling, and I can't allow footage to exist of the first female Solar Flare cowering away from the presence of Mayor William "The Conqueror" Card.

Do your job.

Be yourself.

Open the door, you silly girl.

I wouldn't have thought it possible, but his office turns out even harder on the eyes than the rest of the mansion. Pointless marble pillars turn the room into an obstacle course, while the walls themselves are almost covered floor to ceiling with pictures of him smiling and shaking hands with superheroes and celebrities.

The only picture not of him is to the left, out of frame of the cameras: a giant map of Pinnacle City as seen from space, with sections highlighted by hand in different colors and marked with pushpins.

Next to each pillar is a museum display case of jewels, or some other relics of bygone royalty, each gaudier than the last.

Flanked by two massive oil paintings of him looking somber yet powerful (each cutting a generous ten inches off his waistline, at least), Mayor Card himself sits behind a desk of black marble, looking even more like a slab of melted plastic than he does on TV. His withered face is starched and painted with more Botox and makeup than any of the ladies in my mom's philanthropy club, and his thinning hair is so black that it looks like he's resorted to dipping the back of his head in permanent ink every morning to keep the passage of time at bay. The reflection of his upper half in the desk's bright finish gives the calculated illusion of a reversible, two-headed playing card king.

He's looking intently at something he's writing with a hawk feather quill, as if I've caught him unawares in the middle of some important business, but judging by the cameraman waiting with his lens aimed at the doorway to follow me in, I doubt this.

No fewer than six armed security personnel are positioned around the perimeter of the room, observing.

I don't wait for an introduction this time, just clear my throat. Card looks up and puts his quill in its ornate stand. It's already dripped all over the place.

"Solar Girl," he says, in a voice with the same maxed-out volume he uses on TV. "Great of you to make the time. Just terrific!"

I try to reconcile the *being myself* part of me that's spent years wanting to kick this man in the shins, and the *doing my job* part that probably has to represent the Guardians with a certain level of courtesy and decorum. I ultimately manage to summon an extra dose of friendliness I do my best to save up for people who make friendliness especially difficult.

"Solar *Flare*, actually," I correct him cheerfully, as if it happens all the time. "And no trouble. The PCG take *all* threats of violence seriously."

I shake his hand, which has a pinkie ring with a diamond-shaped setting and smears of spilled ink on it, and then float myself comfortably in the air, because there's no chair on this side of the desk.

"Of course. You're Ethan's girl, aren't you?"

I think my uncle had some dealings with Card back before he went into politics, but we've never been introduced.

"His niece," I acknowledge.

"And even lovelier than he always said you were. It's a pleasure to have you. I'm a big lover of the superheroes, I hope you know."

"No, I didn't know that," I say with a smirk, eying the many superhero pictures on his walls.

"Oh, you'll never find a bigger lover of superheroes than me."

So, in that rant he gave last week about how supers are stealing the natural power of *real* people (his words, not mine), I guess he only meant the supers who aren't famous.

I bite my tongue.

"The kids will feel so much safer from all those animals out there with a superhero on the job," Card continues. "You know how they can be. All the bodyguards in the world just make them feel more singled out, but if there's a cape involved, they know everything's going to be okay, and who can put a price on the best for my kids?"

I almost point out that two of his "kids" are legally adults, but I stop, because I'm invulnerable and they're not, and however ridiculously worked up they may get about having to order overpriced purses from the next city over, maybe it's not fair for me to judge their feelings about their personal safety.

"We do what we can," I say.

"It's nice that you're so close to their age, too. As traumatized as they've been by all this persecution, it doesn't seem to stop them from doing stupid things." He chuckles as if he expects me to join in this indulgent criticism of the intelligence of young people in general, right after he's aptly pointed out that I'm one of them. "Truthfully, they need the most protecting from themselves, and if anyone can give them that, it'd be you. They might even listen to someone like you."

"Mr. Mayor, I . . . appreciate your wanting the best for your family. But you need to understand that the PCG are responsible for an entire city of families. I'm not your employee," I tell him this nicely, like breaking bad news. "I'm also not a nanny, or an actress, or a pet. I'm going to be here until the danger to you is neutralized or subsides, and no longer. You might want to prepare your *kids*. Just so they don't end up disappointed."

"Of course, of course, we'll figure it out if it comes to that," he says, which is the exact opposite of what I just suggested.

"So about the danger *other* than themselves . . ." I prompt, and Card pulls a sheaf of envelopes addressed to himself from the desk drawer and places them between us.

"It's shocking, how these dregs of society will terrorize a law-abiding family," he says seriously.

I pick up the envelopes, and Card turns his quill around once in its stand.

The cameraman takes this as a signal, powers down, and angles his lens to the floor.

"It's off?" Card verifies.

"Yes, sir," says the cameraman.

"All right, tell her the score, Sergei," Card says to one of the guards standing around the room.

Sergei takes a tablet from one of the room's locked cabinets, shows me a map of the estate's extensive security system, and runs me through the various alarms and what will trip them, which I suppose is something that probably shouldn't be detailed on TV.

"Looks pretty exhaustive."

"It is," says Sergei, and I get the sense that Card's dissatisfaction with his protection alone is as irksome to him as it is to me.

"Not against my enemies with superpowers," says Card. "The *bad* supers, of course," he adds to me, as if that explains everything.

"Well, you're set against intangibles and teleporters," I tell him, looking over the security specs. "It doesn't look like anything's going to sneak past your team here, and once any intruders are detected, they won't muscle past me, even if they're bulletproof."

At least the part of this assignment about keeping the Cards alive won't be difficult.

"Do any of the letters suggest anything about the sender having access to particular abilities we should account for?" I ask, starting to open the first envelope of the sizeable stack.

"See for yourself," says Card, opening the laptop on his desk and beckoning me over.

When I get it open, the envelope is empty. Card chuckles.

"The paper looks good on film, but hardly any of these deviants take the time to write their attacks down anymore."

I float around the desk to look over his shoulder and have to lean in close to read the tiny font setting of his inbox.

He takes his hand off the mouse to give me room and rests it instead at the small of my back.

My skin's been crawling more than enough since I set foot in this house, and I have half a mind to tell him to back up and give me some air, but I'm sure those cameras can be turned back on at a moment's notice, and that's one more scene I'd rather not make.

I focus on scanning the screen quickly and find exactly what I was afraid of: a folder full of angry email subject lines, all from different addresses, all angry for slightly different reasons, calling him a Nazi, a pig, an idiot, a villain, a psychopath, and a variety of other titles of varying accuracy.

This isn't evidence of a single stalker or criminal group. This is just the public inbox of an intensely divisive and inflammatory public figure, and not something that's going to change in time for me to get in on the PCG's next big trafficking sting.

"This isn't going to be a simple fix," I warn Card, scanning my cursor farther down the inbox.

"I have faith in you," says Card, sliding his hand farther down my back.

In a protracted instant of unreality, driven more by blind hope than reason, I almost manage to believe that the movement is unconscious on his part, a mistake, that he'll notice and pull away at any second, or vanish into a crowd never to be heard from again, the way my occasional obnoxious fans sometimes do.

Then he slides a fingertip under the back edge of my leotard's oversized leg hole, runs it along the inside of the hem, and finally snaps the stretchy fabric against my skin.

The protracted instant continues, lengthened by my superhuman reflexes. Within that frozen, stunned moment between two ticks of a clock, I'm able to take stock of his hand, still resting on my butt where the spandex struck, now caught in the middle of a follow-up squeeze. I read his face next to mine, observing me, *checking* on me, checking that I understand something.

I do.

Shaking off my shock, I send an energy charge down through my body and into his hand with a firework *crack*. With a yelp synchronized to Card's own, I leap away, all within a plausible human reaction time.

Thank you, reflexes.

Sergei draws his gun a million years late in response to the sound, and I pretend not to notice.

"Oh my gosh!" I rush back over to Card, who's rolling his desk chair away from me, cradling his hand.

I didn't use enough force to break it, but he won't be touching anyone, including himself, with it for at least a week while the blistered skin grows back.

"Oh my gosh, I am so, so sorry!" I lie. "That happens sometimes when I'm startled. Are you okay?"

Before Card can answer me, half a dozen more guards charge into the room, their guns also drawn.

"Is everything all right, sir?" the lead guard asks, looking around in confusion. "I heard gunfire, and screams."

Card's looking at me, and so is the cameraman, and Sergei and his team, all waiting to see what I'm going to make this into.

The truth tempts me for half a second, but I change my mind at the prospect of having to file a report. That would mean Pinnacle finding out, and there's no way I'm running back to him after this morning's briefing to whine about how the bad man who can't physically hurt me touched me in a naughty place.

I answer the guard with a giggle. "Oh, nothing like that. Just a little misunderstanding." I pretend that smiling at Card is the same thing as spitting on him, and smile with according vigor. "But I think we understand each other now, don't we?"

CHAPTER 9: THE DETECTIVE

Even through the rain you can smell all the fires.

The biggest blazes are all in the WPC wreckage, mostly transforming rubble into more rubble, but there are a few fires out here in the Crescent too. Whether they were set by protestors or hate-filled assholes, I can't say.

What I know for sure, though, is that Ruby didn't give the footage I shot to the police.

No, she took the easier path to justice and gave it to the media a few minutes after dumping it all online, and the Internet working the way it does best rolled with it from there.

Mayor Card took the murder of respected EPC citizen Quentin Julian as a rallying cry, calling it a vindication of everything he's said about the danger of gene-jobs and the cesspool they call home. Standing in front of blown-up pictures of the four unidentified attackers, he urged all "true heroes" to not let this crime go unpunished.

He might as well have put a bounty on their heads.

While the Guardians vowed to be vigilant in the wake of such a "terrible crime" (including *her*), a lot of people found a pretty funny definition of "true heroes."

Violent crimes against gene-jobs in particular, but non-humans in general, are all over the place. There are gangs of EPC kids in Card for Senate hats just driving through the Crescent and WPC like goddamn old west posses, stopping and beating the shit out of gene-jobs, aliens, Lemurians, Atlanteans, and any super whose power makes them look vaguely non-human. One of these gangs had the misfortune of trying to take on Petting Zoo, who showed them what it was like to be on the receiving end of a timber wolf attack.

The cops have been out in force, allegedly to deal with the violence, but mostly adding to it, turning a blind eye to the Card for Senate hat-wearing crowd while hassling Crescent people harder than ever. At least three unarmed Crescent citizens have been shot by cops already for "resisting arrest," with one dying.

The way things are going, he won't be the last.

Mayor Card didn't waste any time calling on a special DSA task force to round up and imprison unlicensed supers. While my paperwork's in order, I've seen their heavily armored vans patrolling the streets, and the Lemurian restaurant next door to my office closed down after one raid cleaned out most of their kitchen staff. I fear for Tragedii; she won't be born for another sixty-odd years and is the definition of unlicensed, but she's not taking this as a serious problem.

Considering when she's come from, she's seen worse.

The feeling in the Crescent has been one of defiance, even if no one can agree how to respond. There's a lot of people arguing for peace and accountability from authorities and the EPC crowd, and god bless Fadia for giving them the biggest voice with her program, but even with their peaceful protest plans, there's a lot of others who don't want to stop there.

People in the Crescent are used to fights, and they won't back down.

Their way of demanding peace has been trying to take their fight to EPC by force, staging violent protests that are mostly an excuse to throw things at the police and set stuff on fire. Burning police cars and DSA vans are almost as common a sight as cell phones.

I don't blame them for being angry, because they got every reason to be with all this shit going down, but I want to yell at them that what they're doing isn't helping and only gives more ammunition to Card and his cronies.

I want to believe the rumor Tragedii told me that Milgram's been sending goons out into the Crescent to encourage chaos, but that's probably just wishful thinking.

I know that the real blame sits with me.

There were so many threads to the case I didn't pull on, so many things I thought, *knew*, were off, and I didn't look into them because I just wanted a quick check so I could go home and get drunk.

I didn't vet her intentions well enough. I didn't read her like I should have.

And now the Crescent burns because of me.

I can't fix this.

But I can do my best to drown it out.

✳

The rain's pouring so hard my headlights barely cut through the torrent, but I don't need their light.

Not when I know the way to the Lineup by memory.

It's late, and the Crescent around me is not a Crescent I know. It's dark and, even stranger, it's quiet. I recognize the shops and the streets, but it's a ghost town even by rainy night standards.

Then again, when you see businesses with broken windows and words like GENE FREAKS FUCK OFF spray-painted on them, you get a pretty good idea how things get this way.

A beer can, full by the sounds of it, smashes against my windshield, cracking it.

"Fuck!"

A voice outside screams, "TRAITOR!"

Another can hits my side-view mirror, knocking it almost clean off.

I floor it, getting the hell out of dodge before I find out if the guy bought a six-pack or a case.

It's been like this around here ever since things started going to shit. I don't know how the news spread so quickly, but the Crescent's been letting me know how much it doesn't like me getting the Julian evidence. Mostly it's been people looking at me funny on the street, but some have gotten in my face.

And I can't say that this guy's the first to forcibly redecorate my car.

Whoever slashed my tires this morning got that honor.

This isn't the first home to reject me, but it hurts a lot more than last time.

Speeding away, I'm turned around, not entirely sure where I am, but when I slam on the brakes I know what's before me: chaos.

There's at least thirty people fighting, the flickering flames of some of the attackers' Tiki torches and the dully rotating lights of a few cop cars shining through the darkness. I can't tell who's fighting or why, if it's locals or outsiders, but I can see who's stuck in the middle.

Dissident.

She's fighting with the ferocity of an army, whirling and kicking and striking attackers with her clubs. She tosses explosives, blades, even her own cape at the mob, yet no matter how many she takes down the others get even angrier. She won't give up until there's not an ounce of fight left in her body, but even from here I know she's tiring. She should use her grappling hook gun to escape, catch her breath, but instead she uses it to snare one attacker and whip him into another.

A beefy guy with a burnt-out torch in one hand sneaks up behind her, a large chunk of broken cinderblock in his other hand. He raises it over his head.

I do the only thing I can.

I floor it.

The guy bounces off my hood and rolls over the top. He lands beside my car, still alive, but I'll probably be investigating him for insurance fraud in a year or so.

Dissident whirls on me for a second, the eyes of her helmet sharpening.

I throw the passenger's side door open and yell, "Get in!"

Dissident considers the fight for only a second before jumping in. I gun it in reverse, watching the dark, angry mob continue fighting, some of them throwing things at us as we escape.

"Just so you know," Dissident says, taking off her helmet. "I had that fight in hand."

"Obviously."

Fadia flips down the vanity mirror by her seat, eying the blood trickling down the side of her lip. "Makeup guys are going to *love* me tomorrow morning."

"They still believe your self-defense class story?"

"For now," she says, testing her shoulder's mobility and wincing. "But if it keeps going like this . . ."

"How bad is it?"

"Bad."

"Like, *bad* bad, or *repent all sins* bad?"

"Bad to a point where I doubt there'll be anything left west of the Crescent if this keeps up much longer. Bad where I predict this will turn into a fight for the right to WPC's ashes between Milgram and Mayor Card. Bad where the person who set this in motion will do nothing to fix it, and everything to let it spiral out of control."

She won't look at me.

"So you agree that I'm to blame?"

"For doing your job? No. You're a hired thug with a gift for the past, and you did your job wonderfully. For not using common sense? Yes."

"Thanks," I say, unable to keep the sarcasm in.

"Well, what did you expect? You know how tenuous things are in the Crescent, better than most do, and you hand someone a bomb like this to blow it apart with?"

"Like you said, it was a job. *Just* a job. She said she was going to the cops. I thought she was legit."

"If you'd brought it to me first—"

"I *thought* she was legit!"

"Because you wanted to fuck her?"

"What, you're saying you've never fucked up because you wanted to impress a leggy blonde?"

"No. But I've never let things get this bad because of it, either."

"You're saying I should fix this?"

"Yes."

"How? The town's on fire and, if you haven't noticed, I'm no firefighter."

"This is one of those things you'll have to figure out on your own. But don't be surprised at people's reactions to you either until you do."

Fadia's a friend, but I'm not in the mood for a lecture. All my life I've had people telling me what to do with my powers, and every time I've listened I've wound up in a world of hurt. So if people want to be pissed, fine, let them be pissed, but they can't tell me how to live my life.

"Where're you headed? The Lineup?" she asks after the silence stretches too long.

"Where else? Want me to drop you off somewhere?"

She takes a second. "The Lineup's fine. Lucero should be there tonight; I can probably beg, bribe, or beat a healing charm out of him."

"And Petting Zoo having a shift tonight has nothing to do with this?"

Fadia smiles. "She does? I had no idea."

The humor in her voice tells me all I need to know; the sharp edge tells me I'm far from being off the hook.

I'll take what I can get.

✳

The Lineup's about the closest thing to looking alive in the Crescent tonight, if just by the virtue of having a lit sign. When I pull into the lot, I see what looks like a welcome sight at first. Tragedii's standing in the doorway like she's waiting for us.

It doesn't stay welcome for long.

She runs up to my car, her personal shield generator wicking the rain away in a spherical bubble, and motions for me to roll the window down.

"Can't let you in tonight, Eddie."

"What? Isn't it group tonight? If it's about my tab—"

"That's not why," she says. "Hey, Dissident."

"Hey," Dissident says, helmet back on.

I grip the steering wheel tightly.

"I'm really not welcome?"

"Not tonight. Not when people's blood's up like it is now. Me, I don't care, but I can't have my bar fucked up because of this. People in there . . . they want a safe place tonight, no cops, no DSA, no fights . . ."

I don't want to beg, but I will if I have to.

"Tragedii, come on. You know me. When you had problems with those Atlantean tweakers, who helped you out?" I plead.

"And I appreciated that. But it still stands on tonight. I'm sorry."

A door opens and closes, and Dissident's no longer at my side. She strides past Tragedii through the pouring rain, calling back to me, "Remember what I said!"

Tragedii doesn't have much to offer other than a shrug.

Then she runs into the bar and out of the rain.

I can't tell what I am more, pissed or sad, and by the time I figure out it doesn't matter. I'm just trying not to start punching my car.

Everything I've done, everything I've tried to do, even when I thought I knew what was right and wrong, it all turned to shit. I do one thing, one *stupid* thing that I think might be me making something right, and it fucks up my whole life.

"Fucking figures," I mutter.

I don't want to go home. My apartment's a dump on the best of days, and with the rain like it is and the Crescent not doing itself any favors right now, odds are my power's out.

And I'm out of liquor. I think.

I park the car (or what's left of it) and cross the street to my office. I keep a couple emergency bottles on hand, and the way the building's lit up, I know there'll be power. Maybe I can fire up my ancient computer, watch a movie, get nice and lit . . .

Trying to will the ache out of my left arm by resting it on Harriet, sheathed in one of my coat's inner pockets, I unlock the front door, get in and lock it behind me, for all the good it'll do.

What used to be my front window is now a couple sheets of plywood with some duct tape to give it personality, courtesy of the asshole yesterday who thought a chunk of concrete parking bumper would look better hurled through the glass than out in the parking lot. Whether they were part of the same group who decided to repaint my walls with the conflicting messages of TRAITOR and GET OUT SUPER FAAG (correcting their spelling was my contribution), I couldn't tell you.

I'm just glad they didn't steal anything.

Sitting down at my desk, I boot up my computer and slide open the bottom drawer. From it I pull a tumbler and a bottle of cheap scotch, pouring myself a drink.

"I hope you have a second glass."

The voice comes from behind. I deserve an award for keeping my cool.

"Hello, Miss Herron."

She saunters out of the darkness of my back office. The bright red dress she wears is more fitting for a night out on the town than a cold winter rainstorm. She picks the glass of scotch off my desk and takes a sip, grimacing.

"For what I paid you, you can afford a little better than *that*," she says, putting it back on my desk.

"I have cheap taste."

"Especially in door locks," she says, eying the wreck of my office, amused.

Well, that explains how she got in.

"What are you doing here?" I ask, tightening my grip on Harriet. I don't want to have to pull her out, but I've no idea why Ruby's here or why she keeps her hand in her purse.

"The man I work for was impressed with your efficiency on the Julian issue."

"The man you work for? Found yourself a new boss already?"

She laughs. "It'll make sense when I tell you, but you probably won't like it."

"And why's that?"

"Because I know how much you hate surprises."

"You seem to know an awful lot about me."

"I do."

"You got your own people looking into me?"

"I've been watching you for quite some time now. Seeing if you were as ready as I thought you were."

"Funny, I think I would have noticed if you were watching me."

"Let's just say I'm good at blending in."

"Oh, really?" I say, tightening my grip on Harriet. My left hand aches. I need a pill bad, but I need to end this, too.

"Yes," she says, pulling something from her purse.

I kick away from my desk and am on my feet in a flash, Harriet in hand and about to charge.

She doesn't even flinch as she pulls the folded piece of paper from her purse. I stop in my tracks but don't lower Harriet an inch.

"Are you going to swing that, or would you like me to explain what's really going on?"

"What's in your hand?" I ask, eying the paper.

She unfolds it to reveal an old, well-traveled picture. It takes me a moment to soak it all in, and a moment past that to realize I have a copy of it framed beside my desk: a picture of three teenagers who don't know the horrors their future holds.

"What—" I start to say, before Ruby Herron starts to twist, her body slimming and lengthening slightly, her dress disappearing into her now scaled, light violet skin, replaced by a short-sleeved black leotard. She's taller than the last time I saw her, and has filled out somewhat too, but she is otherwise the same. Still lithe, still with muted features, still with those solid black eyes that always terrified people, but that I fell in love with back in the day.

Anya Rosales.

Bystander.

"Surprised, Eddie?" she asks, her voice now familiar.

I don't know what to do. So instead of knowing what to do, I take her in. I take her in because it feels like if I don't, I may never get another chance. The more I take her in, the less I feel the anger toward Ruby and the more I remember of us as kids. Before I know it, Harriet's on the floor and I find myself with my arms wrapped around her neck, laughing.

The world itself has given in to shit and chaos, but seeing her here, now, makes everything feel like it used to.

I start babbling as more than a decade's worth of thoughts about her all fight to the surface.

"I thought you were—"

"I wasn't."

"But you never—"

"We were on different paths."

"I should've—"

"I'm glad to see you too," she says dryly, pushing away from me. "And there will be plenty of time to catch up later. But I'm here on business."

Reality hits me like a bolt of light. Every memory of Ruby Herron and the Julian job comes rushing back and has me questioning everything that's happened in the past few weeks.

I step back, try not to wobble on my nervous feet, try to keep the hard edge that's served me well all these years, and find it's not as easy as it was moments ago. My shell has become soft, and I'm a teenage boy trying to ask a pretty girl out for the first time all over again.

"You've got some stuff to explain," I say.

"I know."

"Like, now?"

"Not now."

"Then why are you here?"

"To tell you that, whatever you think you know, you don't. That you've become a part of something big. That this job I gave you was actually an audition. You did so well, my boss wants to meet you in person."

The corners of her muted, slit of a mouth curve upward in an unsettling approximation of a smile.

"Eddie, I think it's time you met Mr. Milgram."

CHAPTER 10: THE SUPERHERO

He knew the risks, working out there with those people," Mom reminds me. "I'm sure he accepted that something like this could happen."

"Just like we do in the PCG," Uncle Ethan agrees.

It's just the three of us sitting around the corner table at Dorabella's for lunch, and it seems I was the last to find out about what happened to Quentin.

"Yeah, I know," I say, "but I can't stop wondering what kind of new project he was working on. I keep picturing people out there waiting for whatever kind of help he was bringing, realizing it's not coming. Do you think maybe we could hold a benefit in his honor, for the Julian Foundation? Make sure the shelters don't end up closing down without him?"

"It's a thought," my mother says, noncommittally.

"Might not be a bad idea, once you've had time to make some connections in the big leagues who wouldn't mind you calling in a favor," says Uncle Ethan with overflowing pride, passing me the equally overflowing bread basket. "Nothing would bring people out in droves like a few Guardian guests of honor. How's the team agreeing with you so far?"

Mom snags a tiny end piece as the basket passes her and then leans in over the table to listen.

I take a slice, dip it in the pesto, and take a giant bite. This is my first afternoon off since joining the Guardians, and I was hoping to consume at least half my body weight in refined carbohydrates before having to think about the Card family again, but there's no delaying this question for long.

"It's an adjustment," I say, holding my hand in front of my full mouth.

"How's Pinnacle treating you?" Mom prods.

"He's . . . direct."

Uncle Ethan laughs. "He can take some getting used to, that's for certain. Trust me, if he's already speaking to you at all, he likes you."

I debate for a moment, then decide I'd rather they find out from me than on TV.

"He's got me protecting Mayor Card," I say, drowning another slice of bread while the two of them exchange whatever kind of look they feel like exchanging. "I'm working my way up, I guess."

This is the conclusion I've come to over the past week of babysitting the Card offspring, trying to give Jacob as little usable footage as possible, avoiding being dragged into their conversations about their cars, their vacation plans, their significant others, and how darn *hard* it is being them.

I'm paying my dues. I'm the rookie, so I'm the one stuck with the cruddy jobs no one wants. That *has* to be what this is.

It sucks right now, but it's also a relief, not only because it means things have to get better from here, but also because it means that the other Guardians *know* this is a cruddy job that no one in their right mind would want, which means they're sane, which is good.

Maybe they even have some secret reason why watching Card is more important than they're telling me, something they're not ready to trust me with yet, and sending me to take care of it instead of one of the more senior members is their way of showing him they're only helping under protest.

"Oh, I don't know," says Mom. "Stopping the mayor from being assassinated sounds like a job for a Pinnacle City Guardian to me."

"He's not just 'the mayor,' he's Mayor *Card*," I say.

There's a big difference.

"Which makes it a job worthy of ATHENA herself," jokes Uncle Ethan. "Don't sell yourself short, Kimmy."

The food arrives and I pause with my fork over my veggie linguini. "How did you ever do business with that man?"

"He's a pill, no denying that," says Uncle Ethan. "But he does have a knack for motivating a certain class of people."

"Yeah, bullies," I mutter, twisting my fork around my plate.

Card's practically the official mascot of all the worst people still roughing up the streets more than a week after the details of Quentin's murder went public, the ones shouting things like "burn the gene freaks" and "we want no man's land" and other things I choose not to repeat.

I should be out there stopping them, or protecting one of the peaceful protests that are finally getting organized and gaining steam among all the random violence, but instead I'm trying to catch my breath for an hour so I can go back to watching Card's overgrown brats and boosting his ratings with the novelty of having a superhero on his show, no matter how unwatchable I try to be.

"People will get bored with him eventually," says Uncle Ethan. "And then they'll move on to the next loud voice that validates them. It's how it always goes. But let's hope it's not too soon."

"How can you *say* that?"

"Because as long as they're in his pocket, they're predictable. They'll do what he tells them to, say what he tells them to, wear what he tells them to, so they're easy to spot and, most importantly, *buy* what he tells them to. If there was ever a bunch of people who deserved a good fleecing . . ."

"Positively Machiavellian." Mom rolls her eyes, blowing on her mussels marinara with a discreet puff of her ice powers.

"Say what you want about Machiavelli, he was a hell of a strategist," adds Uncle Ethan.

"Or *satirist*," I say through a mouthful of pasta, recalling a college lit class I probably haven't thought of since finals, and crossing my fingers that Uncle Ethan either hasn't heard this one or has forgotten.

I win my bet.

"Do tell," he says.

"Rousseau theorized that *The Prince* was supposed to be a joke. It might have been like Jonathan Swift's *A Modest Proposal* for its time."

Huh. I must've been paying more attention that semester than I thought.

Good for me.

"Really?" says Uncle Ethan, delighted. "That's fascinating. Look at us, discussing sixteenth century political philosophy over a family lunch. I feel so continental!"

Uncle Ethan has simple enough tastes, but I've never yet discovered the lure powerful enough to distract Mom from asking follow up questions about my day.

"Seriously though, sweetie, he's just a person, right? Mayor Card, I mean?" she squeezes my elbow across the table.

Oh well, it was nice while it lasted.

"Has his good points and his bad points like everyone else?" she pushes. "I mean, no one could ever be that character we see in his speeches."

The urge to tell someone about what happened in Card's office surfaces again, and maybe someday I'll indulge it—with a therapist sworn to secrecy, perhaps—but it won't help anything here and now.

I'm not sure which would be worse, watching my mother and uncle imagining their little Kimmy in that position, knowing that they can't do anything about it, or having them *try* to do something about it.

The image of my famous namesake uncle, or worse, my *mother*, going to ask Pinnacle to transfer me to an assignment better suited to my fragile little feelings gives me worse shudders than the thought of doing it myself.

It'd be freshman year all over again.

Anyway, Card hasn't tried to put his hands on me again after that first time. I've got that part of my problem handled, all by myself.

"I guess so," I tell Mom.

This doesn't wholly assure her, so she tries another angle.

"Well, I'm sure he's very busy," she says. "You probably don't have to see much of him?"

"No, not that much."

"Have you made any friends working there?"

"Well, his son owns the Silver Cowl, so the kids go there a lot when I'm guarding them," I say. "Some of the servers there are pretty cool."

"Oh, honey," Mom puts her hand over her mouth as if that's the saddest thing she's ever heard. "Is the whole family really that awful?"

"Yesterday, Anastasia—that's his wife, she's about my age—she asked me to help her process a shipment of Gucci shoes to a westside shelter. She said if the homeless had some pretty things of their own, maybe they'd stop breaking windows downtown. She's the *nice* one."

Mom keeps a hand over her mouth, now to stifle laughter.

"Did you do it for her?"

"I may have made a teeny-weeny counter-suggestion that the same donation to the Julian Foundation would translate to roughly a bajillion blankets or a half bajillion hours of free legal counsel, but she made it very clear that it was her dime. Then she called in her social media consultant to take stills of us packing the boxes. Did I mention she's the nice one?"

Mom waits for the giggles to subside so she can employ a bit of sympathy when she answers.

"I'm sure they don't make it easy on you. But don't take this wrong now, maybe that's for the best."

I raise an eyebrow.

Mom raises her hands as if she's backing off, but she's not. "I only mean, getting along with people has always come so easily to you. It might be good for you to have to work for it a bit, just this once."

"It's not easy getting along with them, because I don't *want* to get along with them."

"Well, maybe there's a lesson in that, too," she says. "Getting along with people when you'd rather not is a valuable skill. No matter how you feel about them, there'll rarely be a time when you'll be sorry you gave someone good feelings about *you*. Especially someone in a position with as much sway as the mayoral family."

"The *Card* family," I repeat. "Why don't I just stick a Jovium needle in my eye?"

"Consider it the ultimate challenge for your considerable charms?" Uncle Ethan proposes lightly.

I put my fork down.

My throat is stinging and tightening, and I don't want it to. I don't want to dissolve into a sulky mess like Diamond Card when she's told she can't go shopping today, not when my family's just trying to be optimistic for me.

My fragile little feelings in action.

But I'm tired and frustrated and off-camera for the first time in what feels like ever, and if we *have* to spend my break talking about this, can't they at least be on my side about it?

"You're making it sound like I'm not trying."

"Of course you're trying!" Mom backtracks.

"I'm sure you've been an angel of patience," says Uncle Ethan. "I only meant to—"

My phone alarm spares them the effort of coddling me.

God, what now?

At double speed, I check the Card security app that should theoretically eliminate the need for me to patrol the mansion at all, given how quickly I can respond to any problem by air—try telling Card that—and find a red alert.

"Gotta go, there's been a breach."

I don't wait to explain more, and Mom and Uncle Ethan don't expect me to. Even though Dad wasn't super and Mom's never put on a cape of her own, we're still a superhero family. We all know how it goes.

✳

Sergei's already jogging out to the gate to meet me when I get there, suited up, inside of twenty seconds. He's followed at some distance by Jacob and a full camera team.

"Have you seen anything?" I ask Sergei as soon as we're within shouting distance. "Is everyone accounted for?"

"No, and no," says Sergei, disgruntled, releasing the gate lock for me. "It seems Mr. Card the younger may have tripped the alarm on his way out. We currently have no eyes on him." He looks at Jacob as though this is his fault.

"Ace *ran away*?" I ask, landing between the two of them.

Jacob's attending cameraman zooms in on me, and I can already hear my words being edited into the teaser for next week's episode.

"Does anyone have any guesses where?" I ask.

"Not yet," says Jacob, thoroughly enthused by this turn of events. "But all we have to do is watch his film crew's cloud uploads, and we'll know in a few minutes."

"So he didn't leave the perimeter alone?" I ask, relieved. I'm not messing up the easy, keep-everyone-alive part of this mission.

"He didn't bring a security escort," says Sergei, crossing his arms.

"Meaning he gave your team the slip," says Jacob, almost proudly. "But every member of the Card family has their own mini film crew on their personal payroll. That way, no matter what any of them does, they *never* have to hide it from the cameras, because the crews are always on their side. And every one of those crews freelances for me."

I've already learned better than to try to get Jacob to give his stupid show a rest for five minutes and think about a little thing like security.

"Fine," I say. "We check your cloud. Well, what are you waiting for?"

Jacob leads us to his office in the mansion's backhouse, claiming we'll get faster access from his desktop than his tablet.

The chair he offers me is in front of one of the same red curtains as the mansion's confessional stalls, and as soon as he's shown me the cloud folder and its lack of recent uploads from Ace's team, he signals his own trailing cameraman over to me.

"Nothing yet," he says, "but it won't be long. Would you like to share some of what you're feeling while we wait?"

"No."

"Would you say that you and Ace have formed a connection in the short time you've spent together?"

"No, I wouldn't."

"Would you say that you feel a certain professional responsibility for him?"

"Of course I do. It's my job."

"That's good! Good, but remember, contextualize your own remarks. The audience won't hear my voice, so try it again, and this time start with, 'I feel a certain professional responsibility for Ace.'"

"Click the refresh button, Jake."

"Or in your own words—"

"Click it."

Sergei stands in the corner looking so amused with Jacob's frustration that for a moment I forget him standing there in Card's office on my first day, with the cameras off, doing nothing, and doing nothing, and then pulling his gun on me.

But only for a moment.

When Jacob finally refreshes the folder, it's there, a new upload from Ace's team.

Sergei pushes Jacob aside to play the clip before I can do the same. Ace's perpetual smirk dominates the screen.

"This is the best paintball rifle money can buy," he says, holding up said paintball gun to the camera. "These," he opens his hand, "are ball bearings. And *that*," he points over his shoulder at the building ledge behind him, "is what 'asking for it' looks like."

At his direction, his cameraman focuses on the park beyond the ledge, and the demonstrators gathered in it.

Jobs, not cages, says the first picket sign that comes into view.

Humanoid rights.

REGISTRATION = SUBJUGATION

Stop killing our children.

"Damnit, Ace!" Jacob yells at the screen in exasperation. "You know your dad's not gonna let us show you doing that!"

I'm already on my phone, checking the location of the rally.

"Go on," Jacob sighs, waving me off. "Bring him home."

"I didn't ask your permission. Send a car," I tell Sergei, jotting down the address. "I'll meet you there."

✻

Judging by the level of chaos at the rally, I'm guessing there's about a minute's delay on the cloud uploads.

I can't see Ace yet, but he's not the only one here to cause trouble. Another group in Card for Senate hats has converged on the planned rally crowd and is throwing trash and rocks, trying to break up their ranks.

The rally crowd is refusing to disperse, but they're holding up their signs like shields, standing shoulder to shoulder in a mass and chanting with increased ferocity.

"We won't be put down! We won't be put down!"

Most of them are gene-jobs, but not all. I spot some Grays, some Lemurians, a few of what look like unaltered humans, and a little girl who seems to be manipulating the earth to raise a crude shelter around a woman with compound eyes, who's bleeding from a welt on her cheek.

A steel ball pings off a park bench at the front of the mass, and it's not hard to trace where it came from.

The next shot bounces harmlessly off my sternum when I hover level with Ace Card, perched on the roof of an adjacent hotel.

Surprise, surprise, it's a Royal Flush Inn. Card property. The staff probably gave him the run of the place as soon as he dropped his dad's name.

"Give me the gun, Ace."

"Oh, come on, sunshine," says Ace, with the not-quite-sheepish grin he gets when he's caught. "It's not even a real gun. It's a toy, see? I was just playing with—"

I snatch it out of his hands when he holds it up to show me its orange-tipped barrel, and turn it around to aim at his chest.

He cowers sensibly.

"You're right! This is fun!" I give him my sweetest in-lieu-of-spitting smile. "How do I unload it?"

With a breath of relief, he points. "You just slide the—"

I send a crackle of energy through the whole frame of the gun, shattering it in my hands.

"The fuck!" protests Ace.

"Oops." I shrug.

"You know what? This is bullshit!" he exclaims, cheating his face toward the rolling cameras as he points his finger at me. "I'm a grown-ass man and I don't need some Mary Poppins wannabe telling me what to do with *my* life!"

"You're a playful little scamp who doesn't know any better, or you're a grown man who doesn't need a sitter," I say, putting a finger to my chin in mock confusion. "Hmm. Maybe you should pick one lie and stick to it?"

"You should be thanking me, bitch!" He jabs his finger as close to my chest as he can without falling over the edge. "I just justified your pathetic salary! If I decided to be good all the time, you'd spend all your time sitting on my couch, getting fat. Sorry, *fatter*."

"*Thank you*," I say, darting forward a few feet onto the rooftop so that he has to scramble back. "Dragging you out of here by the ear like a bad schoolboy is going to be my favorite thing I've done all week."

I don't even care right now if some neutered version of this footage ends up hitting the air or if it only keeps Jacob up for a few nights, pulling his hair out over not being able to show a good shouting match without incriminating his star.

I point to the roof access doorway. "Downstairs. Now."

Ace doesn't move.

"Fine."

"Hey!" he yelps when I throw him over my shoulder like a sack of potatoes and take to the air.

"You can't take him out of the shot!" his cameraman objects.

"Eat my sparkles, Tom."

"Put me down!" Ace writhes and kicks at me for a few seconds, then realizes how high off the ground we are and changes his mind. "Put me down, I'll walk. I'll *walk*!"

"Too late. Hide your face . . . or don't."

I fly us over the rally and, for a moment, I can almost pretend that I'm taking him to the police the way I would have on the Juniors, instead of home to his mansion. I can almost pretend that I'm protecting the chanting demonstrators from *him*, instead of protecting him from *them*, from being identified or arrested or, horror of horrors, *embarrassed* during his dad's delicate senatorial campaign.

Almost.

I turn back toward the main rally crowd and put my hands over my chest in the shape of a heart, making them glow with purple light.

My heart is with you.

I don't think they believe me.

CHAPTER 11: THE DETECTIVE

The only supervillain I ever worked for called himself Padre Peligro. If you feel bad for not having heard about him, don't. Few have. He could generate concussive waves from his hands that could hurt if you stood still, but his ambitions were greater than his powers. He was probably the only person surprised when the PCG finally caught up to him, and he probably wouldn't have died if he'd just decided to go quietly.

If there's one thing he was good at, it was networking. He viewed himself as the first major post War on Villainy villain, and knew that it helped to have a good network of loyal lieutenants, henchmen, and minions. Since loyalty didn't come cheap, and his startup funds were nothing, he took the budget route to loyalty.

He found a bunch of dumb (and powerful) kids who weren't happy with their home lives and gave them a family they could actually like.

Like me.

I was the fourth of five kids in an almost-but-not-quite-poor family in the Crescent. My folks had jobs with the city, so it's not like we were ever really left wanting, but being that I wasn't the oldest, or the youngest, or even the dreaded middle child, my place in the pecking order wasn't that great. I wasn't as smart, or strong, or talented, or even as *bad* as the rest of my brothers and sisters.

I was just . . . *there.*

When my powers manifested, I was so excited. I had something that could finally show the rest of 'em that I was different. Better.

But I was afraid of messing the reveal up, so I kept it my own little secret. And then the little secret became a big one the longer I held onto it, and then I was so afraid of being yelled at for holding onto it that I just decided to keep it mine forever.

That's the problem with secrets, though. They want to be spilled.

So I told a couple friends I thought could keep it to themselves, and they were about as good at that as I was. Word traveled, and eventually got to Padre Peligro. When he sought me out, telling me he could offer me everything a fourteen year old could want, like money, girls, drugs, friends, and a place to call home . . . it was like God himself was speaking to me, and I'd seen the light.

So I was stupid. I was fourteen. Cut me some slack.

If you've seen any after-school specials, you know how the rest of this goes.

I used my powers to find things to steal, to get information from people (we never called it an interrogation then, that was more the Army's word of choice), and even though I knew it was bad, I was never the one who actually had to do the truly *bad* parts, so I felt pretty clean. I had friends I loved, was earning some money, and life was good.

Until the EPC gig where Bystander and I got caught and Marco got killed.

Then life stopped being good.

Being fifteen sent me to Glamper's Island Juvenile Detention Facility, a hellhole that's still a damn sight better than where they send adult supers.

The last time I saw any of my family was Dad visiting a few days after my sentencing, just long enough to tell me I'd been disowned and that if I even tried talking to any of my siblings or mother when I got out, he'd have me arrested.

Nice guy.

There were two ways my life could've gone after this.

I could've used all the networking and criminal skill-building opportunities available to me at Glamper's Island to make sure that when I got out, I'd be a way more qualified villain than I was when I went in.

Or, I could've taken this as an opportunity to reevaluate my life and work toward getting on the straight and narrow path.

I think you know the direction I chose.

I didn't find God like a lot of the rest of the straight-and-narrow crowd, but I vowed to become a better person. I'd live a good, crime-free life, and no matter what happened, I'd never let myself be taken in by a charismatic supervillain with a good sales pitch ever again.

I mention this because this experience is going through my head on a constant loop the whole car ride to Milgram's place.

They put a bag on my head so I wouldn't see the way, not that it's done them a lot of good. Just being in this car I can tell you everywhere it's been in the last month, and wearing this head bag tells me how many other people it's been on.

I feel honored that I'm only the third one . . . and that they washed it recently.

After all, nothing's worse than a dirty head bag.

Them not trying to stop my power tells me that they're either not prepared to deal with it (which, with Bystander on their side, is unlikely) or they don't care what I do and don't find out and the bag's meant to show me how they normally treat "people."

That's why I'm nervous.

Not nervous that I'm gonna die or anything, but nervous enough that I'm wishing I had Harriet and my coat instead of just a light hoodie and a head bag to protect me.

The SUV pulls to a stop. There's voices outside the car, only barely above the rain. A door opens and I'm pushed outside.

My bag's pulled off.

"Hi," Bystander says. She's holding an umbrella big enough to share. The rest of the guards around us disperse, either back into the SUV or into the large, dark building in front of us to get out of the rain.

"They trust you alone with me?"

"Mr. Milgram understands that I am capable of handling you."

I grin.

"What?" she asks.

"Nothing. I've just never heard you talk like an adult before. I remember when every third word out of your mouth was 'motherfucker.'"

"People change," she says, then pulls me close to whisper in my ear. "Just don't be tellin' any of those motherfuckers back on Carpenter Street I've taken fucking elocution lessons, or I'll cut you from dick to throat. A girl's got a reputation to keep up, a'ight?"

"I haven't been back to the old street since we were kids, so I'd say you're cool there."

"Good." She steps back, dropping back into her professional stance.

"So, this is it?" I ask, eying the massive, darkened building.

"Yes. You're not going to pretend you didn't already get a read on this place and make me dramatically introduce it to you, are you?"

"If you already had a dramatic speech in mind, I won't stop you."

"Save me the trouble and do it yourself," she says, smirking.

I clear my throat dramatically. "Welcome to the Snyder Sanitarium for Lost Souls, one of West Pinnacle City's most notorious mental health care facilities, even before it was closed down because of all of Dr. Tongue's human experimentation projects."

"You got all that off a read?"

"I got the name off the read. The rest I got from true-crime shows."

She rolls her eyes.

"What?"

"You're not taking this very seriously."

"I'm sorry if I'm not giving it all the pomp and circumstance, but, seriously? A supervillain setting up shop in an abandoned mental hospital? Isn't that just asking for the pro-heroes to kick down its doors?"

"Mr. Milgram knows how to deal with the Guardians," she says cryptically, walking toward the entrance up ahead. I keep up to stay under the umbrella . . . and close to her.

"What do you mean by that?"

She ignores my question. "Did you know that back when they were first discovering superpowers, they thought they were a defect in humanity? That instead of bowing down and worshipping us as gods, as you might expect the ignorant masses of the times to do, they'd send us to places like this for *treatment*?"

"No," I say.

"I didn't think so; they like leaving this unfortunate chapter out of the superhuman history books. Because few understood the nature of the *condition*. Most of these treatments were horrible, pointless mutilations, the kind of things you'd hear about in campfire stories. They did this because they feared us. But when the heroes appeared, they called it water under the bridge and tried to make us think that they suddenly didn't worry about the rest of us anymore. But the hatred never went away, did it? It's just been waiting for a new voice to give it strength."

For emphasis, she shapeshifts a CARD FOR SENATE button onto her chest, then disappears it.

"And this?" I motion to the sanitarium.

She opens the door for me. "A different voice."

✳

I had a lot of expectations for Milgram's lair, as the man's reputation demands them.

If you follow the word on the street, Milgram is basically the boogeyman of everything between EPC and the ocean. He rolled into town about a decade ago and took over organized crime almost overnight, eliminating all opposition and assimilating most of the rest; those few independent gangs in town that remain know well enough to pay tribute to him if they mean to keep in business.

He has his hand in pretty much every crime that has a name.

Extortion.

Fraud.

Illegal drugs, weapons, and sorcery.

Human trafficking and prostitution.

Mad science.

His henchmen kill at least two dozen people a year, enough to never let people forget his name.

Since few have ever seen him in person, he's rumored to be an eight-foot tall mountain of pure muscle, with glowing eyes that shoot disintegration beams and sharpened teeth that better help him devour his enemies, constantly surrounded by a harem of a hundred beautiful women he unleashes his lusts and rages upon.

There are a lot of rumors about the man; when you add them all up, of course it's going to sound crazy.

I didn't know *exactly* what to expect when Bystander made this meeting, but I assumed it'd be pretty bad.

It sure as hell wasn't . . . this.

The sanitarium's interior has been cleaned up and refurbished, with not a single rusted bar or straightjacket in sight. The entrance rotunda is decked out for Christmas, with a giant tree in the center surrounded by a pile of presents almost half as high as the tree itself.

In addition to Milgram's well-dressed and ever-present henchmen, there are hundreds of civilians from across the Crescent and WPC, all of whom appear, at least at first glance, to be here of their own free will. Every open room Bystander leads me past gives another sight I wouldn't have expected in a lair like this.

Classrooms and playgrounds full of children.

Gardens lit by brilliant, glowing orbs.

Medical wards with real doctors, as well as sorcerers and healers, seeing to the needs of the most destitute.

Bystander enjoys my confusion.

"Not quite what you expected?"

"Not in the slightest."

"Not every supervillain has to live in a skull-shaped mountain."

"Or the back of an abandoned convenience store," I say, thinking of Padre Peligro's headquarters.

She shudders. "Don't remind me."

A couple kids run past us, kicking a soccer ball. Playfully, Bystander joins in and passes it down a nearby hall.

"This center hosts a number of services for the lower-income citizens of Pinnacle City, from free medical care and drug rehabilitation programs, to education and job placement to help longhairs, and anyone else in need, get on their feet."

"And Milgram gets, what, out of this, exactly?"

"All good things," she teases, guiding me to one of the large indoor gardens. She always liked to play these games, and I always let her because I was fifteen and in love. I don't normally entertain such personalities these days, but with her here, I must be losing my mind.

The garden she's led me into is paradise, with trees loaded down with heavy, colorful fruit, and a half-dozen or so people collecting them in baskets. A wiry, balding, middle-aged man with pale skin and a stringy ponytail notices us and waves. Casually, he slides down a ladder propped against a tree and brings a basket of apples over to us.

"Anya! You're early!" he says excitedly, craning his neck to push his glasses up the bridge of his nose with his shoulder.

"Yes, traffic was merciful today."

"It's not raining too badly outside, I hope?"

"You can hope, but that's about all you'll do on that."

"Well, shit. Thank the sorcerers and scientists for the artificial suns then. Want an apple? They're more pie apples than snacking apples, but really, all apples are pretty fantastic when you get them fresh."

Bystander gladly takes an apple from the basket. The few years of Sunday school my parents tried sending me to come back in a rush, but when I realize an apple's just an apple, I accept one.

He's right. They are best fresh.

"Thanks," I say.

"Don't mention it. Any friend of Anya is a friend of mine," he says, setting the basket down and wiping his gloved hands on his apron.

He then holds out a gloved hand to me. "Pleased to meet you. Hope you guessed my name."

Cautious, I take the man's hand and read it.

I'll say this, he's smart. With gloves on, I can only read the gloves and where they've been the past few days, but from them, I know a hint of the man wearing them.

My blood has turned to ice, but I try to keep cool as I pull my hand away.

"Nice to meet you, Mr. Milgram."

"While it's kind of you to say, there's a glint in your eye that says otherwise. But don't worry about that, I understand why you lie, and I don't blame you. After all, I'm the *Big Bad Milgram*, eater of babies and defiler of virgin's virtues. I drink the blood of superheroes for breakfast out of a goblet made from a president's skull. Isn't that what they say?" he jokes.

"I've . . . never heard any of those."

He laughs. "Well, good! Don't believe half of what you hear and anything you see, isn't that what they also say? I'm not some fairy tale monster. I'm just like you, and indeed, most of the people here: a person born gifted in a world that would rather I wasn't. Would you mind taking a walk with me?"

A thousand different ways to answer that question run through my head, with most of them ending with me running like hell for the door.

Instead of listening to any of those more sensible voices, I begin to follow.

We walk from the garden to the vast, main hall of the sanitarium.

"You come from the Crescent, yes?" he asks.

"Yeah."

"I don't. I'm a WPC kid, born and raised. I remember a time—a time which doesn't feel that long ago but certainly must be—when this place was worth being proud of. This was where honest, hardworking people could make a living and spend their free time dreaming of moving to the towers of EPC someday. It was the *backbone* of the city, until the skies opened up and changed everything," he says, staring off into space.

"My family made it through the attack in one piece, but we lost a lot of friends to the post-Killtron WPC exodus. Dad was an utter bastard, but he had a pride to him that made him almost admirable in his less cruel moments. He believed that the people who turned their backs on WPC were traitors, and that it was the manifest destiny of those who stayed behind to rebuild it by whatever means necessary."

"From what I've seen around here, it's not working," I say. A few members of his entourage eye me angrily, but a wave of a hand from Milgram ends that.

"True progress is never swift."

"And it involves building a criminal syndicate?"

He chuckles. "Crime is an unfortunate byproduct of society, and it will exist no matter what we do. I saw what the vultures were doing to WPC, and I did something about it. Now they all answer to me. I keep criminals honest and fair, providing services as demand dictates and using the profits to better various projects like this across WPC and the Crescent. This is an imperfect process, and occasionally some eggs will have to be broken to make this omelet, but we are doing good work here . . . and we could really use someone like you to help us out."

I think about asking him if he considers the riots and fires consuming the region "eggs" in this case, but know better than to push the point. His attack dogs, save Bystander, all look ready to pounce, and I don't want to give them any reason to.

"So, what do you want from me?"

"Your help with the work that needs to be done. Contrary to what the moguls and tycoons of EPC want you to believe, true power does not lie with money, but with superpowers. He who has the most people with superpowers on his side is truly the one who writes the fate of the world. The superheroes think they understand this, but they only half see it. They think superpowers need only be flashy and destructive to be powerful, but people like you and me, our powers aren't nearly so showy, and are all the more powerful for it. With a touch, you can find out anyone's deepest, darkest secrets, and with a word, I can strip people of all the filters that hold them back. I've seen what you can do, and Anya here tells me you're capable of so much more. Work for me, and I can promise you a plum position in the great things that will soon be taking place in Pinnacle City."

What he says, he says with complete and practiced earnestness. There's not a hint of untruth in his eyes, not a trace of deception in his voice. Every part of me wants to believe the man in front of me. My very soul screams that he isn't the villain everybody says he is, and that he is the exact kind of hero the city needs.

It's because of this I know not to trust him.

His "man of the people" act is too good to be true; it's a sales pitch used to cover what he's really up to. Dissident's told me a lot about Milgram's operations, and I know he does things there are no excuse for.

He's good. Too good.

I need to keep an eye on Milgram but, more importantly, I need to be careful.

"Can I think about it?"

"Please do. Should you ever need to get in touch, Anya will be more than happy to make that possible."

A henchman, a young blonde man with tattoos of flames going up his left arm, jogs up behind Milgram and taps him on the shoulder.

"Excuse me, sir," he says.

"Yes, Effigy?" Milgram says distractedly.

"It's time."

"Oh, good. I'm going to play Santa and hand out presents to the kids in our literacy center. If you'd like to stick around, I wouldn't mind having an extra elf!" he says, cheerfully.

Correction: I need to be *really* careful about this man.

✳

Bystander fingers the fabric of my trench coat, hanging by the door of my apartment.

"Nice coat. Reactive absorption polymers?"

"Something like that," I say, pouring us a drink.

"Stuff'll absorb most impacts, gunshots, knives, fire, cold . . ."

"Same materials the superheroes wear."

"The same *expensive* materials."

"What can I say, I got friends with expensive taste."

This is half true. Dissident got this for me not long after we met on the street, reasoning that if I wouldn't join her in her vigilantism, at least the coat would keep me mostly protected when she wasn't around to save me. I don't tell Bystander this because I want to keep that smile on her face.

"Me too. Mr. Milgram gets my suits made from similar materials so they'll shift forms with me," she says, twirling around to show off her leotard.

"It suits you," I say, handing her a glass.

"Thanks," she says, plopping down on my couch. She looks around at my apartment, at the dim, buzzing lights, the cracked paint on the walls, the leaky spots in the ceiling that collect in the scattered pots and pans I've set out. I sit at the opposite end of the couch, a glass in hand, my other hand unconsciously sweeping some of the crap off my coffee table into the trash can. She knows me, who I am, what I'm like, and I know she doesn't care about shit like this, but I still feel the unconscious need to impress her.

Swirling her glass around after taking a sip, she asks the question I know she's been dying to ask. "So, what'd you think of Mr. Milgram?"

If only I had an easy answer.

I debate how much I want to lie, stalling by finishing off and refilling my glass.

Looking into her black eyes, remembering the long talks she and Marco and I used to have about what we'd be when we grew up, I probably make the wrong choice.

"I think he's a madman who's really good at holding the mad in check when he needs to, who's aiming to take over the city. He gains devotion through his *charitable* acts, but what he's really doing is grooming Crescent residents and children into henchmen while keeping them around to act as human shields. I also think, given how massive and difficult to hide his base of operations is, that he has connections somewhere high up who keep the police and pro-heroes off his back."

"So what?" Bystander says.

"That's . . . not quite the response I was expecting."

"What, you'd thought I'd drunk the Milgram Kool-Aid?"

"Well . . . yes? The man's built an impressive cult of personality."

"Give me a little credit," she scoffs. "I haven't survived this long by following every guy with a superpower and a slick pitch."

"Padre Peligro?" I propose.

"That was *one time*. I've raised my standards since."

"Milgram is raised standards?"

"Padre Peligro was a fool, but Milgram's the real deal. He understands strategy and has better connections than most War on Villainy era villains ever did, and when he says he's going to do something he does."

"But he's exploiting people. Exploiting *you*."

"Again, I say, so, fucking, what?"

"Seriously?"

"Seriously. I'm a superpowered minority woman from the Crescent who has to keep constant mental focus to pass for a normal human being. No matter what I do with my life, I'll be exploited. At least this way, if I'm being exploited, I'll be exploited by someone on the winning side, and I'll get to do some exploiting of my own. For all the shit in my past, in *our* past, I've earned the right to deliver some payback."

I want to say that this isn't the Bystander I remember, but I can't.

When she was a kid, she got picked on a lot for her non-human appearance and powers, and for all the charm she had, this had grown her a mean streak a mile wide.

I remember a time once when the three of us were ditching school, hanging out in a pool hall Padre Peligro took over, playing video games and bumming smokes off some of the older kids who hung out there. We felt like real-life goddamn supervillains.

This was around the time that she started to fill out and receive the attention of the older boys. One of them, Ricardo, always found excuses to get close and touch her and was always pestering her to transform into his favorite hot celebrities. One time, he had her nearly pinned to the wall while Marco and I were playing video games, which worried me but also didn't worry me because both

Ricardo and Bystander were smiling while he whispered in her ear. When he was done saying whatever he had to say, he walked the other way and smacked her on the ass.

Her smile was gone as fast as he was. When she rejoined us, she was trembling, her hands balled so tightly into fists that they bled, and none of our usual teasing about him could get her to tease back.

When we met up with her at the pool hall the next day, she was in a much better mood, which I thought was just because Ricardo wasn't there.

As it turned out, *she* was the reason Ricardo wasn't there. She proudly shared with us how she'd shifted into Ricardo's form and, over the course of three hours, set fire to his parents' place, beat up his girlfriend, stabbed two of his drug-dealer friends in the stomach, robbed a convenience store and, for good measure, hurled a brick through the windshield of a police car. The last she saw, Ricardo was being hauled away by the cops and had at least one gang out for his blood.

She never told us what Ricardo said to her that made her do this, but she told the story with the same casual pride she'd normally have while telling us about learning a new skateboard trick. I think even she knew she went a little over the top with it, but said it was what needed to be done so people knew not to mess with her ever again.

If this were just a story, this would be the part where I'd say how right she was, and that nobody ever fucked with her again.

But this isn't a story, at least, not *that* kind of story.

No one messed with her, for a while, but people's memories are short, and the truly cruel and vicious will fuck with those they think are weaker just because it's in their nature.

Not even two weeks later there was another older boy working the same line as Ricardo. The same easy smile, the same threatening-yet-not-entirely-threatening posture, the same innuendos and whispered comments in her ear.

I'd never seen a person so crushed as she was that day.

I can't agree with what she's doing now, but I can't say I don't understand it, either.

"I'm sorry," I say.

"For what? You're not responsible for how fucked up the world is."

"I meant losing touch."

She shakes her head. "We were both in the system, we couldn't help it."

"But we could've tried. *I* could've tried."

She slides closer to me on the couch. "Well, we're here now. We can make up for lost time."

I don't need another invitation, leaning in and kissing her. She kisses me back fiercely.

I want this to be real. I need this to be real. I want Bystander to be here because she wants to be, not because Milgram sent her to bait me onto his side.

No one makes me do what I don't wanna do. Ever.

That was what she always used to tell us, and for as long as I've known her, it's always been true.

Not even Milgram could change that.

So I allow myself to get lost and just be here, now, with Bystander.

I close my eyes for a moment, and when I open them, I'm kissing Ruby Herron.

I push her away.

"What? I thought you liked this form," she teases. "Would you prefer something more familiar?"

In quick succession, she becomes Fadia, Petting Zoo, and *her*.

"Stop it," I say.

"Why? Isn't that the fantasy? To have any woman you could ever want? I can be all of them, and *more*."

I grab Bystander (*Kimberly*) by the arms and pull her to me.

"I don't want them. I want you."

Slowly, Bystander transforms back to her natural form.

"You want this? You honestly want *this?*"

"Yes."

"Why?" she asks, pushing me away.

"What kind of question is that?"

"Oh, please, you think I haven't heard this one before? 'Oh, let me see your true form, that's how you're really beautiful!' 'Oh, let me call you Anya instead of Bystander, isn't it so much better to go by your true name?' The nice guy lie gets old fast."

Her voice is full of a bitterness beyond what I knew she was capable of.

Mine isn't. "Did I ever claim to be a nice guy?"

"No."

"Then give me the benefit of the doubt, take the fucking lead, and play this how *you* want to instead of how some parade of assholes who aren't here wanted."

"Fine," she says.

Then she's on top of me, straddling me, and I lean forward to kiss her with a ferocity that matches her own. Her fingers tear through my shirt like it's made of tissue paper. She unzips my jeans, fumbles past my underwear, pulls me out forcefully, and places me against her.

"This *is* the me you want?"

"So long as it's you, it's all I've ever wanted."

Surprisingly calm, given the intense look on her face, she slides me inside of her.

We're past fighting now, long past fighting, as we've got much better things to be putting our passions toward.

✳

It's three hours later, and for the life of me I couldn't say all of what just happened, or how we made it to the bedroom, or where my pants are for that matter, but I know that it sure as hell felt right what we did. I watch her as she gets dressed in the corner of my room, and I can't keep the grin from my face.

"So, better or worse than you were expecting?" she says, rubbing a hand over her bald head.

"Not bad," I joke.

"Not bad?"

"Yeah."

"I think it was sure as shit better than 'not bad.'"

"Thanks for letting my neighbors know that, by the way," I say, glad that I don't like my neighbors much.

"You're welcome. We really should've done that ages ago," she says.

"Well, don't run out on me so soon and I think I can go round three," I say.

"I wish, but I can't."

"Milgram?"

"The one and only." She finishes pulling on her leotard. "And I'm pretty fucking late as is."

I watch her as she dresses, torn between how happy I am she's back in my life and how scared I am of the company she keeps.

I want to tell her both of these things, so of course I tell her neither.

"This wasn't weird for you, was it?" I ask.

"No. Maybe. Sort of, I think? It's been so long since we saw each other, and we were kids then, so, definitely strange. And . . ."

"And?"

She purses her lips, looking uncertain of what she's going to say next. "Look, I've been with a lot of guys."

"So?"

"And I'm pretty good at observing and judging people's behavior. You have to be to take their shape convincingly. I know when someone, especially a man, is telling the truth or not, and . . . and

I couldn't believe it, but you're the first man who ever told me he preferred me like this and meant it."

"So I was your first?"

She rolls her eyes. "Don't let it go to your head."

"It's kind of hard not to."

This is precisely the worst time for my phone to start ringing, so of course it does. It buzzes almost off my bedside table.

"You should get that. I'll see myself out," she says, leaning across the bed and kissing me again.

"Can I see you again?"

"Count on it. We've got a lot to talk about."

She leaves the room and I pick up my phone, cursing my arm as I feel the pills wearing off.

The number isn't one I know. I can let it go to voicemail, deal with it tomorrow while I try and figure out just where the hell my life's taking me.

But it could also be a client, so I pick it up.

"Finders Keepers Investigations," I say, hearing the front door close behind Bystander.

"Eddie Enriquez?" a raspy, quiet voice asks.

"Speaking."

"I'm one of the guys that killed Quentin Julian. I need your help."

And I thought today was already full of surprises.

CHAPTER 12: THE SUPERHERO

Leah: Gonna disappear soon. Dinner smells like it's almost done.

My stomach growls at the reminder of dinnertime at Juniors Ranch, and I try to quiet it with another petal of this deep fried onion appetizer that's the closest thing the Silver Cowl has to a non-liquid specialty.

Ace kicked me out of his VIP room, and it wasn't as if I really felt like sitting there watching him try to flirt with the servers anyway, so I'm keeping watch from outside the door, sitting on the stairs, watching Jackie and her three man security detail at the bar down below.

Kimberly: What are you guys having?

I ask this half to torment myself with the answer, half to stall Leah from logging out of messenger and leaving me alone.

Leah: Cory's making tofu lasagna.

Kimberly: Ha, nice try.

Cory's tofu lasagna is my favorite, and Leah knows it, but I could barely even get the meat-eating other members of the team to let him make it for my birthday. No way is he making it on a random Friday night without me there.

Leah: No, for real.

My phone is still for a moment, and then the next message carries a pic of Cory holding the gooey, cheesy pan with a guilty-nervous look on his face.

Leah: He's all sweaty about impressing this new girl. She's veggie too.

Kimberly: You guys replaced me already? :p

Emojis are the only cure for how not joking I am.

Leah: Relax. She's a musician, not a superhero. Wait, I didn't say that. She's completely moving in on your turf and you should be jealous. Very jealous. Want to come kick her out of your room?

Kimberly: Now THAT'S a nice try :)

I hide behind armies of smiley emojis.

I knew the team would survive me, theoretically, but knowing is different from suddenly finding out that there's a new chapter to the twisting, turning soap of Cory's love life that nobody thought to fill me in on until now.

Kimberly: Is

I erase the message and retype it five times before hitting send.

Kimberly: Is Mason seeing anyone new?

It takes Leah a moment to respond, no longer than it takes me to inventory all the reasons she might need that moment. Is she laughing at me? Deciding how to break bad news gently? Has she already disappeared into a plateful of tofu lasagna, not to be heard from again until morning?

> Leah: *Bad Kimmy. You're not shoveling any more coal into that train wreck.*

That's not an answer.

> Kimberly: *Of course not. Just curious.*

Pause.

> Leah: *Fine, you twisted my arm. I'll tell Mason you'll only come home if he's waiting on your bed in ten minutes in that tight pair of jeans you like and nothing else. But you'll owe me.*

> Kimberly: *Talk him into a kilt if you want, it still won't make me move back.*

It takes me longer than it should to press send.

God, I'm homesick. I miss Cory's cooking, and the way half the appliances are always disassembled at any given time from Derek's constant tinkering, and I miss talking to Leah from inside the same room, sharing a bag of peanut butter pretzels.

I even miss Mason, and not only because he looks unreasonably good in skinny jeans and even better out of them, or because he can actually be a pretty good friend sometimes when push comes to shove, or because I've been kinda in love with him on and off since I was sixteen . . .

Mostly, I miss him because even when he's being a total ass, there's a reliable ceiling on it.

I miss imagining that jerking me around with a little go-away-come-back was the ceiling of asses.

> *Leah: Whipped cream mankini. That's my final offer.*

> *Kimberly: Make it happen, then we'll talk.*

Then, because I've learned never to underestimate what Leah can make happen,

> *Kimberly: Totally kidding, by the way.*

I could be there in a matter of seconds, in time for dinner, in time to meet Cory's new girlfriend or crush or whatever, and maybe we could even pretend I'd never been gone.

Tomorrow's headline: "First Female Solar Flare Resigns in First Month, Cites Unexpected Job Pressures."

Yeah, no thanks.

> *Leah: Going once ... Going twice ...*

> *Kimberly: Just tell me what happened with*
> *Bowerbird yesterday.*

Leah spends a while typing.

> *Leah: Oh yeah, we caught him, got the kid home*
> *safe and sound. Turned out birdbrain didn't*
> *even mean to kidnap him. He thought the*
> *baby carriage was empty when he stole it. You*

should have seen the rest of his stash though.
Mostly a warehouse full of straw and garbage,
but the whole missing lapis lazuli display from
that traveling gem exhibit was in there. He
never even tried to fence it.

And this is the part I miss most, the real reason I've been keeping Leah on the phone longer and longer the last few evenings. I've been shamelessly pumping her for my vicarious heroing fix.

Trouble is, she's catching on.

Leah: So, what did YOU do yesterday?

I don't even remember the last time I did something good. Was it the Seaside Shopping District mission?

Has it been that long?

Kimberly: Don't ask.

Leah: Uh-huh. Hey, Mason! Come over here a sec!

Kimberly: You're typing. That doesn't even make
sense.

Leah: You don't know that. Maybe I'm using speech-
to-text.

Kimberly: Punctuation's too good.

Leah: Damn my impeccable grammatical skills!

"Hey, Miss Flare?"

I look up reluctantly at the bouncer trying to attract my attention, probably to tell me I'm not supposed to be sitting on the stairs.

"Sorry, Winters, I'll move." I pick up my fried onion from its spot next to me.

"You come here with the owner's personal staff, right?" He points down the hallway to Ace's VIP room.

". . . Sort of?"

"He's blocked the door with something," says Winters. "I know he likes his privacy, but I've got a fire code inspector downstairs, and I can only stall for so long. I thought he might listen to you."

"Not likely," I say. "But don't worry, I'll get it open."

Kimberly: G2G.

Sergei stands outside Ace's room, making no move to either help or interfere with me.

I wait for Winters to go about his business, just so I don't have to explain to Mayor Card tomorrow how I allowed his son to get busted for drugs or whatever else he's doing in there, and then I bang on the door hard enough to rattle it in its frame.

"Ace! Open up!"

"Fuck off!" he shouts back drunkenly.

Like clockwork, Jacob comes sprinting down the hallway, wiping powder off his nose.

He's carrying his close-quarters handheld camera, presently off, and motions me to be quiet.

"Ace finally got Anna to accept a drink with him!" he whispers excitedly, motioning to his camera, which presumably captured the earlier phases of this proposition. "Who knows what we'll get from him in the morning? Tearful confessional about his betrayal of Jessica? Glowing discovery of a new love?"

I have no idea who Anna is, and I really don't care.

"Either we open this room, or the fire department does," I say.

"We can't get in the way of this storyline," says Jacob.

"Yeah, well, when have you ever let what really happened do that?"

I enter the code to unlock the door, feel for the spot where Ace has braced some piece of furniture against it, compensate for the slight extra resistance of Jacob's hand trying to hold me back, and push in a smooth, firm motion to open the door without breaking anything.

When I see him, I drop the fried onion half that's still in my hand, and the half in my stomach makes a reappearance in my mouth.

One of our regular servers is keeled over the armrest of a couch, the skirt of her knockoff supersuit hiked up her hips. Her mask is off, showing the smattering of gene bomb scales across her face. She's drooling unconsciously into the cushions, and her breath comes in the whimpering gasps of a nightmare that's not just a nightmare.

Ace doesn't even bother to pull out of her when he glares at me. "Unless you wanna join in, get the fuck out, and shut the door behind you!"

I hit him with a firework blast that knocks him backward into the wall.

"You can't do that!" he slurs from the ground. "You're fired!"

"Sit in the corner," I tell him. He starts crawling back toward her, his ankles tangled in his own jeans, and I hit him with another blast, trying to keep it small, keep it measured.

I'm too angry to yell, too angry to fight. If I start now, or if I have to look at his repulsive face for another moment, I might kill him. Actually kill him. And I don't do that. Justice Juniors don't do that. Maybe Pinnacle City Guardians do, when they have to, but not me.

"Sit. In. The. Corner."

"God! Why can't you just leave me alone?" he sulks.

"Face the wall."

He snorts in disbelief.

I charge my hand to a bright, threatening glow, and he turns around.

Oh god, oh god, oh god, when I said I missed real heroing, I didn't mean *this*.

I flit back and forth for a moment, trying to figure out where to start. Nothing this horrible ever happened on the Juniors, and whenever anything came close, Cory would already be transporting survivors directly to the hospital and Mason and Derek would take care of recording and preserving the crime scene while Leah and I fought off any bad guys in the area . . . but there's nothing here to fight, just that little glass-jawed prick in the corner, and no one to help with the rest.

There's only me.

But I'm Solar Flare, and that'll have to do.

I take the unconscious woman by the hands and pull her the rest of the way onto the couch, rolling her to the side so she won't drown, and carefully adjust her skirt, trying to preserve as much of her dignity and the evidence as I can at the same time.

"Stupid *mudak*," Sergei mutters as he and Jacob follow me in, closing the door behind them.

I pull out my phone and find the Superdirectline app.

"What are you doing?" Jacob asks sharply.

"What's it look like? Calling for backup."

"From the cops?"

"No, the Easter bunny. Yes, from the cops!" I snap. "We've got an unconscious victim and a violent criminal in custody. We need an ambulance and a squad car, unless one of you wants to wait with her while I take him in myself, and—put those down, that's evidence!"

I pocket the phone to grab Sergei's arm and make him put down the two glasses on the table next to the couch. One of them probably has residue of whatever Ace drugged her with.

In the instant I'm busy prying the glasses from Sergei's hands, Jacob reaches into my pocket and throws my phone into a melted ice bucket.

"What the hell is wrong with you two?" I crack a light energy blast at each of them, knocking them to opposite sides of the room.

"Kimmy, baby, just listen," says Jacob, bobbing up and down on his feet with the jitters of whatever he's been snorting on his break. "Ace is dating a *Runway Races* finalist."

"So?"

"So, no one's going to believe he'd throw that away over one of *them*." He gestures at the server's exposed scales.

"He's left his DNA all over her, and he was caught in the act by three eyewitnesses!"

"Kimmy, look at her."

"I am looking at her!" I shove Jacob two paces to his right so he can better see the stain of blood-tinted fluids on the armrest. "Are you?"

"Yes, yes, it's tragic," says Jacob, "but people won't accept it. That's not how the story goes."

"Ace *raped* someone! Do you even get that?"

"You see how she's dressed, she was advertising it!" Ace protests from the corner. "I offered her a drink! *She said yes!* Everyone knows what those signals mean!"

"Face the *wall!*"

He grumbles into it inaudibly.

"*In the Cards* is over," I tell Jacob. "At least it is for him, and if you two don't help me help her, it will be for you too, because I will personally make sure you're both charged as accessories."

"We are helping her," says Sergei, removing his suit jacket and draping it over her. "Ace isn't the only one who needs this all to go away."

"Yeah!" says Jacob. "Anna won't thank you for—"

"Ella!" I shout. "Her name is Ella! She has a five-year-old daughter named Liza, and she dances in the 59th Street masked ballet in the winter season!"

"That's a neat party trick you do, isn't it?" says Sergei. "Always knowing everyone's names. Collecting their lives like trading cards in a hundred and forty characters or less. Do you think it means you know them? Does it make you an expert on what she'd want us to do?"

"I don't have to be her friend to send him to jail for her!"

"He's not going to jail," says Sergei simply. "Boys like Ace never do. It's not an option."

"But the story can go two ways from here," says Jacob. "The Cards can either pay Collingwraith and the rest of their army of lawyers to clear Ace in court by annihilating Anna's—"

"*Ella!*"

". . . *Ella's* credibility, and making sure she spends the rest of her life remembered as that ugly gene-job slut who tried to blackmail Ace for a slice of the family fortune," Jacob continues without missing a beat. "*Or,* they can put that same money toward . . . What did you say the kid's name was again?"

"Liza," I repeat through my teeth.

"Right, a nice college fund for Liza, plus enough to make sure her mom can dance all the ballet she wants and never has to serve another drink, in exchange for her signature on a tiny little non-disclosure agreement. They're going to want to go with option B. It's quieter, less fuss, but the moment this becomes a headline, or a criminal case file, that storyline gets a whole lot harder to play out."

My own fingernails are digging into my palms, and I can't seem to make them stop, or douse the purple heat radiating off my fists.

"That's sick."

"The sick part's already happened," says Jacob. "We can't change that."

"Which would you choose?" asks Sergei. "If it were you?"

I want to punch him right in his calm, creepily understanding expression.

He already knows what I'd choose, what I *chose*, given the chance to stake my career and reputation on my word versus a Card's. He was there.

I didn't even need a payoff to make me want that whole humiliating instant of my life to just go away.

"If she doesn't get every penny she—"

"It won't be a problem if you don't make it one," says Sergei, picking up the glasses again and heading for the wet bar sink.

"I . . . I'm not doing this."

"Who said you had to?" says Jacob, clapping me tentatively on the shoulder, wary of my glowing parts. "You think the rest of us are just here to look pretty?"

"Consider the situation handled," says Sergei. "Go put in an expense report for your phone, and take an early night. You'll feel better in the morning."

✳

I can't go home—any of my homes.

I can't go to Juniors Ranch and ruin Cory's meet-the-girlfriend dinner with the way I'm feeling now. I can't go to my mom's house and get into another discussion about why I can't just try harder to get along with the Card family, and I can't go to Guardian Tower, not even to change my clothes.

I don't know if the Guardians would blame me more for letting this happen in the first place or for not helping Sergei and Jacob clean up, and I don't even know if I can ask them without jeopardizing Ella's option B.

But I can't go flying around in my Solar Flare outfit, either. Screw the headlines, I can't.

If I did what Solar Flare is supposed to do tonight, if this is what it meant when I pledged myself to protect the people of this city, then I can't be Solar Flare, because I can't ever do that again.

And if I didn't do what Solar Flare is supposed to do, then I don't deserve to be Solar Flare anyway.

Eventually, I end up flying down to the beach and wrapping myself in an abandoned towel so I don't have to see the circles of red and gold on my chest while I'm puking the rest of my bar snack dinner into the sea.

I don't know if Sergei was right or wrong about the rest of it, but he was wrong about one thing: I will not feel better in the morning.

This is never, ever going to feel better.

CHAPTER 13: THE DETECTIVE

Red and blue lights behind me.

Instinct tells me to run.

Common sense and newsfeeds of people who tried to run getting shot tell me to stay put.

So, standing in the rain, I turn to face the DSA van as it pulls up to the curb and the agents step out.

I know the steps to this dance better than I'd like to admit.

"Pleasant evening, officers. What can I do you for?"

"Hands where we can see 'em," the one nearest me says, a hand on his piece.

They know the opening steps to this one too; they know they've got the lead, and are hoping I don't know how to follow.

The one on the driver's side shines a floodlight in my face to blind me, while the one closest to me approaches.

We exchange the pleasantries one always does in situations like this.

Who are you? Edgar Enriquez, I'm a private investigator following a lead.

What are you doing in West Pinnacle City? Like I said, following a lead.

Do you have your documentation? Why yes, officer, of course I do.

This stuff looks fake. It's real. Phone it in if you want.

You showing us attitude, boy? No, just stating facts.

What else you got in that coat? A baseball bat, my medicine, and about ten dollars in small bills and change.

What's with the bat? Have you noticed I'm taking a stroll in West Pinnacle City?

Hands on the hood.

They're not the gentlest friskers in the world, but they're not the worst, either. I get a read on the guy frisking me, the one who doesn't want to take his hand off his gun, and I know that he wanted to check me out to up their arrest numbers.

A shady-looking non-white guy walking the streets of WPC at night, in a storm, on his own?

Must be guilty of something.

They confiscate my pills for looking suspicious (which, being stored in an unlabeled pill bottle, they kinda do). Irritating, since they weren't cheap, but since I dry-chewed a couple about an hour ago, I'm pretty mellow and just go with the flow.

They're itching to bring me in for something, anything, and when they get the call on the radio that all my paperwork checks out, you might as well've told them that Santa won't be coming around this year.

They debate back and forth in their car, trying to figure if the pills are enough to haul me in (or, perhaps, if I'm about to "resist arrest"), but it sounds like it's not gonna be worth the paperwork for them.

Soon enough, I'm on my way, sans an almost empty bottle of my pills and more than ever wanting this night to be over.

The gene-job didn't give me a lot of details except for claiming he was both innocent and guilty of killing Quentin Julian. He was desperate and scared, and that was probably the only reason I decided to meet with him on his terms in one of the worst parts of WPC.

I don't dare drive here, as while my car is in pieces I'd rather it not be stolen (or worse), so I took a bus that stopped within half a mile of the meeting spot, and I've hoofed it from there. Working street lights are few and far between, so I'm mostly navigating with my phone's light and hoping the batteries hold out. With the rain this bad, I can only see a few feet in front of me.

All told, even that's probably more than I want to see of WPC.

I don't know what this part of the city held before, but right now all I see are ancient storefronts with boarded-up or smashed-in windows on the few intact buildings, and piles of rubble everywhere else. The streets are lifeless but, unlike the Crescent, I think this area's usually like this.

It doesn't take long to find where I'm supposed to go. It'd be hard to miss it, really.

Mission Camp 31 stands in an abandoned grocery store parking lot. It was one of several set up by FEMA in a time when the government tried to step in and fix things up after Killtron's attack. They abandoned it after about six months and left their assets in place. Now it's a shantytown of old FEMA trailers, tents, and a bunch of hovels improvised from scrap wood, cardboard, and sheet metal. They've got some electricity, but there's also a lot of fires and stoves keeping the place lit.

Spray painted on the outside of the nearest trailer is GENE FREAKS F, with a trail of paint leading off after the final F. Whoever tried to paint it left in a hurry.

Or was made to leave.

I walk down the aisles of the camp, seeing no one and feeling every eye on me. Save the paint, this place is untouched by the violence of the past days, but I get the impression it isn't for a lack of trying. These are people who've learned to protect themselves, and I'm a stranger here. I have to tread lightly if I don't—

"Are you the detective?"

A little girl appears in front of me, wearing a well-worn, probably second-hand hoodie with some cartoon cat on the front. Maybe ten, eleven years old at the most, her twin braids are dirty blonde and reach past her shoulders, but she does everything she can to hide her face from me.

"Depends on who's asking."

"My papi called for you. He said you were the one who's supposed to help him even though you made everyone hate us. You have to follow me," she says, running off.

This feels like a trap, but lately everything does, so I follow her.

She leads me to a particularly rundown trailer, flush up against one of the former grocery store's crumbling walls, and knocks a few times, then once, then twice.

The door opens a crack.

"This him?" a woman's voice asks.

"Yeah," the girl says.

A long, clawed hand swings the door wide open, ushering the girl and myself inside.

The trailer is small and cramped, lit mostly with candles and with rooms made from sheets hung from the ceiling. The woman's a gene-job with blonde hair, the left half of her body twisted with sharp, reptilian features and an unnaturally long arm with clawed fingers that almost reach the floor. In her right arm, she holds a misshapen baby to her breast, who feeds eagerly.

"So you're the piece of shit who brought this hell down on us?" she hisses with contempt.

"Mama, please," the little girl pulls at her mother's sweater.

"No, sweetie, this man deserves a piece of my mind. We didn't have it good before all this, but at least we had a life! It wasn't a good life, but it was a life, and now—"

"Honey, love, *mi amor*, he may be the only one who can save us. Can we at least save the yelling at him for when we need it?"

A man comes from behind one of the hanging sheets. His face is one of the most horrible things I've ever seen. His skin, if he has any, is transparent and waxy, showing off white bone and bits of muscle connecting his angular, asymmetrical head. His teeth are sharp fangs and his eyes are large, yellow, and thick with green veins. What little hair he has is long, black, and greasy, hanging around his shoulders in clumps. He is an ugly monster of a gene-job that every natural instinct tells me to look away from.

I've seen his face on the news.

I should know, since I put it there.

He strides toward me, a bit awkwardly, and holds out a clawed, three-fingered hand.

"Max Mendoza. Thank you for coming. You've already met my wife, Jeanine. The parasite sucking on her tit is our youngest, John, and Kaley here's the one who brought you in. Say hi to the detective."

Shyly, Kaley turns to me, still hiding her face in the hoodie. Now, though, enough light shows the lower half of her face that I can see she takes most after her dad.

"Hi."

"Hello."

Slowly, like a Polaroid developing in reverse, she becomes invisible. One of the sheet walls then pulls itself aside, and I hear footsteps running behind it.

Mendoza shrugs. "Raising kids is a challenge. Raising super kids . . ."

"I'm sure."

His hand's still out.

"You know what I can do if I shake with you, right?"

"Yeah," he says.

I take that as informed consent. I shake his hand and get a read off the man. I hold on for a while, but I see little new, mostly him hanging around the trailer, talking with his wife, playing with his kids, worriedly talking with neighbors wondering if anyone else was looking for him, finally getting a burner cell phone from someone to call me with. Nothing illegal, nothing more than what a guy normally hiding from the law would do.

He takes his hand back. "You willing to talk with me?"

"Sure."

"Good." He motions me to a nearby couch, or the fraying remains of one. Jeanine looks at us disapprovingly, but says nothing, disappearing behind the sheets with Kaley.

"So you're the guy who retro-filmed the murder?" he says.

"That's right. And you're one of the guys who killed Quentin Julian."

"That's right. But I bet I can tell you something you don't know about it. A whole lot of things, actually."

"Like?"

"That I'm the only one who did it that's still alive."

He's right, that is news. Or, more appropriately, it's news that it *isn't* news. This is the sort of thing they'd be all over.

"You know there's not much I can do about this, right? I just recorded what happened. I don't got any sway with the cops or heroes or anything like that."

"No, but you look into things for money, right? Well, I got some money. It ain't much, but I can pay you. Pay you to help me clear my name. What do you say?"

I could say a lot of things to this.

That he should save the world a lot of trouble and tell his story to the police.

That I'm not worth his time.

That I don't want to get any more involved with this than I am.

I could even say sorry.

"Tell me what you gotta say," is instead what comes outta my mouth.

"Then you'll help me?"

"That all depends on what you gotta say."

"You brought this down on us! You can do a lot more than see!" Jeanine calls from behind one of the sheets.

"Please, honey, I'm trying to fix this!"

He stands up, hands held behind his back.

"I believe in the American dream. Having a family, a job, a good home. That's why my folks moved us here after the gene bombs in El Paso made them like this. They thought things'd be better here. They both died when I was a kid, but WPC here's been otherwise good to me. I met my wife, had my kids. This place is my home. I work hard, when I can, manual shit mostly, building, gardening, and I provide. But I still always wanted that American dream. And that's why I went to Mr. Julian."

"You killed Quentin Julian for the American dream?"

"No, no, no, please, no, I didn't do that for that. Mr. Julian . . . I would never hurt him. I wouldn't."

I have a hard time believing that, remembering the savagery Julian was killed with, but the sheer sadness on his terrible face makes me give him the benefit of the doubt . . . for now.

"I wanted to do more when Jeanine got pregnant with John, so I attended one of the work placement programs that Mr. Julian held. He helped me create a résumé, build references from previous guys I'd worked with, even helped me and Jeanine get signed up for a program that'd get us discounted health insurance. He *helped* us, so much, but it wasn't enough. I wanted to do so much more for them, and I told him this. And he looked at me like he had a secret he wasn't sure he wanted to give up, and wrote an address on the back of his business card and told me to go there if I wanted some off-the-books opportunities. Now I've lived a God-fearing life, never once broke a law I didn't have to, but I didn't even have to think to say yes. So I went to the address, an old hospital, a place all the kids think is haunted, and I met Milgram."

Milgram, Mendoza, and Julian. A frightening picture forms.

"Milgram, he seemed like a good guy, not a monster like everyone said. He said things like—"

I interrupt, "Like he's not as bad as everyone says. That he does bad things for a good reason. That more than anything else, he wants to help everybody and rebuild WPC into something great again?"

"So you've met Milgram too?"

"I got the sales pitch."

"He paid well, and he put me to work right away. Me and three other guys, Jaime, Mike, and Billy, we got put on this team of couriers. Drive packages from place to place, moving people, things . . . things I didn't want to know what they were. We didn't ask questions, we got paid, and things, they were looking up . . . or so I thought. I thought that because it was better than really thinking about what I was doing, because I knew it had to be bad, but I would've kept doing it anyway for the money. It went like this for a while, enough that I was thinking I might be able to swing a good Christmas for my family, when Mr. Julian found me one day and told me to stop working for Milgram."

The picture gets sharper, but I'm still missing a lot of the pieces.

"He found me here, talked with me. He was scared, but really trying to hide it. He kept apologizing for putting me with Milgram and said he was going to make it up to me, and to the city. Then he took a video of me talking about what I'd done for Milgram. He thanked me, saying to keep my head down and that he'd be in touch. That he was putting something together to make Milgram, and everyone who kept him in business, pay for what they were doing to the city. This was the day before he died."

"What happened next?"

"Next day, I got a call from Milgram's people, saying they had a special job for my team, and because I was supposed to keep my head down, I showed up. I think Mr. Julian had talked to Mike, Jaime, and Billy some too, 'cause they looked as scared as me, but none of us talked about it. The four of us, and one of Milgram's guys, we took a moving van over to an apartment building in EPC, real early in the morning. They put us in these coveralls that'd cover up what we were, and guided us up to an apartment, and inside . . . it was a mess. Everything torn up like they were looking for something. And, the woman."

"What woman?"

"She was dead. On the floor. Stabbed in the stomach a couple times. I'd never seen a dead person before."

He hunches over, wrapping his arms around his chest for support.

"Did you get a name?"

"For her? I don't remember. I think it began with an R."

"Ruby?'

"Yeah. Ruby."

Son of a bitch.

"Billy threw up. I wanted to as well, but then this . . . person came out of the bathroom."

"Person?"

"Look, I know it sounds funny, but I'm not sure who or what I saw, okay? I thought I heard another woman humming to herself in the shower, but then a man like any other one of Milgram's guards came out of the bathroom."

Bystander.

I knew she was tight with Milgram, and that she'd replaced Julian's secretary, but I never thought to ask her what they'd done with the real Ruby Herron.

What she'd *done to the real Ruby Herron.*

"The guards told us to clean up the apartment, so we did. We put everything back in its place, took everything broken out to the garbage, put her body in the van and cleaned up all the blood. Then the showering guard stayed behind, and the rest of us were sent back to Milgram's hospital. We all wanted to quit right then, because this wasn't the kind of work we'd signed up for, but then Milgram himself brought all of us aside, and said he had an important job for us. When we still said no, he used his powers on us.

"It was like, nothing mattered anymore except what he told us to do. He gave each of us five one-hundred dollar bills, right out of his own wallet, and told us that tonight we had to go to this spot and kill Quentin Julian. I knew this was something I wouldn't do, not normally, but it didn't just feel right, it felt like what we were put on this earth to do. And so we did it. We all took our money, and we killed Quentin Julian. But there was one thing we messed up."

"You were supposed to record it," I say, remembering the vision.

He nods. "When the other guys started dying, I thought it was maybe because we messed this up, but it's to keep us quiet, isn't it?"

"Maybe," I say.

It's all starting to make sense. Quentin Julian was involved in some kind of conspiracy with Milgram, but wanted to back out and probably go public with it. Milgram decided to cut his losses with Julian, find out what he had on him and then send a few lackeys to take him out. They were supposed to record it, and it was supposed to leak out, so Milgram could turn public opinion against gene-jobs specifically, and WPC in general. When they didn't, he had Bystander hire me to do their job for them. He even managed to get most of the press to sit on the story until he could spin it his way.

But what kind of conspiracy? To what end? WPC is a tinderbox as is, they didn't need to go this far to destabilize it. There's something else in play here. Something . . .

"Do you have any of that money still?" I ask.

"Yes," Mendoza says, pulling a crumpled bill from his pocket. "Why?"

"I can read you to verify your part of the story, but to find out more, I need to read something that was with Milgram," I say, taking the bill.

"So you're going to help me?"

"Maybe. I might get weird for a few minutes. Make sure I don't swallow my tongue, okay?"

He looks confused. "Wh—"

I'm reading the bill before he can say anything.

I'm following it around in his pocket, pacing throughout the trailer for days. Then back to the murder. Then to the moments before the murder.

Then when it was in Milgram's possession.

I follow him back, watching and listening as he talks to a bunch of his people, none of them about this.

Then he's in his office, making a phone call, when I hear the name Julian and stop rewinding. I can only hear his side of the conversation, but it's more detail than I could've hoped for.

Calmly, Milgram says, "Look, I understand Julian's a problem. No, I haven't been able to lock down the file yet, it wasn't at his office or with his secretary, but that's not gonna matter. I've already put one of my best in undercover. All good things come to those who have patience, right? You want him dead? Well, that would save a lot of work. No, I'm not saying we still shouldn't find the file, but what are the odds that he put that kind of safety on it yet? He doesn't know we're onto him. We'll do it tonight, I got some guys who're outliving their usefulness; they'll be perfect. It'll get done, Mr. Collingwraith, don't worry about it. When have I ever let you down?"

I know that name, Collingwraith. It's not a common name, so when you hear it, you remember it, and while I know there's a chance it could be another Collingwraith, I know in my heart of hearts it's Jeremy Collingwraith, celebrity lawyer and darling of the eleven o'clock news for his over-the-top defenses of his primary client.

Mayor William "The Conqueror" Card.

"Motherfucker," I whisper, falling out of the vision.

"Language!" Jeanine calls from behind a curtain.

My phone vibrates. I go to silence it, but look at the name on it first.

When I see who it is, I answer.

"Bystander," I say.

"I'm betting, where you are, that things aren't looking so hot right now."

"Shit," I say, running to a window and inching a curtain open. All I see is dark and rain.

"What?" Mendoza asks.

"We're being watched. You need to get out of here."

"I wouldn't do that if I were you," Bystander says.

"Oh no?"

"There's a lot going on you don't know about but, before I can explain, I'm going to need you to live through tonight, and the only way you're going to do that is if you, and you alone, right now, run out of that trailer and don't stop until you reach the Crescent. If you do that, the operative Mr. Milgram sent has orders to let you pass freely."

"And if I don't?"

"Then you're going to find out why he's called Effigy. Be smart. Let's work together on this, like we discussed."

"We never discussed anything like this . . . especially not murder."

"Certain moral compromises must be made on the road to progress."

"Like Ruby Herron? Or the rest of Mendoza's team? Were they just *moral compromises* when you killed them?"

I don't know that she killed anyone beyond Ruby, actually, but the pause on the other line confirms it.

"Don't," she says.

"Don't what?"

"Don't get so fucking sanctimonious on me. I've seen your army record. I know the horrible shit you've done. We're not that different."

"That was war," I say, now the defensive one.

"And this isn't?"

I can't say no to that.

"Don't do this to me. Don't make me choose like this."

"Sooner or later you're gonna have to get off that fence and make a choice. All I want you to do is make the right one. Please."

She hangs up.

In a flash of lightning, I see a figure standing in the aisle outside. I remember him from Milgram's place: the young, blonde, tattooed guy.

He stretches his arms out.

And suddenly there's more of him. Duplicates that begin walking away from him in every direction like his own personal zombie horde.

And one after another the duplicates begin to ignite, burning with brilliant blue flames that cut through the rain.

I know, at once, that I still have a small window to escape, one that shrinks every second I stay, and that I have to decide how I want to play this.

I can walk out right now, cut my ties with something I never wanted to be a part of in the first place, and come out of this one the same side with Bystander, letting all these people die.

Or I can try to do something about it, and almost certainly die myself.

Two flaming duplicates begin to sprint toward Mendoza's trailer.

Time to get off that fence.

CHAPTER 14: THE SUPERHERO

Hey, you're the new Solar Flare, aren't you?" asks the sales rep, peering around my sunglasses and frayed hoodie.

"No."

"Are too!" he says, pointing at my info on his computer screen. "You're Kimberly Kline! I have—I mean, my little sister has all your posters."

I glance at his nametag, merging it permanently with his face in my memory, and feel icky when I do.

My shallow "party trick" habit.

"Lance," I say, taking off the glasses to show him my puffy, mascara-free eyes. "I've had a really long couple days. Can I please, please just buy a phone?"

Lance looks disappointed but goes ahead with clicking around my account.

"It looks like you're not authorized for an upgrade until next month. If you can wait until the 21st, you can get the contract discount."

"Can't," I say, "but it's fine."

"Something happen to your old one?"

"Dropped it in the toilet."

"Huh, guess it happens to superheroes too."

"Guess so."

After a ten-minute pitch for a supposedly waterproof case that weighs twice as much as the new phone itself, Lance finally takes my credit card and activates the phone.

Thankfully, I'm one of the last customers of the day, and he's prodded along by his coworkers' impatient stares.

I don't know if I'll file for reimbursement or not. I'm torn between not wanting to take a cent from the Card family and not wanting to leave them a cent that's in any way mine. And it *is* their fault I have to spend an extra five hundred dollars to upgrade early.

Maybe I'll expense it to them and then donate the check to the Julian Foundation, or another worthy cause they'd hate even more.

The thought almost makes me smile, but it's like counting pocket change toward a private jet.

Nothing I do tonight is going to level the scales with what I didn't do last night.

The rain's been coming in fits and starts all day. It's pouring at the moment, so I tuck the new phone into the pocket of my badly fitting new jeans and pull the waistband of the hoodie down over it as an extra shield while I run to the little burger place down the street.

I must have eventually dozed off on the beach last night, because that's where I woke up this morning. As soon as the stores opened, I wandered, draped in a towel, into this thrift shop on the backstreets off the waterfront, the first place I could find where the staff wouldn't recognize me.

I changed in the dressing room and dropped my Solar Flare outfit in the trash on the way out, which would've been a whole lot more satisfying if there weren't a closet full of identical copies of it back at Guardian Tower.

Since then, I've spent the day avoiding . . . pretty much everything.

It's easy to tell myself I'm quitting when I'm flying laps of the North Pole or sitting alone in a New York deli, but the moment I have to tell someone, here in Pinnacle City, I know there's a good chance I won't have it in me to stay quit.

Sitting at one of the corner tables of the burger place, I finally do what I've been dreading. I turn on the new phone, connect to the Wi-Fi, and start the sweeping sync of my apps and accounts.

First comes the backed-up wave of texts and voicemails.

Pinnacle asking where the hell I am and why I didn't check in to my assignment today.

Mom and Uncle Ethan asking the same in more measured words, letting me know how "worried" Pinnacle sounded on the phone and asking me to assure them that I haven't somehow come in contact with Jovium and been incapacitated.

Jacob asking me to come in early for a confessional and then taking it incrementally more personally when I'm not early but late, and then absent.

Leah sending more pics of tofu lasagna and then asking if I'm mad after I stopped answering her.

Sergei letting me know it's no skin off his nose if I never come back, but that in case I'd like to, he's informed the others that my phone and I were both under the weather last night.

He was never so nice to me before, and I'm starting to think he might have more experience than I thought in keeping people quiet.

Last night probably wasn't the first time something like this has happened.

I don't answer any of them, not yet.

I should have picked a different shelter. The volume's too high on the TVs in here, and since there's no major game on tonight, half of them are set to the news. The current story is about Rickie Maroon taking an indefinite administrative leave, pending investigation into allegations made by over a dozen female interns.

I want to be shocked. I *try* to be shocked, to care the way I should, but there doesn't seem to be room left inside me to take it in.

Once the reporters are done gloating over their rival station's scandal, they move on to reviewing the sound bites from Mayor Card's latest interview.

"Do you have any comment on the recent rash of hate crimes citing your leadership as inspiration?" asks the reporter. I open one of the menus tucked between my table's napkin dispensers rather than look at Card's face as he responds.

"Well, you know, people are scared, and they're angry, and I think it's been a long time coming. We've got these communities, these cultures of aberrant violence existing right on the doorsteps of people's homes, and I think people, they're just sick and tired of it. It's been one of my top priorities as mayor to give law enforcement and the people the means and freedom they need to fight back and protect their families, but we've been so sabotaged with just, just an unprecedented amount of malice from our enemies, that we obviously haven't been able to come far enough. I can promise you this, though, when I can advocate for Pinnacle City above the mayoral level, it's going to be so safe, so protected, everyone's going to want to raise their families here."

"By 'cultures of aberrant violence,' you mean the residents of WPC?"

"Look, someone's starting the violence, and everyone knows who it is. Everyone. You look at the peaceful family homes on the one side, and the streets full of drugs and robbery and murder and rape on the other, and it doesn't take a genius to do the math."

I watch my apps download, three at a time.

Translator.

Music.

Library.

Three different messengers.

Villscan.

Superdirectline.

DistressFinder.

When it finishes installing, I tap DistressFinder and let it run in the background, searching and cross-referencing all emergency calls, infrastructure damage, and the hashtags of mobile uploads in the city to pinpoint likely locations of supervillain activity and disasters.

Anything that might be a job for a hero.

I don't know why I bother. Maybe because it feels normal, feels like before all this. It was the first app I opened when I turned on my phone every morning as Glitter Girl.

"I'm glad you brought up family," says the reporter. "Your 'Family Restoration' plan has been one of the more controversial points of your senate campaign. Would you—"

"Oh, there've been a lot of false reports going around about all this huge opposition, but they're really just a few bitter, lonely, angry old ladies making a fuss. Tremendous exaggeration."

"You believe the media has exaggerated the response to your promise to eliminate legal protections for women in the work-force?"

"Actually, I never said that," says Card. "There's a lot of slanted news out there about me. You should do your homework more carefully."

The reporter checks his notes. "Here's the quote we received: 'The Equal Employment Opportunity Commission is one of the most serious and sinister modern threats to both the economy and the family unit.' Is that incorrect?"

It's correct. I was standing in the wings behind him waiting to dive in front of snipers when he said that.

"What I said or didn't say isn't important," he continues. "The point is, I'm going to bring back family and the American dream, no matter how my enemies try to tear it down. Children need a mother. Employers need reliable, focused employees. But I respect the role of women in the workforce. I do. Nobody does more than me. There are certain women, young ladies without the distractions they'll have later in life, who can be more valuable than any man in certain positions. Take my relationship with Solar Flare, for example."

Oh god.

I scroll down the alerts on DistressFinder, past the bank and jewelry store robberies I know the other Guardians will reach before I could, trying not to hear Card's voice.

"She's a girl, and a *super* no less, a big role model to girls everywhere, and she's become like a member of the family looking out for us the way she has. People don't think I care about the ladies, but I love them. I love them like crazy."

Far toward the bottom of the DistressFinder listings, there's a cluster of reports of a structure fire. Given the rain, it's almost certainly superhuman arson.

The location is deep in WPC, far outside the core response radius for either the Juniors or the PCG.

Another text comes in from Pinnacle, asking me to clarify my need for a sick day, given that my application listed no known weaknesses.

I don't answer.

I don't know who Solar Flare is or what she's supposed to do next, or if she even still exists, but I know who Kimberly Kline is, and she's going to go put out a fire.

It's a shantytown that's blazing in spite of the downpour; trailers, tents, shacks, and an old abandoned grocery store all dripping with wet ash even as they burn.

There isn't a superhero or a police car in sight, but a half-dozen figures glowing with blue flame are circling the wreckage, adding to the fire wherever it begins to go out.

Some of the inhabitants are still around, several of them throwing buckets of rainwater at the figures and structures, others standing off to the side, huddling under whatever blankets, tarps, or clothes they could grab, watching in an attitude of inevitable gloom.

Okay, Glitter Girl, g—

No, I mean *Kimberly*, go!

"Hey, Matchsticks!" I shout to the glowing blue arsonists, floating over them and the epicenter of the destruction. "This little gang of yours got a name?"

Not that it matters, but old habits.

The figures all answer in perfect unison without deviating from their work.

"We are Effigy."

Huh. Pretty good name.

"Are you going to move away from the homes, Effigy? Or am I going to move you?"

The Effigies don't answer, which in this case is answer enough.

Swooping down in a long, fast arc, I grab two of them, one under each arm, and dangle them over the fruits of their efforts, waiting to see if that'll be enough to make the others back off.

Didn't think so.

The Effigies squirm without concern for their altitude, burning through my secondhand sweatshirt, and it takes me a moment to realize they're not only squirming and burning. They're multiplying.

When I'm holding three of them under each arm instead of one, one of them slips and falls into the charred tent below, splitting on impact into three more.

New strategy: burst of speed.

Two at a time, I start grabbing copies and flying them out to the ocean, dropping them about a half mile offshore, close enough that they won't drown even if I leave them there, far enough that they won't make it back to land before I can take care of the fire and figure out what to do with them.

It seems for a while that I'm making progress, relocating them faster than they can multiply, but the copies left in the shantytown are getting angrier, meaner, turning their flames on the people wielding buckets as well as their homes.

"Heroes have no business here!" all of Effigy shouts together, one of the copies grabbing me with a flaming hand that can't hurt me but sets the cuff of my jeans on fire.

A young family standing guard over their dilapidated lean-to abandons their defense, scooping up their children and making a break away from the encampment.

I relocate the copies laying into their possessions next.

The deeper I go into the wreckage, grabbing copies along the way, the worse the news gets. People have died here already, skeletons charred beyond recognition holding each other or raising their arms in defense against the flaming Effigies that set their homes on fire.

I might be sick again, but not 'til this is under control.

Why is no one else here?

No. No one answer that.

No matter how many copies I move, this isn't working. The fires are too hot. Nothing's going to be left on this spot by morning but ash.

I leave the Effigies alone and go for the residents instead, flying anyone who'll take my hand out to the edge of the destruction and blasting aside the copies trying to block off their escape routes on the ground.

An elderly man with the beak of a hummingbird emerges shakily from one of the trailers, dragging an oxygen tank and a mask jury-rigged to fit him with trash bags and duct tape. He raises his cane defensively when I fly for him, and I try to explain that his tank's in danger of accelerating the fire, but eventually I have to scoop up both him and it and drop them off before we get a live demonstration.

I'm confused by why the Effigies hardly seem to be trying to stop me anymore, until I realize they're converging on one trailer in particular, cornered up against the grocery store, abandoning the rest to their evacuation.

"If this is what Milgram calls a recruitment package, you can tell him *fuck off*!" shouts a man in front of the trailer in question.

There's a hole burnt clean through the side of it, and there are people inside, hissing urgently to each other. Through the hole I see a little girl frantically gathering things into a bag.

A man swings a baseball bat that connects with an Effigy's head, forcing it back.

There's soot on his clothes and sparks in his long, wet hair, and oh sugar cookies, it's Eddie.

It's the guy whose name I didn't want next to mine in the tabloids, shielding a family from supervillains with nothing but a baseball bat, while Mayor Card babbles to a national news audience about how he's going to quarantine this whole neighborhood and what a great endorsement my friendship has been.

I thought coming here would make me feel better about myself.

I was wrong.

Eddie looks up, and in the several, squinting seconds it takes for the recognition to reach his face, I'd like nothing better than to hide, but the Effigy in front of him is glowing brighter around the hands, and there's no time for my embarrassment.

I pluck the copy off the ground before it can reach its burning hands to Eddie's face, tossing it only a few yards away so I can grab the next one and do the same.

All at once, the Effigies part as a non-burning copy runs through their midst toward Eddie. He swings his bat at it, but it dodges easily, grabbing him in a chokehold. They exchange some words and I want to help him, but there are too many of them between us, and they're on me like a wave.

Spreading his legs out for balance, he manages to flip the unburning copy over his shoulder, taking a swing at it with his bat, but before he can make contact it rolls out of the way and disappears back into the horde.

"I don't want to hurt you!" I shout at the Effigies, doing my best to clear them away from between us with nonlethal blasts. "*Please!*"

"The real one's long gone!" shouts Eddie. "Nothing you do to these fuckers'll hurt anyone!"

I hope he's right.

No light, I tell my fingers, rerouting as much as I can of my usual, reflexive type of energy direction. *No light, no heat, just force.*

The shockwave I send forward cuts the Effigies closest to us in half at the waist, and there's a brief whiff of excrement and burning meat before they extinguish, then dissipate into nothing.

Those farther back are knocked down with a variety of injuries, some dissolving like the dismembered ones, others, the farthest away, beginning to multiply to replace them.

This is the best chance we're going to get. I turn to look at what's left of the trailer. Most of the base still looks sturdy enough.

"Everyone get down!" I shout through the hole in the wall.

Eddie considers for a moment, looking at the regrouping Effigies, then drops, and I hear three bodies inside the trailer do the same.

I take aim at the blaze eating through the trailer's roof.

No light, no heat, just force.

My next, smaller shockwave extinguishes the fire, mostly by knocking off the top third of the trailer, preserving as much as I can of the inside.

The girl crawls to the hole to look out, her eyes wide under her hood. Her frightened face is secreting some kind of mucous, and she clutches an armful of comics to her chest like her dearest friend. I recognize the *Adventures of Glitter Girl* logo, big and bright at the top of the covers.

When she sees me looking, she vanishes into thin air.

No, not vanishes, turns invisible. I can see the smoke and rain avoiding the space her body still occupies.

"Climb aboard and hold onto something," I tell Eddie. After a brief hesitation he steps through the hole, beckoning the invisible girl away from the edge.

A couple, presumably her parents, peer over the top of the wall I broke. The woman's holding a baby, and the man . . . I hope for a moment that I'm imagining things. Maybe it's just a similar mutation and the firelight playing tricks on me, but no, the sick feeling in my stomach is sure of it. I've seen the girl's father before.

He helped murder Quentin.

There are about a million things I'd like to say to him, but the Effigies are closing in. I bend my knees and brace my fingers, lifting the bottom of the trailer off the asphalt, holding it level over my head. I take off, flying Eddie, Quentin's murderer, and his family along inside.

When exactly did doing the right thing get so complicated?

CHAPTER 15: THE DETECTIVE

I guide the hero to the Crescent and hold on for dear life. The trailer half she carries us all on wasn't meant for this kind of travel, let alone at high speed, through pouring rain, late at night. I don't have it as bad as Mendoza and his wife, trying to help two kids hold on as well, but I'm not having fun either.

Credit to her, though, she gets us there quick and we're all alive. Better than things would've been if we'd stayed at Camp 31.

I can't say for sure how many other residents got out alive. I can hope, but I can't believe it was very many. We got out by what has got to be some of the greatest dumb luck in history.

Or I've got a pissed off one night stand who's looking for a pound of flesh.

For once, I'm hoping for dumb luck.

She sets us down around the back of the Lineup. Though she didn't respond to my texts, Tragedii is waiting for us, rain pouring around her shield bubble.

She gives the trailer half, then us, then the trailer half again all one quick look before saying, "Just what the hell happened?"

"Long story. I'm trying to fix things, and these people got caught in the middle. Can we stash them in the Well for a few days?"

I've said the magic words.

"Let me get the keys."

She presses a button on her mechanical wrist, opening a small compartment farther up her arm that reveals a small key card, which she takes. Her mechanical eye swivels on its own and locks onto the hero, glowing bright red.

"What about her?" Tragedii asks.

That's not a bad question.

Solar Flare, Kimberly Kline, whatever she wants to be called, stands in the rain with us, and yet not with us. She knows she's somewhere she's not welcome. This is new for her, I think, and I don't think she likes it very much. I could take a lot of pleasure in just kicking her to the curb, here and now, like any other pro-hero would do to us under the circumstances.

But she *did* save us when she didn't have to, and on her own time, if her lack of uniform means anything. The other Guardians, they wouldn't go to WPC unless there were headlines in it, and there *aren't* headlines in saving a bunch of homeless and gene-jobs from a shantytown fire. There's an actual chance, however much I don't want to believe it, that she may actually believe in all that heroing shit.

"She's with us, I guess," I say.

"Okay. You got any designs on that trailer?" Tragedii asks.

"No."

"Excellent. I've been meaning to give my disintegrator ray a good workout," Tragedii says, waving us over to a stairway leading to the basement behind the bar. Mendoza, his family, and Kline all head down.

Tragedii waves her key over a brick near the base of the basement's dingy-looking door and it disappears, replaced by a swirling green portal.

With the others looking at it warily, I step through, and into the Well.

✳

The Well used to be Tragedii's time travel ship. According to her, it's no bigger on the outside than a small van, but on the inside it's about the size of a pretty decent condo, with living quarters, medical facilities, and entertainment enough for close to a dozen people. I've never seen the outside of it, because Tragedii refuses to tell anyone where, or when, it currently is, making it one of the safest places in the world as far as I know.

With her future no longer existing, Tragedii uses the Well mostly as a place to rest her feet between shifts, but occasionally for more altruistic purposes. She's opened it up to runaways dodging the system, junkies looking to detox, and women fleeing from abusive husbands, boyfriends, and stalkers on more than one occasion. I don't think she's ever had a group this big in it before, but I'm glad she's cool letting us hole up here for now.

Mendoza and his family take two of the bedrooms, and after a few rounds of thanks that I don't feel I've fully earned, they disappear for the night with an escort from Kline.

I park myself in front of the big screen in the ship's media room, surfing around the news and finding nothing about Milgram's attack on Camp 31. I'm not surprised when it's all gossip about which pro-heroes are sleeping with which pro-heroes (and rumors that working with the Cards has made the new Solar Flare crack), so I finally settle on some nature documentary, where a British guy narrates lions picking off weak wildebeest from a herd.

I'm watching without watching, because what I'm really doing is waiting for her. Waiting for a conversation I don't want to but very much need to have, because, like it or not, there's a chance I can trust this girl, and a chance that I'm going to need more of her help.

But the conundrum is whether to tell her everything or *almost* everything. Do I leave out Bystander in the naïve hope that I can still save her from the mess she's gotten into with Milgram, giving her what I want her to know as opposed to what she probably should know?

Bystander came for me, during the attack. Tried to save me from the Effigies while disguised as one of them. She tried to choke me out and drag me off (very romantic, I know), and for her trouble I flung her down and tried to hit her with Harriet.

I haven't seen her look that hurt since after the Ricardo incident. Even with her wearing a stranger's face, my heart broke for doing that to her.

I wish it hadn't. I wish it were easier to think of her as just another Milgram thug if that's what she really wants to be.

After what seems like hours of waiting, Kline's back in the room.

"Have you ever tried the showers in here? I've never had water this hot with that much pressure before," she sighs, wrapping her hair in a towel. She's wearing a bath robe that was clearly made for Tragedii's size, baggy on even her impressive frame and dragging on the ground, even though I'm pretty sure she's hovering by a few inches.

"Did it smell a little funny?" I ask, amused.

"Like sulfur? A little bit."

"Then you got the shower plugged into primordial Earth. Tragedii doesn't like paying for utilities or anything like that so she's wired the Well to all kinds of time travel shortcuts. Try not to shower for too long next time or you might prevent life from existing. Did you toss your clothes in that thing that looked like a dryer?"

"Yes. Why? It's not a dryer?" she asks, dubious.

Suddenly, I'm very grave. "No, it isn't. In fact, you just threw your clothes into a machine that might unravel the very nature of reality itself."

Her eyes go wide as saucers, and in a streak of light, she disappears, only to come back a fraction of a second later. By this point, I can't help but laugh out loud.

"The Maytag logo on that dryer says you're lying."

"Sorry. Couldn't resist. In any case, how're the Mendozas settling in?"

"Good. I don't think the parents trust me."

"You're a pro-hero, and they're from WPC. What'd you expect, a parade?"

She has nothing to say to this. "Kaley's a sweetheart, though. She wants to be a superhero when she grows up."

She doesn't meet my eyes when she says this, looking to some faraway place of hurt. The part of me that grew up in the Crescent wants to push and prod, to scratch open that hurt and pour salt on it, but I don't.

"So," she says.

"So," I say, letting the word hang there.

Believe it or not, this isn't the most awkward conversation I've had after running into an ex-one-night-stand.

"Should I be asking you what you were doing at the Camp tonight?" I ask.

"Should I be asking what *you* were doing there with one of Quentin Julian's killers?" she asks back.

"You caught that, then?"

"Kind of hard to miss with his face all over the news."

"It's a memorable face," I admit. "So, why haven't you arrested him? And the rest of us, for that matter?"

She still won't meet my eyes, instead staring at the TV, through it even.

"I used to think I knew what good and evil looked like. I thought I could fly into any situation and know right from wrong. Lately, it hasn't been working out that way. But tonight, I knew. I could see the men burning everything down, killing people, and I knew that was evil. Then I saw you. You were protecting those people because you knew it was the right thing to do, putting your life on the line, and I knew you were good. And I knew that if you were doing this because it was good, then things couldn't be so simple about Mr. Mendoza. So that's why I'm here, talking to you and trying to figure out what the heck to do next."

She's put me in one helluvan awkward spot. It would be a lot easier, and safer, to blow her off with a half-ass excuse about why I was protecting Mendoza. It would have been easier and safer not to invite her into the Well in the first place. But if she means what she says, she could be my ticket into circles I'd never be able to infiltrate otherwise, places even Fadia can't go (though won't she be pissed when she hears about this).

If she hasn't been kicked off *In the Cards* yet, she may even be able to get me access to the Conqueror himself, and wouldn't that be something?

Maybe she can help me find out what the hell the connection is between him and Milgram, and what the hell that has to do with the death of Quentin Julian.

Or maybe, she really is just a spoiled EPC starlet out for a cheap thrill. Maybe she's even on Milgram's payroll too, just like the cops.

There's only one way to know.

"Give me your hands," I say.

"Why?"

"Are you really gonna tell me you've never looked up my record and R-SAL info?"

"I . . . might have done some research."

"Then you know why. If you're worried about me stealing your deepest, darkest secrets, relax, I'm better with inanimate objects, people are never as reliable. But if you give me a few minutes I'll get enough of a reading to know if I can trust you."

"And if you decide you can't?"

"Then I guess we're both shit out of luck."

She doesn't hesitate long before offering up her hands. I try to shake the feelings of revulsion I had in the days after our tryst, and take them without too much hesitation of my own.

And then I see what she's been up to.

I see a woman trying to be a hero and being blocked at every turn.

I see someone regretting actions not taken and wanting to fix that.

I see an EPC princess stopping a jackass from shooting up a peaceful protest.

I see a superhero who actually believes in the word and isn't just in it for the fame.

That's all I need to see.

"So you want to be a hero?"

"Yes. Yes I do."

"I don't just mean like a pro-hero, I mean a real hero. You want to make a difference, do something good no matter what it takes and how it might blow up in your face?"

"Yes."

"Good. I think I do, too. So let me spin you a story."

And then I lay it out for her.

Milgram and what he's doing to WPC and the Crescent.

Everything Mendoza told and showed me, and how that led to the discovery of a probable connection between Milgram and Mayor Card and the violence that's been taking place.

I pause when it gets to my part in this.

For a moment I almost give Bystander up, but ultimately decide against it. I just . . . I can't. I tell Kline that Milgram sent a shapeshifter looking like Julian's murdered secretary to set me on the trail to find Julian's killers.

She doesn't quite react the way I expect.

"I knew it!" she exclaims, standing up.

"Really?"

She paces back and forth in front of me, so distracted she doesn't even seem to realize her feet aren't touching the floor.

"I knew before I knew, I mean, *really* knew what they were, that the Cards were bad people. You don't have to see much to know that. But working for them, being in their house every day, shadowing them like a flipping puppy . . ."

"Everyone knows they're assholes. That's why they voted for the guy."

"I didn't."

"Well, then that's something else you and me got in common."

"I've seen things, though, that I think might be a part of what you're talking about."

Now she's got my attention.

"And what might that be?"

"He's got a map of Pinnacle City on the wall of his home office with a lot of markings on it. Sometimes when he's watching TV, I sneak in and look at it."

"What kind of markings?"

"Misspellings, mostly, but most of them are over the west half of the city. Like a new map on top of the old one. Kind of a grid, with some sections empty, and some of them holding company names. Some of them were his, some I know belong to other people—"

"Other people in your circle?" I finish.

She doesn't say yes, but she doesn't say no.

"It makes sense, though, doesn't it?" I add.

"Card and Milgram stage the murder of Quentin Julian because he was building a case against them, and to demonize West Pinnacle City," she says.

"Two birds with one stone," I confirm.

"Probably to set the political scene for Card to push through his no man's land project," she goes on. "That fits. But then why all the map work? It's not like he cares what happens in WPC once it's cut off. And what does Milgram get out of it?"

"I don't know yet, but I don't think they're the only two with a stake in this." I'm sure this is a delicate question, but it has to be asked. "Is there any chance the other pro-heroes are in on it?"

The way she looks at me, you'd think I just told her Christmas was canceled.

"No." she says, her hands glowing with energy, and I'm not sure she's really talking to me. "No way. The others, they're not perfect, but they're not criminals."

I could go on about this for a while, but I've learned better than to antagonize a pro-hero, especially when their blood is up like this.

"So, what do we do now?" she asks.

"We?"

"Yes, *we*. You told me all of this, and if any of it's true, I'm as much a part of this as you are."

"For now, I'm going to go upstairs and get a drink," I say, feeling a tug in my left arm. I need my pills and I need them bad; I'm just hoping Lucero has a fresh stash upstairs and is willing to let me get some on credit.

"You're getting drunk?"

"It's late, and there's not a lot that can be done for now, so, yeah, I'm gonna get drunk and surround myself with a bunch of even drunker ex-supervillains who no one, not even Milgram himself, would dare fuck with. You go home, get a good night's sleep, and go back to work."

"Back. To. Work?!" she says, punctuating each word as if it were a curse.

"Yeah?"

"The Cards are monsters, and every moment I'm with them I feel like I need to scrub myself clean. Why would I go back to them?"

"Because the best idea I've got right now is building a case to prove all this and making it go public. We can't just go around killing the mayor (I have it on good authority it might destroy the future, or something), but we can tell everyone the evil shit he's done and take a stab at getting him arrested. I've got a friend in a pretty good place with the media. I think if we get enough proof that they can make stick, maybe if we can find Julian's file, there's a chance we can clear Mendoza's name and get the right people put behind bars. But to get that proof, we could sure use someone like you on the inside."

I don't know when I became we, but there you have it.

Her fury, though, is unstoppable.

"That's not good enough. I want to—I *need* to hit something. I want to fight some bad guys."

Looking at her, remembering how well she fought against the Effigies and how little they could hurt her, an idea forms.

"If you can't take on Card," I suggest, "why don't you take on Milgram?"

Her eyes brighten at the idea. "Take the conspiracy out at the ankles. Make it so they can't walk."

"Exactly. I know his home base, and I have a friend who can probably show you where the rest of his operations are if you ask real nice. If I help you do this, will you help me look for Julian's file?"

She looks thoughtful for a moment. "Only if you'll do something for me, first."

"Other than setting you up to give Milgram a hard time?"

"Going back to the Card family is worth two favors."

I didn't think she had it in her. "Go on."

"You know Ace Card?"

"The mayor's son? The one who looks like he needs a good punch to the face? You want me to rough him up for swatting you on the ass or something? 'Cause I don't need that much of an excuse."

She's not amused. Maybe I hit too close to the mark.

"Working for the Cards is about ninety percent covering for everything they do," she says. "*You* have the ability to *un*cover things, in a way that'll stand up in court. I need you to help me fix a mistake."

She chews her tongue, preparing for an uphill battle of convincing me, of justifying what she's about to say.

"Last night, at the Silver Cowl, Ace drugged and raped—"

"Done," I say, without hesitation. I meant it when I said I didn't need that much of an excuse to go after Ace Card, but proving *this* is something I'd do pro bono.

She's speechless for a moment, tripping over the unnecessary remainder of her pitch. "Thank you."

Finally, she sits down and holds her hand out to me. "So, we're going to save this city?"

"We can try," I say, standing up. "But if we do this, it might be the end of your heroing days."

"If I can't be a superhero and a hero at the same time, I don't deserve these powers."

I clasp her hand in mine.

I know this is insane, and I know this is risky, and I still don't want to like or trust this woman, but I also know that she's likely my, and this city's, best hope.

Now here's hoping we can both do even half of what we promised each other.

CHAPTER 16: THE SUPERHERO

The meeting spot Eddie named is on the corner of a homeless tent city and a street of businesses crushed under Killtron bot-sized footprints. I'm dressed again in jeans and a hoodie, a better-fitting set after what Effigy did to my thrift shop ensemble, but as inconspicuous as I can be.

I've been counting the hours all day until I could get out of my Solar Flare outfit and slip away from both Card Mansion and Guardian Tower, away from all the concerned and disappointed glances lingering from my no-call no-show day.

It's only now that the nerves are starting to set in.

"You're here," says a voice behind me.

I jump and whirl around, energy charging up my fingers, but I know the instant I turn that it's no mugger. It's her, the contact Eddie told me to meet for my first of our self-assigned rogue heroing missions.

Dissident.

She looks exactly like all the grainy photos of her you see on the evening news, covered from head to toe in black. Black body armor, black cape, black holsters and belts for a million different weapons, and a black helmet that reveals nothing but digital, glowing eyes and the faintest glow of the electronics inside.

Her voice comes out distorted, digitized, and without kindness.

"Put it on."

She holds out a plain, store bought ski mask.

"I never wear one," I tell her.

Glasses when I don't want to be noticed are the closest I let myself get.

"That face of yours is worth most as a mole," says Dissident. "You're here on the condition that you keep it clean."

She shoves the mask into my hands, and rather than argue and be left behind I pull it on. In her helmet's reflective faceplate, I look like a common robber.

Uncle Ethan always said real heroes don't need masks. He said we were the trustworthy ones, the ones who give our names and faces to the world, the ones who accept true responsibility and allow ourselves no reasons to hide, no reasons to be ashamed of what we do.

Now I'm wearing one to do the first thing I've been unashamed of since taking his name.

"It also has filters to shield you against Milgram's verbal mind tampering," adds Dissident.

"You know, you could have led with that."

"Stop. Right now, or I send you back where you came from."

"Stop what?"

"Stop playing Glitter Girl."

"I'm not playing—"

"*You are not here to inspire children's comic books.* You are not here to out-dance, out-gimmick, and out-banter this man. You are here to bring pain and take names and ruin the days of people who smuggle bioweapons and rent out kidnapped women and children to the highest bidder. You're here because Eddie says you can be trusted, and because I've been waiting for so long to have the muscle to fuck this place up that I'm willing to risk putting a superstrong rookie in the same room with a mind controller to do it, and you are *not* going to make me regret that gamble."

"No regrets." I hold up my hands. "Promise. And you don't have to worry, I've been fighting crime for fifteen years."

"Kittens in trees aren't crime."

I want to tell her that pet rescues only make up about two percent of the calls the Justice Juniors go out on, but the memory of the charred corpses in that burning shantytown resurface, along with a layer of bile at the back of my throat to suggest that maybe she has a point.

Without another word, Dissident turns, walks, and gestures for me to follow.

"So, you think he'll actually be there?" I break the silence. "I mean, personally?"

"His personal schedule varies without warning, but I'd give us good odds."

We traverse several shattered city blocks at her painfully deliberate walking pace, and I have to ask.

"Where are we going?"

Dissident finally nods up the slope of weeds ahead. "Where else?"

I take in the stark, crumbling façade of the old Snyder Sanitarium and wonder for a moment if I've only traded in one superteam's hazing for another.

"Seriously?"

"Deadly," Dissident answers.

"He's operating out of an actual abandoned mental institution, and he somehow hasn't been exposed yet?"

"You can afford to be audacious when you've got the whole PCPD either on your payroll or terrified for their families' lives."

"And maybe the mayor," I mutter.

The sanitarium's front gate is still padlocked under its faded CONDEMNED sign, and I charge up my hand to break through it, but Dissident blocks me at the wrist.

"Element of surprise."

"Up and over then?" I ask, holding out my arms.

"Do not pick me up," says Dissident.

She pulls what looks like an extra baton from her belt, holds it to the side, and pushes a button to extend it into a vaulting pole, propelling herself over.

I lift off, swoop down next to her on the other side—no smashing, no lights—and follow her up the sanitarium's former lawn to the front door.

She pulls a set of metal picks from her belt and sets to work on the lock. I try to stand still and not overthink what's going to be on the other side of that door until it finally creaks open into a dark, empty lobby.

"Now what?" I whisper.

"The offices are upstairs on the left, and there are some storerooms in the basement. Go find out what they're running through this place and see if you can find anything to link your buddies in the mayor's office to it."

"And you?"

"Milgram. You hear my voice in your mask, you come in smashing to back me up. I won't ask twice." She runs silently down the ground floor hallway while I start up the stairs.

And I thought Pinnacle was bossy.

Though, on the other hand, Pinnacle's never trusted me to come along to bust up organized crime in the first place, so this is a net improvement.

The offices Dissident's pointed me toward are empty for now and weirdly . . . normal.

I don't know what I expected the offices of an infamous crime syndicate operating out of an abandoned mental asylum to look like. Skull-shaped desks, caged puppies and straightjackets hanging threateningly on the walls, maybe, but they're just offices, with wastebaskets, computers, coffee mugs, even in and out mail trays, though I'm sure there's no official mail service out here.

By the dates on some of the papers—invoices for off-brand sticky notes—someone was working here earlier today, and when I concentrate hard enough, I get an inkling of patches of energy nearby that probably mean not everyone's gone home for the night.

Without knowing if Milgram is even a real name (*probably not*), I don't know how I'm going to recognize which office is his . . . until I see it.

I know it by all the crayon drawings taped to the walls and desk. They're all different, all signed with different names in rough block letters, but about half the artists have labeled their subjects, the way kids do.

"Mr. Milgram," reading to a full classroom.

"Mister Millgrum," working in a garden.

"Mr. Milgrim," holding a jump rope while kids skip over it.

They sure do love to draw him.

"My gallery's bigger," I mutter to no one in particular, while I start searching the room for I'm not sure what.

I'm rummaging through his desk full of more drawings, some actual photographs of him with the children, more invoices for thoroughly boring office supplies, when my phone buzzes.

Hard as I try, I don't quite manage to shut it off without seeing that it's Mason.

I don't have to answer.

I'm not going to.

I'm kidding myself again.

I accept the call and press it to my ear with my shoulder, still digging through the drawers.

"Little busy right now," I whisper.

"That's okay, this won't take long." Mason has a habit of saying this whenever it isn't true. "I just thought you should know that I'm quitting the team."

"Oh, jeez, okay, can I call you when I get home? Or tomorrow? Whatever happened, I'm sure it'll look better in the morning."

"It's a done deal this time. Like I said, just wanted you to know."

"Oh. Well that . . . that sucks." I run out of more specific words of sympathy when my fingers fall on the thing I didn't know I was looking for.

An invoice for "consultant services rendered" from Jeremy Collingwraith.

I know it's not conclusive. Milgram and Card using the services of the same lawyer doesn't prove any further connection between them; it's not even illegal, but it fits with what we've put together so far. If Collingwraith's done more for Milgram than just make some calls to him on Card's behalf, he's looking more and more like the person to talk to about them both.

"I'm leaving tonight," says Mason.

"Leaving for where?" I ask automatically, shoving the invoice into the back pocket of my jeans.

There's nothing else here, so I start back down the stairs toward the storerooms.

"I'm not sure yet," says Mason.

The lights don't work in the asylum's basement, so I light up my free hand to look over the maze of shipping crates down here.

" . . . I'm at the pancake house," says Mason. "In the parking lot."

He lets the information hang there, without having to specify which pancake house.

"*The* pancake house" means the one where we shared cinnamon French toast on our retroactively official first date, and the sequence of "I'm quitting the team," "I'm leaving tonight," and "I'm at the pancake house" means "Come to the pancake house and talk me out of it."

I pull the lid off one of the crates and get the immediate urge to wash my hands.

I'm no connoisseur of narcotics, but I know this stuff from the PSA the Justice Juniors had to film after something like fifty kids up and down the West Coast overdosed on it.

It's called Catch, and it's basically synthetic heroin in fruity flavors, with some stimulants mixed in. I pry off another lid and find more of the same. There must be over a million doses in here.

"It hasn't been the same since you left," Mason continues, and it sounds like every word has to be pressed out of him with a vice. "I think I finally realized you were the only real reason I stayed this long. Without you there, I just don't see a lot of point in staying."

My heart swells up into a sore, familiar lump, and I almost tell him not to go anywhere, that I'm on my way, that I'll be there in two seconds.

I can see my mother's knowing smile as she waves me on my way to yet another tumultuous reconciliation, picture the paparazzi shots of the two of us alone together off duty again, the lines around the block for the next issue of the comic, and suddenly the prospect sickens me.

I do miss him, and I miss the others, and I miss the work, and the possibility of going back someday has crossed my mind about a hundred more times since I clocked back in with the PCG so I could spy on the Cards.

But maybe Dissident is right. Maybe all we were really doing, in the grand scheme of things, was saving kittens from trees.

Cute, safe, photogenic kittens.

Kicking open another crate and spilling the rainbow-colored Catch gummies all over the floor, I know that even if I exhaust my usefulness on the Guardians and get to quit permanently, I don't want to go back.

I want to go forward.

This woman in the ski mask, destroying a Catch smuggler's cache, I don't even know if she has a name, but she's who I want to be now.

"Mason," I start, not sure how I'm going to explain all that.

Dissident's voice blares out of the tiny speaker sewn in next to my ear.

"South wing, now!"

Protecting my phone between my chest and hand, I charge the rest of my body with enough energy to light the room up ten times over and release it all in a single blast, shattering every crate to smoldering splinters and leaving the contents a molten mess of sugar and plastic wrappings.

"You okay?" asks Mason.

"I have to go," I say, taking off and orienting myself to the south.

"Oh." I hear the roar of Mason's motorcycle starting in the background. "Yeah. Me too. Goodbye, Kimberly."

"Goodbye, Mason."

Dissident said to come in smashing, so I take a few shortcuts through walls to let whoever she's found hear what they're up against if they hurt her.

Goodbye, Mason.

Did I really just say that?

Following the sounds of screams and arguing, I find Dissident standing in a large, tidy cafeteria, facing down a double-thick row of rather well-dressed men with automatic weapons, one man who appears to be made entirely out of menacingly revving chainsaws, and a few who appear to be unarmed.

Those ones worry me most.

She's already disarmed one of the gunmen and is holding him in front of her as a shield, his throat pinned with her extendable staff, his weapon under her foot. The others appear hesitant to approach her, but they're not backing off, either.

In one swoop, I clear away the first row of guns, pulling them from hands, bending them out of shape, deflecting the few bullets that get loose in the process.

Dissident charges into the resulting shock and confusion, dropping her human shield to the floor, beating away the guns still in hand with her batons, as certain and unfazed as if my power were an extension of her own, not a rescue she required.

"We're close," she tells me, fighting her way to the staircase at the cafeteria's far end.

I move to follow her, but one of the unarmed men raises his arms toward me and his fingers shoot out like silly string, stretching and dividing across the distance until they wrap around me in the form of a hundred steely tendrils.

I send out an energy charge that seems to paralyze the tendrils for a moment, but not long enough for me to wriggle out of their grip. They grow and lengthen, pinning down my arms and reaching up toward my face.

Okay, energy's not doing it, and I'm in a disadvantageous position for strength. Running down my checklist of options, I take off for the ceiling and start to spin, reeling in the stretcher like spaghetti on a fork, and then dive bomb the chainsaw man.

The revving blade of the chainsaw man's head digs into the fleshy strings of the stretcher, not cutting them, but sucking them into the gears of his neck like shoelaces in a bike chain.

"Ow!" the stretcher says to the chainsaw man. "Let go!"

"You let go!" the chainsaw man replies, powering down his engines and trying to pick the stretcher out of his chains with yet more chains that make up his hands.

In their struggle to extricate themselves from each other, I pull free of the stretcher's loosening strands and fly straight into a stone statue that was a man a moment ago.

"Hold still," he says, slowly changing from gray to green to gold. "There's gotta be something on the periodic table that'll slow you down."

I dodge a swing from his stone arm, feel myself buffeted by someone's telekinesis, and smell the sole of my shoe melting when Effigy reveals himself from among the thugs in a blaze of blue flame.

A dart hits my shoulder from somewhere behind, sticking in my hoodie, unable to pierce my skin. I shake it off and reach back to grab the nearest body to where I think it came from, and find myself dragging a small, scaly, violet woman by the wrist.

"Don't hurt me!" she begs with open palms, her pure black eyes wide. "Please, they told me they were an exotic modeling agency!"

Bracing her against my chest, I fly backward out of one of the front windows and set her on the lawn.

"Go," I tell her, before turning back inside.

Where did she spring out of, and how did I miss her at first? Never mind.

I dodge the next wave of powers and bullets and rocket myself straight through the cafeteria ceiling to go find Dissident. The rest of them can wait.

I catch up with her sprinting down an upstairs hallway between cells.

"Where the hell were you?" she asks.

"Drawing their fire, apparently."

Up here, the way is deserted. I can hear the cafeteria full of thugs following us the long way up the stairs, but they're several seconds behind.

"Shit." Dissident skids to a stop at the doorway of an old dayroom, and I stop beside her.

Just like in his photographs, Milgram is surrounded by children. Here and now, those children are dressed in pajamas and nightgowns, rubbing their eyes and squinting against the dayroom lights, looking recently frightened out of bed.

"You're outgunned, Milgram," Dissident tries anyway. "Come with us, and no one has to get hurt."

The children huddle closer to him, and he pats the nearest girl on the head, then lifts her up onto his lap, making it doubly impossible to get a clear shot.

"It's okay," he tells them soothingly. "It's all going to be okay."

Then he looks at me, right through the eyes of my mask, as if none of what it covers matters in the least.

"We're not the ones they want to hurt," he says.

Something's wrong. Something's wrong with me, with the way his words coax to the surface a million tiny, half-forgotten irritations.

Mason.

Cory's unmet new girlfriend.

A dozen-odd fans who've turned mean after I brushed off their petitions for a closer relationship.

So many other people I wasn't thinking about at all two seconds ago, and now I want to find and hurt them so much more than I want to be here.

Milgram opens his mouth again, but my mask emits a deafening, high-pitched whine, and I don't hear a word of it.

In a few seconds, the feeling mercifully passes.

"Move away from the kids," I back Dissident up, hovering forward, ready to swoop over the top of them and snatch Milgram up, as soon as there's enough room to keep him from dragging one along for the ride.

Milgram looks at the girl on his lap with good-natured disappointment.

"If you wouldn't mind, my dear?"

The girl screws up her face in concentration, and in a flash of light and a puff of smoke that smells like daffodils, Milgram and the entire roomful of children vanish.

Dissident kicks the door of one of the room's craft supply cabinets in frustration and then makes for the window.

"Come on, then," she says.

The thugs from downstairs are closing in down the hallway we entered through.

"I thought you wanted to ruin Milgram's day," I say.

"There'll be other days to ruin worse than this one."

"Or we can arrest a cafeteria full of his guys, *today*."

"He owns the Pinnacle City police!" shouts Dissident. "Did that just go in one ear and out the other?"

"Then I'll drop them off with the Amber City PD."

"You think Milgram doesn't have the reach to deal with a little change of venue?"

"Maybe he does, but at least in another city, they'll get booked, and he'll have to go through channels. Even if he gets every one of them back out, it'll cost him time and money." I hold up my phone and pull up the VillScan app. "C'mon, I'll handle sorting and transport, just help me out a little with the giftwrapping?"

In a blaze of heat, Effigy makes it through the door first, leaving a trail of smoldering footprints behind as he lunges toward us.

With a guarded nod, Dissident pulls a pair of weights on a cable from her belt and throws them at Effigy. The cable wraps around him and he trips, igniting the carpet as he tries to duplicate himself out of its grasp.

The cable doesn't budge.

CHAPTER 17: THE DETECTIVE

I push the cart of cleaning supplies up to the Silver Cowl's rear loading dock. The door's heavy and locked, but doesn't have a guard outside, one of the rare benefits of the mid-morning hour. The rain isn't as heavy as it has been lately, but I'm glad for it anyway.

It allows me to wrap my arms around myself theatrically, shivering in my coveralls, after I press the intercom button by the door.

"Who is it?" a female voice responds.

"*Hola*, I mean, *Hello*, my name is Diego Dominguez. I am from Axis Cleaning Management. I am to clean here?" I say, smiling up at the security camera above the door. Laying on the accent extra thick isn't necessary, but I've found it helps sell the act, at least in EPC.

"Your team isn't due until ten," the voice says.

"I am hour early, I know this. But today, you see, my first day. I want to look good. To show I can be early and helpful, yes?"

"You have an ID?"

"Yes! I do!" I say, holding the ID up to the camera, shivering to show how cold and wet I am and to cover any imperfections in the fake ID Tragedii made me.

After a moment, the door buzzes and swings open.

It's hard not being a little smug that this worked, but I think I hide my smile as eager gratitude well enough to the tired, middle-aged morning manager who lets me in.

Piece of cake.

Watch enough TV and you'll come out thinking that the easiest way to sneak into a place is to have a janitor's uniform and keep your head down. While there's some truth to this, bein' how most places that can afford to hire outside janitorial services are the kinds of places that don't want to look the help in the eyes, there's a little more to it than that. Come in wearing the wrong uniform or on the wrong day, and no matter how much people want to ignore you they're bound to notice something's off and start asking the wrong kind of questions.

So, while Kline and Dissident have been tearing through Milgram's empire a piece at a time, I've been working the phones.

A quick call to the Silver Cowl saying a truck from their janitorial service dented my Maserati got me the name and number of Axis Cleaning Management.

A call to Axis Cleaning Management, this time as an angry supervisor from the Silver Cowl wanting to know who changed up all their cleaning schedules, got me their scheduled work times for the week.

Another call and a promise of a favor got me the backup I need in case anything goes wrong while here.

After that, everything's just gravy.

The manager shows me around, and I try to look suitably impressed with a place I've already been to more times in my life than I'd like to admit. She talks to me like a five year old, and I let her, nodding whenever she says something that sounds even vaguely important.

I'm brought upstairs with plenty of warnings about what to do should I find anything personal, incriminating, or illegal in any of the open VIP rooms (which all boil down to "give it to a manager") before being left to my own devices. She looks tired and in need of coffee, and doesn't want to spend any more time talking a new-hire janitor through the process.

So far, everything's going according to plan. However, as I know all too well, there's still plenty that can go to shit.

As soon as I'm alone upstairs, I drop the act, pull out my phone, and call up Kline.

She answers before the second ring, "You're in?"

"Yeah." I check over each shoulder. There're security cameras at either end of the hall, dark and well hidden, but no doubt active. "Anything you can do about the eyes in the sky?"

"Not from outside. But the VIP rooms themselves are camera free, so get inside and you should be safe."

Makes sense; the rich and powerful don't pay to have people looking over their shoulders. But two words in what she just said have my attention.

"*Should be?*"

"Well, the *club* doesn't have cameras in there, but I wouldn't put it past Jacob to hide some for *In the Cards*. He loves his candid shots."

"And covering up for his golden boy by deleting the worst of what he does in there," I say, still searching for the right door.

"Exactly."

Finally, I've got it. The VIP room with the locked door made to look like an Ace of Hearts. The keypad by its handle glows a dim green.

"Okay, I need the code," I say.

"Ready?"

"Yeah."

"Because you're not going to believe it."

"Try me."

"11111."

She's right. I don't believe it. But I type it in anyway, and the door handle clicks unlocked.

No one ever accused the Cards of being too smart for their own good.

I swing the door open and swiftly push the cart inside. The room looks empty, but all the same, I like having insurance, which is why I reach into the trash can on my cart and pull out the hamster ball.

I roll it into the corner, hoping I won't need to break it open.

Now, you hear a lot about the mythical VIP rooms, and you expect them to be something special; hidden palaces where the rich and famous (or at least those who can scrape together enough money to pretend they're either of those things) can hide away from us mere mortals in the kind of splendor they live for.

What I'm seeing here is just a small, dark lounge. Sure, the furniture's posh, made of velour and some kind of gold-painted hardwood, and there's a large neon ace of spades hung in the corner of the room, but as the Card family goes, it's downright restrained.

It hasn't been cleaned since the last time it was used, with empty glasses on tables and some odd bits of trash on the floor. The mirrored surface of the coffee table next to the couch has a white film of hastily wiped up coke on it. It looks like a hell of a party happened here, but I know, even at a glance, that there's something off. That for all its attempts at appearing glitzy, there's a sheen of grime. Not the kind of grime you find in my end of town, the kind of grime the people who come to clubs like this try to forget exists, no, this one's just a feeling of deep wrongness.

I don't need my powers to tell me bad things have happened in this room.

"Classy," I say, pulling the top of my coveralls off. My left arm cries out in agony, but I hold it at bay. I'll crunch a couple pills soon, after I put the pain to work.

"Tell me about it," Kline says. "You should see what it's like over here."

"You're at the Card mansion?"

"For now. When the girls wake up, I'm supposed to take them out shopping. 'Ratings gold,' Jacob calls it."

"Well, if we get their brother arrested for being a rapist, that should make the episodes more exciting, shouldn't it?"

"I doubt it, but if justice is done, that's all that matters."

"I can live with that. Gonna hang up now and get to work on that."

"Thanks," she says.

"No problem."

"No, really, I mean it . . . I'm not proud—"

"We've all got shit we're not proud of, believe me, I know. We can't fix what happened here, but let me do my thing and we can try to make sure it doesn't happen again."

"Okay."

Kimberly Kline. Solar Flare. She's not like anyone I've ever dealt with before.

I'm still trying to figure out whether or not that's a good thing.

She's a superhero, but like one of the ones out of the comic books and movies—not the ones writing the comic books and starring in the movies—righteous and seemingly incorruptible. I looked into her the old-fashioned way after our all-star team-up night, part of me still hoping to find something, anything about her that'd justify how much I wanted to hate her, and I couldn't find a damn thing. Aside from her family having a lot of big business ties in town (some with Card-owned businesses), she's squeaky clean. This alone was enough to make me even more suspicious of her, but every time we talk, I realize all over again that, no, she is just this nice.

This puts me in a hard place.

I want to hate her. *Really* want to hate her. She's a superhero from one of the richest families in EPC. She's everything a hard life in the Crescent has taught me to be repulsed by. She's teammates with people who did nothing while one of their own burned Marco to cinders and took my families from me. I look at her and see fake, vapid, pro-hero excess. She shouldn't be helping me protect WPC and the Crescent; she should be getting shit-faced and leaking a sex tape to make sure people haven't forgotten about her.

But she's better than that, isn't she?

Much as I hate to admit it, that might be true.

I don't think she'd have sent me here otherwise.

I pull a memory stick from my pocket and plug it into the port in my left arm. It burns going in, sending bolts up my arm that make even my hair hurt. I grit my teeth, put my hand on the nearest couch, and go to work.

✳

I want to vomit.

I've seen a lot of fucked up shit in my life, but I think this room's seen even more. Most of it's the kind of stuff you'd expect in a room like this: drinking, drugs, sex, backroom business deals, fights; stuff I'd usually ignore.

After all, people need hobbies.

Ace Card transforming this room into his personal rape chamber, that's something I can't ignore.

I find and record Ace's entire attack on the server Kline told me about. As much as I want to turn away, I make sure to watch every horrible detail. If I can't ignore it, then nobody else watching it can either.

There's something, though, that makes me stick around in this vision longer than I have to. Something about the practiced way he pours the drink from the wet bar, about the half-empty bottle of pills he pulls from the hidden panel in the back of a chair.

So I look further back and see the whole routine happen again, days earlier.

Then again, days earlier than that.

Another time nearly a week before.

All told, by the time disgust forces me to quit, I think I've watched him rape five separate women over a three week period, and I doubt they're the only ones.

They couldn't possibly be.

Usually he was alone, sometimes he was with his frat boy friends who took their turn after he was done. The girls were usually unconscious or close enough to protest weakly. He always got a kick out of that. By the way they were dressed and made up, like they were trying to fit in but couldn't quite afford to, I'd wager they were all from the Crescent, maybe even WPC.

The kinds of girls no one would believe if they came forward.

I've been out of the vision for about five minutes now, and I'm still shaken by what I've seen. I want to crunch a few pills, blot this all out, but I can't stay here. I gotta get out, pass this footage to Fadia, let her break this, make Ace pay, and—

There's someone at the door. Shaking the handle and typing in the code.

I've only got a couple seconds. I stash the memory stick in my cart and pull my coveralls top back on, just in time for Ace Card to open the door.

"—and I don't care what he says, you can tell him to kiss my ass!" he laughs. Then, finally noticing me, he says, "Who the fuck are you?"

Get back in character.

"Janitor, *señor*," I say, rubbing the accent on thick.

"And you are . . .?" he asks expectantly.

"I clean, *señor*."

Angrily, he stalks up to me, all two hundred pounds of swagger, douche and entitlement, getting within a few inches of my face.

"Then let me ask you something, *Pedro*." His voice is dripping with menace. This guy's a lot bigger than me, but if he thinks this'll be an easy fight, I've got a trick or two up my sleeve I'm dying to share.

"Yes sir?" I ask, tensing.

He smiles. "You haven't by any chance found a pair of Edge Industries *Cutter* sunglasses around here? They cost something like fifteen hundred a pair, and I've been looking all over for them. Help me find 'em and there's five bucks in it for ya, buy yourself some tacos."

He laughs at his own joke. Of course he does.

Be cool. You got what you need, just get the hell out of here.

"Sorry, *señor*, I see nothing. I will leave you alone to look."

I grab my cart and start pushing it toward the door.

Ace is quick to jump in my path.

"What's the hurry, Pedro? This room doesn't look very clean to me."

"Not in your way?" I ask.

"You're not in my way. But I'm wondering why you're hurrying so much," he says, eying my cart. "You don't got a pair of sunglasses in there, do you?"

"No, *señor*."

"Then let me take a look."

"No, *señor*."

I move to push past him, but he stays in my way.

"You know we're about to have a problem here, right?"

So this is gonna happen.

"Yeah, I guess," I say, dropping the accent and shoving my cart into him.

He's stunned, momentarily, long enough for me to pull Harriet from her hiding place in the trash can. I'd have much preferred to get out of here quietly and not create a scene, but I can't say I won't enjoy beating on Ace Card.

I pull back, line up a hit, and swing for his arm.

I'm pretty sure things aren't going to plan when he catches the bat, casually.

I know they aren't when he wrenches Harriet from my hands and sends me sprawling on the floor. He kicks and stomps my chest a few times, not enough to do damage but enough to hurt like hell.

"Cape Fu, motherfucker!" he taunts. "Got trained by Pinnacle himself! Now, give me my fucking sunglasses before I break your motherfucking legs! Whaddya got to say to that, bitch?"

I've got two words for him, not that he'll like them very much.

"PETTING ZOO!"

The hamster ball rolls out of the room's corner, the pale blue hamster inside bursting out and transforming into a pale blue tiger that's all too eager to sink her claws and teeth into Ace Card. With one strike, she slashes him across the chest, getting a surprisingly high-pitched scream out of him. With another, she pins him to the ground, her teeth inches from his neck.

"Oh god, oh god, please don't kill me!"

"Can I eat him? He looks tasty," Petting Zoo taunts. Given that she's a vegetarian, she's never actually eaten anyone, but the threat of it is always fun to watch.

"Just knock him out. We gotta get out of here," I say, finding my feet again.

"Well, if you insist," she says, transforming from a tiger into an anaconda, wrapping her powerful coils around Ace until he passes out from lack of oxygen. When he's out, she transforms back into her usual perky self.

"You get what you need?"

"Yeah," I say, pocketing the memory stick from the cart.

"And he's gonna burn for this?"

"Yeah," I say, picking up Harriet.

"Good." She kicks him once for good measure before transforming into a praying mantis and flying onto my shoulder.

I open the door enough to see there's one other person in the hallway. He looks familiar from the pictures Kline showed me, slightly skeezy and jittery, glued to his phone, but I need to be sure.

"You Jacob?" I ask, strolling out of the room with Harriet held behind my back.

"Yeah?" he says, confused.

That's all I need. One powerful swing of Harriet to his jaw and he's out like a light, collapsed on the floor and bleeding. Two small plastic baggies fall from his jacket pocket and I pick them up. One's full of white powder, the other various pills.

"These are very bad for you," I say, pocketing them.

My hair and the high collar of my coveralls allow me to conceal my face from the cameras as I make my escape. I don't run, because running would attract attention, but I do walk purposefully for the door with Harriet concealed by my coveralls and Petting Zoo on my shoulder. Every step of the way I'm convinced I'm going to be seen and stopped and have to fight my way out, but no, it's still early and nobody wants to be here let alone acknowledge a random janitor running out into the rain, so I make it outside without any trouble.

Finally free, I send two quick texts.

To Kline: GOT IT

To Fadia: HAVE I GOT A STORY FOR YOU

When I'm out of the back alley behind the club and a good enough distance away to be sure I'm not caught, I finally allow myself to smile.

Things are looking up, aren't they?

CHAPTER 18: THE SUPERHERO

Jeremy Collingwraith lives in a downtown penthouse.

Naturally.

Thankfully, that means there'll be no one else on his floor to hear when I break the glass. I haven't touched it yet, and already we can hear his stadium-sized voice.

"I'm doing everything I can, Will, but your boy doesn't make it easy." Collingwraith leans back in his desk chair, holding his phone to his ear with one hand, picking up a drink from next to his laptop with the other.

Eddie's holding tightly to my back while I float silently outside the window. He holds up a finger asking me to wait and listen, and I nod.

My thoughts exactly.

"I'm going to need his transcripts, documentation of all his extracurriculars, anything we can use to humanize him to the jury, and yes, like it or not this *will* go to trial. He's the boy next door, we'll play that up as much as we can, and if we're lucky, we can talk this down to a few years with good behavior and keep him out of gen pop."

My skin begins to heat up, and I have to take a breath to cool it, keep it from burning Eddie.

Eddie notices and shifts his strictly functional grip to give my shoulder a squeeze of sympathetic fury.

It's an infinitely awkward gesture, a distant, overly formal echo of the casual intimacy of our last flight together, and hanging here in the air together with him clinging to me for life, I can't simply lean closer to indicate that I feel him. I do appreciate the sentiment, though, so I put my hand equally awkwardly on top of his, which is freezing from the winter air whipping past us at this altitude.

I let my skin heat up after all, this time to a careful, hot water bottle hundred degrees.

"What are you paying me for?" Collingwraith repeats incredulously. "You want to find out how much worse things could get for Ace under some mail-order degree public defender, be my guest. He got caught with his dick in the cookie jar. It happens, believe me, I know it, you know it, but take my advice, Will. If you're still interested in that senate seat, I'd start disassociating yourself from your son's actions now."

By the way Collingwraith holds his phone away from his ear, Card's pride in his son is no more flexible now than ever.

The police weren't initially that receptive to Eddie's recording, in spite of his power's legally certified infallibility, but once his anonymous friend leaked it to every major news outlet on the West Coast, Ace was arrested within the hour, right there in the private hospital where he was being treated for multiple fractures sustained in what he insisted was a "giant snake attack."

Less than two hours after that, Card was live on his favorite cable news channel, ranting about how disgusting it was that these socialist vultures would persecute Ace this way at such a vulnerable time, for the sake of using him as their own political scapegoat, and might even go so far as to use a bit of youthful mischief as an excuse to rob him of the best years of his life.

I can't watch the complete footage of the interview without gagging, but three of Card's top corporate donors for his senate campaign have since abruptly withdrawn their support, so maybe that's for the best.

Ace is already home on bail for now, but he's going to trial for at least four of the five rapes on the video, and a dozen more women have already come forward since the evidence broke. Ella isn't testifying—god knows what she must have been forced to sign—but payoffs and NDAs seem to be a special contingency for when there are liabilities like me involved. The women without witnesses on their side apparently weren't even worth what it would cost to quiet them on the spot, although I suspect the Cards are regretting that policy now.

Ace won't get all of what he deserves. When I saw him this evening, he was most upset about the picketers blocking the entrance to the Silver Cowl and how difficult it was for him to maneuver through doorways with two arm casts, but at least now everyone knows what he is, and if Collingwraith is trying to prepare the family for the inevitability of *some* jail time, then I'm hopeful there isn't a lawyer on earth who could get him off with less.

Ace now hates me more than ever, convinced I somehow had something to do with his sudden change of fortune. However, in light of the public backlash, his dad insists that the family "appreciates my friendship in this difficult time." I even overheard him admonishing Ace to be nicer to me—at least in public.

Meanwhile, since our mass arrest at Snyder Sanitarium, Dissident and I have been busy, sometimes together, sometimes separately, blowing up Milgram's drug and weapon caches and liberating his human trafficking network, one drugged-out batch of survivors at a time, getting them back to their families when there are any, to shelters when there aren't.

No one knows, no one sees our faces, but I don't think I've hated myself this little since my first PCG mission briefing.

Eddie says his power will be useful tonight, for investigating the possible link between Card and Milgram in person, and I'm sure it will, but I think the real reason he's here in Dissident's place is because he wants to carve off a piece of Collingwraith himself.

"I'm telling you," says Collingwraith. "No, I'm just explaining, probation isn't going to be on the table this time."

Eddie pulls his bat from his coat, cranes his head closer to the window over my shoulder, and grins under his ski mask.

"Ever played good cop bad cop?" he whispers.

I haven't, but I can't think of a better time to try it out.

"Which one do I get to be?"

Eddie laughs. "Yourself."

He gestures with the bat, and I hover closer, until he can tap it against the penthouse's glass wall.

Collingwraith sets his drink down and squints at us, unable to see clearly past the glare of the interior lighting.

When it looks like he's about to shrug us off and return to his call, Eddie taps again.

"I'm going to have to call you back," says Collingwraith, getting up and squinting harder, shading his eyes but not reaching to turn out any of the lights. "No, I'm not bullshitting you. I'll be *right back*."

He cuts off Card's response.

As soon as the call ends, I touch both palms to the glass and shatter it inward in a controlled, heat-shifting *crack*.

Eddie leaps off my back as soon as the path to Collingwraith is clear, swats the phone out of his hand with his bat, and kicks it away across the floor.

I wrap Collingwraith's face in the crook of my arm before he can scream, letting him bite down on my unbreakable skin like a pacifier.

"You're not going to die, okay?" I tell him. "Be cool, you're okay, you're fine."

He only had a second's glimpse of my shape when we burst in through the window, and he looks briefly surprised, even disoriented to hear a soft, female voice coming from under my mask.

Good cop is off to a good start, I guess.

Eddie goes for the desk, bats the drink aside, shattering the glass against the floor, and sits down at the computer, shaking the mouse to stop the screen from locking.

"I know that Mayor Card and Milgram are working together," says Eddie. "I need to know who else is involved, what they're planning, and how to access any records of their communication. I can find that out either from you or from your computer. You get to stay in one piece after sharing. Can't promise the same for this overpriced porn theater."

He twirls the bat casually over the laptop's keyboard.

Collingwraith makes a noise into my arm, and Eddie gives me a nod.

I put a finger to my lips and loosen my hold on Collingwraith's mouth.

"I can't discuss my clients," he says, quietly enough that he doesn't seem to be trying to summon help. "If I do that, my life's over anyway."

"Your professional life, or your actual life?" I ask. "If you're worried about retribution from Milgram's people, we can protect you."

I try for sympathetic and comforting, but really I'm thinking about how much I'd enjoy putting the man who's making a fortune off minimizing Ace's sentence into witness protection.

No more Jeremy Collingwraith, attorney to the stars. Just some guy with a new name he didn't pick in a new nowheresville town, not allowed to appear in the news ever again.

"Yeah? Who the fuck are you?" snorts Collingwraith.

"The people who could've killed you by now if we felt like it," Eddie points out.

"So you're super," says Collingwraith. "I can neither confirm nor deny any relationship between myself and the underworld figure known as Milgram, but general wisdom is that he has plenty of supers of his own. If I *were* in Milgram's employ, and two masked supers entered my residence to entice me to betray him, wouldn't you consider it equally likely that they'd been sent by Milgram himself as a test of my loyalty?"

"He's got you living in fear, doesn't he?" I ask, my arm still around him in a half choke hold, half hug. Whatever product he uses in his hair is leaving grease stains on my sweatshirt.

"Whatever you're hoping to find, it won't be on that hard drive," says Collingwraith to Eddie, who's still clicking away. "All confidential materials are kept on secure servers."

"But you can never really clear your browser history," says Eddie, taking a USB cable from his pocket and plugging his implant directly into the laptop. "Not to me."

He sets the media player to full screen, then rolls the chair to the side, leaves his fingers touching the keyboard, and lets his eyes slide out of focus.

In real time, the computer shows us its own past, exactly as Eddie sees it.

Backwards and in fast motion, Collingwraith sits at his desk, talking on the phone. He checks three different email accounts.

Eddie slows down and shifts his angle of perspective to catch each username, each password as it's being typed. He zooms in on snippets of conversations, and I catch some advice to Card on offshore accounting, some mentions of the names, and outstanding charges of a few of the Milgram thugs Dissident and I brought in.

Then, for kicks, he focuses in on Collingwraith picking his nose.

Time elapses backward a night or two, Collingwraith's pants are off, and Eddie pauses the image.

"You gonna make me watch the whole director's cut, or can we get to the cliff notes?" he asks.

Collingwraith gives us a bleached, toothy smile, adapting on a dime. "You two can still walk away, you know. We can forget the window, I'll go back to doing my job, and you can go back to whatever it is you do, without knowing enough to make every power player in the city want you dead."

Eddie and I swap an instant's glance, confirming what we both already knew coming here.

"You let us worry about that," I say.

Eddie drums his fingers impatiently on the laptop, and finally, Collingwraith gives.

"It's no story you haven't heard before. Mayor Card wants to move up the political ladder and needs money no law-abiding man ever had to make it happen."

"He was on the cover of *Forbes* last year," I say.

Collingwraith shrugs. "Campaigning is expensive."

"So he's subsidizing it with a cut of Milgram's profits, in return for turning a blind eye," says Eddie.

"No!" says Collingwraith. "No, Card's the one paying Milgram."

"For what?" I ask.

"For turning WPC into a warzone."

"Fucking typical," says Eddie, spinning his bat around in agitation.

"So that he can convince everyone to let him wall it off?" I ask.

"No, so he can be the one to *rebuild* it," says Collingwraith. "He's got all the investors he needs lined up to clear out the wreckage and foreclosed buildings and build luxury condos and modern offices in their place, all aboveboard. As soon as the project's finished, Milgram will get to peddle his wares to a more lucrative class of clientele, under a police force handpicked to leave him alone, and Card'll personally be raking in the rent of half the city, and sitting on the platform of the man who made Pinnacle City whole. But before he gets started, he has to prove to the investors that he's not leading them into another of his PR nightmares. Chasing poor people out of their homes gets you boycotted. Flushing out a nest of well-documented depravity makes you a hero."

It makes me sick to admit it, but Card might be smarter than I thought. No less evil or crazy, but smarter. After all his rants about walling off WPC, he'll be able to spin buying it out, knocking it down, and starting over from scratch as the reasonable alternative.

"Who are the investors?" asks Eddie.

"The list's in the mail folder marked 'PCR Prospects,'" says Collingwraith.

Eddie finds it and scans through names.

"It's the usual," says Collingwraith. "Companies that want a monopoly on the new class of residents the project will bring in, a chance to stamp their name all over it, under Card's, of course. Clothing importers. Diamond dealers. The—"

"The Pinnacle City Guardians," Eddie reads aloud.

"Yeah, the Guardians want to set up a sister team in the West." Collingwraith nods.

I grab him by the front of his shirt and turn him around to face me. "Which Guardians?"

He chuckles nervously.

"Your partner over there just said. *The* Pinnacle City Guardians."

"Specifically!" I realize I'm shaking him, but I need to know. "Which members agreed to this? Who have you talked to?"

Collingwraith shrugs grandly. "Some personal assistant. I don't know whose; she was representing the interests of the team as a corporate entity."

"That's not good enough!"

"Hey, hey, ease up!" says Eddie, crossing the room in a blink to get between us.

My handprint is burned into the front of Collingwraith's shirt and still smoking when I let him go, but he's unhurt.

"Whoa," Eddie whispers, tugging me away by my sleeve, avoiding my skin. "What happened to my good cop?"

"You said to be myself."

"Well, tell yourself that we got what we need," he says, grinning as he closes the laptop and tucks it under his arm. "No matter who was supporting this thing, we have enough to stop it."

I take a breath, let the sting of betrayal, the confirmation of what I've feared ever since getting the Card assignment, dissipate. I let the heat go with it, and try to absorb what Eddie's saying.

We can expose Card and the so-called heroes who've been using me to pave the way for their investments. I can stop waiting among them for chances to snoop for this exact evidence. No more of Jacob's camera in my face, or my barely-there Solar Flare leotard riding up when I fly, or Card's press conference rants citing me as his complicit representative of womankind.

I'm free.

I wrap Eddie in a quick hug before taking the computer in my hands and turning for him to hang onto my back.

"Hey! You're not taking that with you, are you?" Collingwraith calls after us. Inspired by his indignation, Eddie grabs a mostly full bottle of cognac off Collingwraith's bar as we fly past it, leaving the same way we arrived.

✺

Between sips from the bottle, Eddie gives me directions for that flight home I offered so half-heartedly on the morning of my first PCG briefing.

I'm glad to get to make good on it now.

"Can you explain to me why this stuff is so expensive?" he asks, wrapping his bottle arm around my neck so he can pull his mask off.

"I don't know," I admit, following suit and tucking mine into my sweatshirt pocket. "I've never bought it. Snuck some when I was twelve, though."

"And they call you a role model," Eddie tuts, taking another long gulp.

"Mom just about cried when she caught me."

"Her little girl growing up too fast?"

"No, her little girl cutting the good stuff with Pepsi."

Eddie cracks up and holds the neck of the bottle toward me. "And what does your sophisticated adult palate think?"

I shake my head. "It's wasted on me. I'd need about a case to get a buzz."

"Too bad, 'cause you know how much this set me back."

Holding the computer and his free arm tightly to my chest, I roll back in the air so he can pour a sip into my mouth.

"It's awful," I discover out loud, choking on my swallow.

"Good stuff my ass," Eddie agrees, and drinks one last swig before dropping the bottle into the night.

I land us in front of his building on a street I'd have called dilapidated not too long ago. It still is, of course, but my perceptual threshold of dilapidation has been drastically redefined lately.

He finds his balance and reaches for the computer, but the goodbye doesn't come on cue, and our hands both dawdle maybe a few seconds longer than it takes to make sure he has a secure enough grip to carry city-saving evidence.

It could be my imagination, but that stifled edge of righteous disgust since he learned my name seems to have gone dull—or maybe it's only become submerged in a tide of cognac.

He clears his throat and wipes a droplet of the drink from his lips. The night we met may be one of the more abstract snapshots in my mental album, but suddenly I remember those lips touring the sensitive spots of my body, the softness of them between the occasional stick of stubble, with a startling spike of clarity.

"I, um, I was going to bring some groceries over to the Medozas tonight," he says, and some piece of tonight's victory has slipped out of his smile without explanation.

Right. Well, that makes this nice and simple.

"Do you—"

"Yeah, I should probably go take care of a couple things too," I say, before it can un-simplify. "Get stuff in order for my resignation."

There are few things I'd like more right now than to help Eddie drunkenly carry grocery bags to the safe house until the wee hours and then maybe see where I wake up tomorrow, but Collingwraith's information, however useful, has left me with homework, and I know I won't be able to give anything else my full attention until it's done.

"Right." Eddie nods with what might be disappointment, shifting the laptop to a more comfortable position in the crook of his good arm. "I'll get the history recorded and start organizing it tomorrow."

"Cool," I say, though this is much more than cool. Before I can overthink it, I kiss him briefly on the cheek and then back away, floating my feet off the ground. "I'll check in then."

✳

Mom's phone is off when I try calling. It's long after the house-keeper's shift, and when I ring the doorbell, I almost expect, maybe almost hope, not to get an answer.

I don't want to ask her this question.

But I don't want to go back to Guardian Tower and pretend that I can sleep with it unasked, either.

She's at the door in her aquamarine dressing gown before I can debate whether to ring again, looking equal parts worried and pleased by my unannounced appearance.

"Kimmy! Is everything okay?"

I nod, change my mind, and shake my head.

It's closer than it's ever been, maybe, but it's also not okay. It's never been okay.

"Can I sleep here tonight?"

Mom simultaneously hugs me and pulls me inside so she can close the door against the cold I always forget to feel. "Of course. What happened? Are you and Mason having problems again?"

I laugh, louder than I mean to. Crying to my mom about Mason feels like an old dream, and somehow even that fact makes me feel oddly sad.

She sits me down at the breakfast nook, puts on the kettle, and carries on quizzing me while I try to form the answer she'll never guess.

"Is there another boy?"

I shake my head. I don't need to explain Eddie to her today, if there's even anything to explain. This isn't about him.

"Work then? Is Pinnacle still giving you a hard time?"

This is as close as we're going to get.

"I think . . . I think Pinnacle did something," I start, testing the waters. "Something bad. I think all the Guardians might be part of it."

She sits down across from me and puts her hands on mine. "What kind of thing?"

Take a breath.

"I think the Guardians are supporting organized crime in WPC."

This time, she laughs. "What? The Guardians are fighting the gangs every other week."

"Yeah," I say, voicing the pattern that's been adding up in my head since long before I wanted it to. "Because they're eliminating competition for the Milgram syndicate."

Mom's expression dips toward serious. "Where's this coming from?"

I swallow. "Actually, I don't exactly think it. I know it. And it's not just the Guardians. It's Mayor Card and the police department and god knows who else, and I'm pretty sure it's been going on for a while. I just needed to ask you . . ."

My throat is so dry.

"Do you think there's any chance Uncle Ethan was involved in this?"

Mom bites her lip uncomfortably.

Pain—real pain—explodes in both my hands, as the freeze power in hers suddenly activates. It takes her only seconds to drain all the energy from mine, my hands which can comfortably make snowballs at the South Pole without gloves.

Even with my forearms encased in a block of zero-degree ice, it takes me a moment to understand that this is an answer to my question.

Mom stands, and from the box of hot cocoa waiting on the counter, she pulls an already prepared syringe full of the unmistakable red-orange glow of Jovium.

As soon as it's free of its airtight container, a wave of wooziness overtakes me, cutting short any attempt to charge my hands back up to break free.

"Mom?" I croak, asking for any kind of explanation.

The kettle is whistling, and I can only think how good a mug of hot cocoa would feel in my hands, until Mom sticks the needle in my neck, my skin already softened by the Jovium's ambient presence, and I stop thinking all together.

CHAPTER 19: THE DETECTIVE

This was a bad idea.

I shouldn't have tried carrying so many grocery bags in one go, but at least this way I don't have to make another trip. I'm barely able to pull the Lineup's front door open, but I manage to squeak inside without spilling any of the bags. The regulars look up at me, but instead of trying to kick me out or lob insults or kill me, as they might've done a week ago, they're back to their drinks and badly sung Christmas carols in a hurry.

All told, I'm having a pretty decent day.

The work Kline and I've been doing has calmed down WPC and the Crescent some, to a point where the smell of smoke and roving gangs of EPC assholes are no longer a constant and more an occasional irritation. With Card busy attacking the "liberal media" for "sullying his son's name" and Milgram's forces scattered and shrunken from Kline and Dissident's attacks, the city feels at peace for the first time in a long time, or at least as at peace as it could ever feel.

I waddle over to the bar and set the bags down. Tragedii, cleaning a glass with her eye laser, wanders up to me.

"These for me? You shouldn't have."

"Not quite. Just came to drop them off at the Well."

She nods curtly, sliding me the Well's hidden key. "Good."

I glance around and notice a face missing. "Isn't Petting Zoo supposed to be on tonight?"

"Yeah, but seems she had a big bachelor party coming into the club and is gonna be late. Like those frat boys'll tip better than our people," she says, waving at the Lineup's mess of regulars.

"Her loss." I pick up the key and grocery bags, making my way for the rear exit.

"Hey, Eddie?" Tragedii calls after me.

"Yeah?"

"It's good having you back."

"It's good being back."

She wants to say more. I can see it in her human eye, but she doesn't. She doesn't have to. These past weeks have been crazy for all of us; we've all done things we're not happy about.

It's not raining too badly tonight, yet another way this day continues to go well, and as I head down the back steps and open up the Well, I'm smiling.

Is it because of Kline?

I don't know. Maybe. Probably.

God help me, I think her impenetrable optimism is starting to rub off.

We've been working this case together now and making some good progress, and with what we got from Collingwraith tonight, I think we're just about ready to bring down this whole damn conspiracy. What it'll mean for the city I can't say, because power vacuums like this don't tend to stay empty for long. But if we can get the Milgram and Card organizations in jail, along with whatever superheroes they got working with them, well, that's gotta stand for something, right?

And then there's the *us* question.

When we're done here, then what? Do we go our separate ways, her back to EPC and me back to the Crescent, or do we stay in touch?

What are we then?

Acquaintances?

All-star team up partners?

Friends?

More?

Doubtful. The two of us couldn't work long term; we're just too damned different. I won't say there's not a spark there, but that's all it is.

A spark can start a fire, even burn for a while, but in the end it'll burn out.

But while it burns, at least it'll be hot.

I could live with some more of that.

Maybe that's why I'm a little let down she had to run out like she did. It felt like we might've been able to pull something tonight, but, hey, she's got her own thing. We'll have other nights.

Now, I do my good deed for the day.

When I get inside, Mendoza and Kaley are still up in the living room, him watching TV while she plays with some dolls on the floor.

"Detective," he says with a nod as I pass by.

"Mendoza," I respond. "Just come by to drop off groceries."

"How's it going out there?"

I don't look at him, and not just because I still have a hard time looking at his terrible face. Clearing Mendoza's name was always part of the hope of Kline's and my plan, but even with my powers and Collingwraith's computer it's going to be hard to completely exonerate the man, especially with the rest of Julian's killers dead and unable to offer up any corroboration.

The courts might go lenient if mind control can be proven beyond a reasonable doubt (no small task with every criminal and his mother using the "I was mind-controlled by a supervillain" defense), or if Milgram confesses, but given how unlikely both those possibilities are, this story'll probably end with us smuggling the Mendoza family out of town.

But what the hell do I tell him? He's got so damn much hope pinned on what Kline and I are doing, and his family's really settled in here in the Well. Do I break the illusion, tell him the truth, or just let it ride until we've got Milgram?

"It's going well," I finally say. "I think we'll have everyone where we need them before New Year's."

I pull the date out of my ass, but it makes him happy.

"Thank you so, so much. I don't know what my family would do without you and Solar Flare and Miss Tragedii protecting us," he says, the corners of his terrible mouth curling into a smile.

"No problem," I say, trying to make my exit. I don't, no, *can't* meet his eyes as I pass, don't want him to know that I'm lying my ass off.

Of course, I can't make it to the door without an insistent, small hand tugging on my trench coat.

"Are you gonna be seeing Solar Flare again?" Kaley asks.

"Yeah."

"Please give this to her?"

She hands me a folded up piece of paper. Unfolding it, I see a crude drawing of Solar Flare and me flying, holding Kaley between us.

"I'll do that next time I see her," I say, trying to ignore the twist of guilt in my gut.

"Thanks!"

"Now, honey, it's way past your bedtime, and if you don't go down soon, your mother *will* kill me in the morning."

In a huff that makes her go invisible for a moment, Kaley runs off.

"Kids," Mendoza says.

"I wouldn't know."

"You don't got any of your own?"

I laugh. "I sure hope not."

"You gotta give it a whirl, man. The world can be all sorts of shit, but when you got kids, it makes even the worst times not so bad."

I don't know what to say to that. "I'll call you if I find anything."

"Thanks. Drive safe, man."

Outside again, the rain's coming down harder than it was before. I pull up the collar of my coat.

Tragedii meets me halfway down the stairs, rain dripping down her armor.

"Hey again," I say.

"Hey, I need to pick up something downstairs, can I have the key?"

"Sure, I was about to bring it back anyway," I say, passing it to her.

"You weren't planning on heading back in, were you?"

"I was thinkin' about getting a drink or two."

"Don't. Louie just came in, and between all his speechifying about the glory days of the Gray Empire, he's still pretty sore with you for what you brought down."

"Still?"

"Hey, you know those Grays; they know how to hold grudges."

"Fine," I say, running a hand through my rain-slicked hair.

She looks at me, concerned. "You still got some work to do back at the office?"

"Stuff I was putting off, but yeah, why?"

"Well, head on over there. When I'm done down here, I'll bring over a bottle."

"On my tab?"

"On the house."

I raise an eyebrow. Offers of free booze from Tragedii are few and far between. You gotta jump on them when they come up. And I was looking forward to something a little more exciting than Collingwraith's cognac.

"Only if you take a shot or two with me."

"Sounds like a night," she says, heading into the Well.

I drive across the street to my office, heading inside and immediately locking up. Content after a quick sweep of the office that it's empty (*fucking Bystander, I shouldn't be this paranoid*), I set my coat out to dry, head to my back storeroom, and empty out the box of reams of printer paper to find the treasure hidden at the bottom.

Collingwraith's computer.

I'm hardly what you'd call a hacker, but with my powers and the necessary device in hand, I can pretty much tear apart anyone's secrets. I've no doubt I'll be able to find any offsite data storage he has, as well as access any and all files on the hard drive itself. None of what we find will stand up in court, of course; recorded visions of people caught in the act are one thing, recorded visions of illegally accessed personal correspondence are another. But if we dump it all online and let the court of public opinion take apart the people named as co-conspirators, well, that wouldn't be so terrible, would it?

God bless the Internet.

Then again, there's a chance Collingwraith might've been given access to the Julian file itself. People have shown crazier things to their lawyers. Julian was almost certainly preparing it for legal action, and if I can download an anonymous copy, maybe we *can* do this the official way.

I set the laptop on my desk and sit down, getting ready to glance into the world of a lawyer to the disgusting, when I feel it.

Three stabbing pains in my right arm.

"Fuck!" I exclaim, wrenching away from the armrest.

There are three small punctures on my forearm, each welling with a bead of blood.

I look closely at the armrest and am just barely able to see what I'm pretty sure are three small needles sticking from it, but before I can be sure, everything turns black.

✳

I'm woken back up by a sharp, stabbing pain to the side of my neck, and the sudden feeling that my body is ready to run a marathon.

Adrenaline. Low dose, but a damn strong wakeup call.

As my eyes clear and feeling comes back to my body, I know I'm still sitting in my office chair, now turned so I'm staring at the picture of me, Marco, and Bystander when we were kids.

I try to stand up, to get away from the chair, but my legs are still weak, and, and . . .

Shit.

My left wrist is handcuffed to one of the exposed pipes in the wall. I test pulling at it and the cuffs hold firm.

There's someone behind me, and though the list of people who might want to drug and chain me to a wall is getting longer by the hour these days, I make a guess.

"If you wanted to bust out the handcuffs, Bystander, you only had to ask."

She doesn't laugh. She does, however, spin my chair around, wrenching at my arm painfully.

"You really should've taken Mr. Milgram's offer," she says, pulling the bottle of pills from my trench coat and setting it beside me on the desk. Collingwraith's laptop is gone, replaced now by an empty can of gas. Growing dread fills me as I see a couple more cans around the room, the stink of gas-soaked carpet filling the air.

"Did you honestly expect me to take it?"

"I expected you to be smart."

"Well, that was your first mistake."

"Eddie—"

"You think smart is joining another supervillain? After that worked out so well for us last time?"

She punches me in the stomach, hard. My left arm twists behind me, pain shooting through my entire body. I feel like I'm dying, and feebly, instinctively, I reach for my pills. She pushes them away, just out of reach.

"Smart's coming out on the winning side, and those sides will be determined sooner than you think."

"Not if we break your organization's back first."

She laughs. "So you've jailed some minions and henchmen and aired the mayor's pervert son's dirty laundry, and you call that a victory? You're just taking down small fish, hoping to build a case or stumble upon Julian's file so a dead man can do all your work for you. Well, I've got news for you: small fish are cheap and replaceable, and *we've* found Julian's file. The mayor's all set to throw a big 'destroying the file' party. You've lost."

I don't want to believe her, but I can hear a lot of the old Bystander in her voice, the Bystander who takes glee in ripping to shreds the lives of people who've wronged her.

"I'm not alone. There are other people who know, who'll fight, if you kill me," I say, in part to taunt, in part to squeeze more information out of her.

She smiles down at me, pulling a cell phone from her pocket.

"Not for long," she says, showing me the screen.

The image cycles between several live hidden camera feeds, each more terrible than the last.

The Lineup, Tragedii working behind the bar, completely unaware of the bomb planted in a small alcove by the camera.

Petting Zoo's strip club, similarly wired with hidden explosives.

A dark alley in the Crescent. Dissident darts in after a dealer, unaware of the hit squad armed to the teeth with machine guns waiting for her.

Kline, unconscious and tied to a chair in a fancy-looking room, a glowing stone on a table nearby.

Mr. and Mrs. Mendoza, beaten and tied to chairs in the Well. Somewhere in the background, little John wails inconsolably.

"Thanks for the key, by the way," she says, tossing the Well key onto my desk.

"You *bitch*," I say, hating how bitter the words feel. Even like this, I still want her to be the Bystander I thought I knew, not the one in front of me.

"Oh, you haven't seen anything yet," she says, putting the phone to her ear. "Light them up."

She drops the phone back in front of my face, and one by one I watch the screens go black.

The Lineup and Petting Zoo's strip club explode, the Lineup's explosion rattling my office windows.

The hit squad opens up on Dissident, the flashes of their weapons blinding the camera.

Milgram walks into frame beside Kline, smiles, and turns the camera off.

A final, cruel explosion engulfs the Mendozas in flames.

I scream and fight, struggling against the handcuffs like a wild animal, reaching for Bystander as I throw every curse known to man her way, to hell with the agony in my arm.

Bystander stands tauntingly out of reach by just a few inches, unflinching and still wearing a spiteful smile as she pockets the phone.

"Hate me all you want, but this doesn't have to be the end. I forgive you for everything you've done, and Mr. Milgram is willing to do the same. With nothing holding you back to this pitiful life, you can start over. *We* can start over. With Mr. Milgram, we can finally have the power we always wanted."

I spit in her face. She easily dodges out of the way, but her expression of hurt is back, and this time it doesn't cut me so deep.

So she knows how it feels, too? Good.

"So that's how it's going to be, then?"

"Yeah."

"Don't make me do this."

"I thought nobody could *make* you do anything, Anya."

She runs a hand over her scalp in frustration. "You know, this has always been your problem. You're so fucking stubborn you don't know a good deal when one's right in front of you."

I have to get out of here, have to help my friends that can still be helped. The way the footage cut out, I might still be able to save

Tragedii and the Mendozas, maybe call Petting Zoo and Dissident to see if they're still alive, and if a quick death were all Milgram had planned for Kline, he would've left the camera rolling . . . wouldn't he?

"Let's run away," I say.

Bystander looks like I've started speaking in tongues. "What?"

"You and me, right now. Let me go, let me help my friends, and we can just leave this city. You want to start over? Then let's start a new life together someplace else, away from all this."

I mean every word, and she knows it.

She considers me for too long before saying, "It's a nice dream, but I can't do that. I've worked too long and hard to get what I've made with Mr. Milgram, and I'm not going to throw that away."

"Then fuck off."

"Eddie . . ."

I thrash out and reach for her again, yelling, "FUCK OFF! GET THE FUCK OUT OF HERE OR KILL ME ALREADY!"

I may be mistaken, but I think that's a tear in her eye.

She approaches me, easily batting away my free hand, and kisses me on the lips, hard, before stepping out of reach again.

"It's because I love you, Eddie, that I left the pill bottle on your desk. Swallow them all and you should die pretty quick, or at least be out for the rest of this." She nudges the bottle back within my reach and starts for the door. She pulls a lighter from her pocket and lights it up.

"I love you too, Bystander," I say when she opens the door. "Remember that when you think about killing me. Remember you killed the only person who ever loved you the way you are."

She pauses, but still drops the lighter. The carpet ignites quickly, and she's out the door.

Shit. I really hoped that would work.

I consider the pills for a fraction of a second, but that's all. I may've made a life of taking the easy way out when things went to shit, but there's too much Sunday school left in me to seriously consider that way out.

What I do consider, though, is thanking my landlords for being as shitty about maintenance as they are. When I pull with both hands, I can feel the ancient pipe shift. When I pull even harder, I feel a little give. Bracing against the wall with both my legs, I feel it start to give way.

The fire licks at my back as I put every bit of strength and pain I have into the pipe and break it free from the wall. The pain in my left arm is so blinding that I worry about losing consciousness, but the fire is enough to keep me focused.

With all the strength I've got left, I stumble through the flames and first grab my pills, then my trench coat, putting it on to help avoid the fire, then Harriet, before flinging myself through the flimsy plywood where my front window should be.

The air is fresh and wet, a nice change from inside. A luxury car with blacked-out windows speeds away, no doubt one of Milgram or Card's, carrying who I assume to be Bystander.

I hobble across the street toward the split-open, flaming crater that used to be the Lineup. A few of the regulars are outside, standing around in shock or lying down and moaning.

A great shape looms over the burning building, reaching inside and sifting through the ruins, plucking Louie up and setting him down next to the other survivors. It's when I get close enough to get a good look at the beast that I feel joy for the first time since coming to in my office.

It's an elephant.

A pale blue elephant.

"PETTING ZOO!" I cry out.

The elephant turns to face me, then transforms down into my old friend. I hobble-run to her and pull her close in a bear hug.

"I thought you were—"

"I was running late. Never thought I'd say thank god for bachelor parties, but—"

"But they got your club, too."

"What?"

"They hit your club. My office. Everywhere."

"They?" she asks, dubious.

"*They*. Milgram. Mayor Card. Everyone in between."

"Motherfucker."

"Have you heard from Dissident?"

"No. Have they gone for her too?"

"Yeah. Can you call her?"

"I'm on it." She pulls out her phone.

"Have you seen Tragedii?" I ask.

Petting Zoo lowers her head.

I don't need to ask again to know the real Tragedii's dead.

"FUCK!" There's a soft whimpering behind me. I take it for one of the regulars until I feel a small hand tugging at my coat. I turn to see a small absence standing behind me, rain curling around the form of what should be a little girl.

"Kaley?"

"They told me to hide and run. Daddy, Mommy, they told me to hide and run, and I did, and, and, Mommy and Daddy and Johnny . . ." she whimpers, collapsing in a cross-legged position next to me, still invisible save for the rain that curls around her like a million tears that don't seem adequate for the horrors she's just witnessed.

Petting Zoo grabs my shoulder. "Dissident's alive, which is more than can be said for all of the hitters who tried to take her out."

Looking down at Kaley, she asks, "Is that—"

"Yeah."

"Her parents?"

I shake my head.

"Fuck," Petting Zoo whispers. "What the hell are we gonna do?"

Rain starting to pour down around me, surrounded by misery in all its forms, the entire life I've built collapsing, all I can say is "I don't know."

CHAPTER 20: THE SUPERHERO

I'd forgotten my body could hurt this much.

Cramps and spasms run the length of my arms, up my neck and down my spine. Something rigid digs into my wrists, and my fingers are numb. Realizing that the way I'm sitting is part of the problem, I coax my head upright and find my senses of motion and direction off-kilter in a way I haven't felt since the end of lab testing when I was sixteen.

Mom took me out for sorbet the night after the last test was done, to celebrate the fact that the only weakness the doctors had been able to find was a substance that could be patented so that only my own family could ever access it.

To celebrate being safe.

Mom.

Recalling the last few seconds of my consciousness, I blink my sore eyes open to find her.

She's still sitting next to me, but we've been relocated to the dining room, and are no longer alone.

Gathered with us around the table where I learned to play *Risk* are a jarring juxtaposition of the people who've plagued my life for the last month and my city since before I was born.

Mayor Card, with Sergei standing behind him.

Milgram.

Pinnacle.

And across from me, at the table's head, Uncle Ethan is pouring them all tiny glasses of sherry.

Glowing in the middle of all this, like a gaudy centerpiece, is a chunk of solid Jovium the size of a grapefruit.

"Mom," I try to keep my voice level over my rising dread, giving her no reason to dismiss me like some tantrum-throwing child. "Mom, please untie me."

I look at her, and keep on looking at her, hoping she'll eventually return the courtesy. I stare at her concerned but unyielding face, exactly the way I remember it from whenever I got in trouble sneaking candy or bringing animals into the house as a kid. I trace her familiar nose, which tapers down to a delicate point exactly like mine; not because we share blood, but because we share a surgeon. I inventory her perfectly pressed skirt suit that she found the time to change into and accessorize with matching brooch and earrings somewhere between poisoning me, zip-tying me to a chair, and inviting her friends and associates over for drinks.

"Mom, listen to me. These are not good people."

"I told you," Card booms. "I told you I didn't come here to be insulted!"

"Oh, *please*. She said you're not a good person. Considering the . . . *colorful* company she keeps these days, you should be thankful she didn't use far more vulgar terms," Milgram chides.

Card huffs, "I will not stand for—"

"Give her a moment," Uncle Ethan tells the guests amiably. "She's still coming around."

Mom finally looks at me, but not in the eyes.

"You know I wouldn't hurt you, right?" I ask her.

She forces a chuckle. "Of course you wouldn't, sweetheart."

"Then I need you to pick up that rock, and throw it as far as you can."

She chuckles again as if this idea is equally ridiculous.

"I don't know what they've told you," I continue. "I don't know what you think you have to do here, but you don't. You're not like them."

"I guess I'm supposed to keep my head down and plan charity balls and keep my nose out of where the real decisions are made?" she challenges.

"No, you're supposed to be better than this!"

"Why?"

"Because you're my *mom!*"

"If I might interject?" asks Uncle Ethan.

Mom straightens up, leaning away from me only too readily, and Uncle Ethan raises a scrap of black fabric above the table for everyone to see.

The ski mask from my sweatshirt pouch.

Without moving, I can tell that the rest of my pockets are empty as well.

"Would you mind explaining this, Kimmy?"

No. No way. I am not the person at this table with the most explaining to do.

I nod at the combination of Milgram, Card, and Pinnacle, who are watching me like a reality show panel, except they've all designated themselves as the mean judge.

"You first," I say.

"Combined with your current attire," says Uncle Ethan, "it looks very much like the disguise worn by two of the gang of unlicensed vigilantes who've recently been sabotaging certain business interests in WPC. An employee of Mr. Milgram's has identified a similarly dressed vigilante as former Glamper's Island inmate, Edgar Enriquez. Would you like me to read you his priors?"

My face is transparent. There's no point in not asking.

"Where is he?"

Mom pinches the bridge of her nose, deeply embarrassed by my question. "Honey, please, I know you've hit a rough patch with Mason, but this isn't how you handle it."

Milgram answers me.

"Mr. Enriquez is being offered the same opportunity you are. As soon as we finish here, I'll be free to check on the results of his interview."

"What kind of opportunity?"

Milgram's smile is disconcertingly friendly. "How many kinds are there?"

"Don't be too hard on yourself, Lizzie," Uncle Ethan comforts Mom. "You knew this phase might come eventually. No matter how well you try to raise a girl . . ."

"You can't undo the allure of the boy from the wrong side of the tracks," says Mom.

"Wrong side of the . . ." I repeat, disbelieving. "Says the woman with a *mob boss* in her house!"

"What on earth could have made you think this would be okay?" Mom asks me reproachfully. "After what they did to Ethan, what they did to your *father*, how could you expect me to risk losing you to the supervillains, too?"

"Dad was killed by an incompetent corporate ransom collector in homemade spandex, who couldn't measure sedative doses!" I shout at her. "Uncle Ethan was stepped on by a giant robot! Eddie worked for some guy who wishes he were that guy," I jerk my head at Milgram, "and quit after he was busted in high school! There's no *pattern*! There is no 'the supervillains.' There are just people who do different bad things for different bad reasons, but if you want a secret clubhouse full of powerful, scheming, interconnected evildoers, *look around this room!*"

Pinnacle watches this overdue family conference in silence, his arms crossed stiffly over his chest.

"I can't listen to much more of this, Ethan," says Card, refilling his sherry glass all the way to the rim. It looks perversely comical raised to his wide, jowled face.

Uncle Ethan ignores this and rests his chin on his clasped fingers, observing my face.

"Kimberly, we've been very patient, waiting for you to outgrow this . . . this Girl Scout phase. It's probably my fault for indulging it for so long, letting you grow up on that Juniors team, building an identity out of simple-mindedness. It seemed like a harmless enough way for you to build your platform, and I was hoping you'd reject it in your own time, but the clock was ticking, you'd already run out more than half of your marketable career, and you were still just as stubborn and oversensitive as you were at eight years old. I thought if I removed you from their influence and put you in Pinnacle's capable hands, maybe he could ease you into the real work you were supposed to inherit, let you get to know the people who keep Pinnacle City running on a personal level, establish a sense of loyalty."

He smiles at Card, then back at me.

"*You* volunteered me for the Card job?" I realize aloud. "Was any of the stuff you said about him real?"

"You been talking shit about me?" Card says, glaring at Uncle Ethan.

"Of course it was real," says Uncle Ethan, utterly unembarrassed. "I said he can be a pill, but that he's good at appealing to a certain class of people."

"You're a pill!" says Card. "Now break out the spurs and make with the filly-taming. You all promised if I kept her on until the time was right, she'd pay for what they did to my son."

"Your son dug his own grave," Pinnacle speaks at last. "And you should be thanking us all for appointing her to you. Until Ace's indiscretion, your polls were up eighteen percent among women voters."

"If I'm not mistaken," says Milgram, "isn't privacy the reason you still keep a head of security *other* than Miss Kline?"

Milgram smiles at Sergei, who stares stonily back while Card turns on him.

"There's blame to share for letting this get out of hand," he says.

"I apologize," says Sergei, and I expect him to leave it there, but he continues, with an edge of contempt under his professional deadpan. "I failed to instill a preventative respect for women in the boy, in his father's unavoidable absence."

"Don't you give me that shit!" roars Card. "I've been getting ten helpings a day from the liberal media, and I don't need it from you! You don't stop people from walking all over you by going around *respecting* them. Is that the advice you'd give him if you could start over? Huh? What would you tell him?"

"That a woman is like a loaded gun," says Sergei, looking at me with a twitch at the corner of his mouth like we're sharing a private joke, though I'm not laughing. "She's beautiful and powerful and dangerous, and if you can't treat her with enough care to keep her from blowing your *myachi* off, you don't deserve to keep either."

"So not at all like a person, then," I say.

If his face can look taken aback, this is it. "My metaphor was—"

"Get me out of this chair, or suck an egg, Sergei!"

My mother looks at her drink and pretends not to notice the discussion taking place.

"If you're quite convinced of the efficacy of the Jovium . . ." Uncle Ethan hints at Card.

Card calms down enough to nod. "Yes, fine. Sergei, you can go. We'll discuss your performance review tomorrow."

Sergei nods and leaves by the patio door without another word.

I'm waking up enough to start running down my list of possibilities.

No strength, no speed, no energy. Not much I can do but talk.

"So do you all, like, work for my uncle?" I ask.

"Not in this fucking lifetime," says Card.

"She's baiting you," Milgram points out mildly, then turns to me. "I'm sure each one of us believes we're the one in charge, but none of us are stupid enough to imagine the others don't feel the same, are we?"

Card backs down grudgingly. "We'll all see who makes out the best for themselves in the end."

"Precisely," says Uncle Ethan. "Nothing to be gained by arguing about it in the meantime, is there? I admire the effort, Kimberly,

I really do. That question might be the most Machiavelli I've ever seen in you. But you don't imagine we're all held together by how much we enjoy each other's company, do you? We need each other, whether we agree on every little ideological detail or not. That was another lesson I was hoping your assignment might teach you. Possibly, that was another of my misjudgments."

"Big time," I mutter.

"I should have been direct with you," he says. "I'll accept that. Will you allow me to remedy it now?"

I don't offer an answer, and he doesn't wait for one.

"The smear file that was being prepared against the people at this table and our plans for the future has been located. The danger will be neutralized. That's a good thing—for us and for you. You're special, Kimberly. Naïve, for now, but special."

Dizziness from the Jovium makes my answering eye roll particularly dramatic.

"You are," says Uncle Ethan, sounding saddened by my disbelief. "You were born with a combination of advantages that few others can boast."

"Yeah, believe me, I *know*."

"You have the strength, the looks, the family name, and even if you resist using them most of the time, you have the brains. People like us are the ones who move mountains. We're the ones who shape the world, and the world owes it shape to us. Without us, mankind would still be grunting to each other in caves. You don't owe anyone more than that. You do the future a service simply by existing and acting out your will. The only way you could fail would be to destroy the potential you've been handed. To waste what you *will* be handed when your mother and I are gone. I need to know that you're strong and savvy enough to make the most of your position before that happens."

Now I'm laughing, because I'm tired, my head hurts, and my family are villains in all but name, and I really, really wish I were still at Eddie's apartment right now. Not that I could have avoided all this that way, not with thugs being sent for him too, but we might've had a better chance of fighting them off together.

"Why do you find it so difficult to believe that you're special enough to deserve better," asks Uncle Ethan, "and so easy to believe you're special enough to deserve *worse*? You swallow your own press so easily, but you won't take the word of someone who's been in the game a lot longer than you have. You are not the ordained savior of Pinnacle City, Kimberly. You're not the one and only chosen hero, destined to bring peace and perfection at the price of your own life. There's no rule that says you have to be a better person than anyone else, except in all the ways you already are. You are not condemned to unreasonable selflessness. You do not carry all the world's problems and trivial little injustices on your shoulders. What cruel, brain-addled force of destiny would choose you for that?"

"I did," I answer, and Uncle Ethan looks disconcerted to hear anything but rhetorical silence in response.

"Excuse me?"

"I'm not the one and only. I don't *want* to be the one and only. But for the task of giving two figs about anyone other than myself? *I* choose me."

Uncle Ethan sighs with great disappointment, then nods to Milgram.

"Do your work. I believe I'll adjourn to the kitchen, if anyone would care to join me."

"Mom, don't, please," I try.

Mom gives me a regretful backward glance that changes nothing before hurrying out of the room.

"Mom. Mom! Mom! MOM!"

Pinnacle stands silently and follows.

Uncle Ethan's floating chair rotates toward the doorway.

Milgram finishes his glass and turns his chair toward me.

Mayor Card moves into my mother's vacated chair, his eyes locked on me with impatient hunger.

"Uncle Ethan," I call out, unable to keep the nerves from quavering the anger in my voice. I say it as plainly as I can. "Mayor Card assaulted me. On my first day working in his house, he grabbed me.."

It sounds even lamer out loud than it always did in my head, but I push onward.

"I shoved him away with my powers then, and I'm asking you now, as your niece and protégé, not to leave me defenseless in a room with him."

I know by the look on Milgram's face that Card is the least of my worries at this moment, but if my uncle deliberately handed me over to these partners of his when he handed me his mantle, I want him to know exactly what he did. I want him to think about it while he's doing it again now.

Uncle Ethan turns to Card with a faintly scolding look.

Card looks only mildly embarrassed. "I might've made a few off-color remarks that could have given her the wrong idea," he allows. "But I would *never* do what she's describing. Not ever. On my honor, I'd never mix business and pleasure like that."

Maybe Uncle Ethan doesn't believe me, given the convenience of my belated timing, or maybe he doesn't care, but he gives Card a nod of understanding and his chair floats onward.

"He wasn't the first!" Any matter-of-fact composure in my tone shatters as I try to explain to the chair's high leather back why those two revolting seconds even matter now. "But he was the first one who made me feel it."

I stare at my uncle's chair and only my uncle's chair so that I don't have to watch Card's face twist that into some kind of compliment.

"He was the first one who ever scared me, because even though I could have squashed him like a bug like any of the others, I thought he could squash me, too. He was my mission, and I thought he could make me fail in front of the Guardians. In front of *you*."

I might as well be taking a knife to my clothes, to my skin, spilling my squirming guts onto this table in front of people who have no business in the world watching, just for the chance of making my uncle understand a fraction of what that moment felt like.

But he's not even looking.

"Please!" I rattle my chair in a frantic underscore. "If we're still family, you won't leave me here!"

The kitchen door closes.

And then I'm alone between Milgram and Card, with a Jovium stone on the table and my hands tied behind my back.

Uncle Ethan has taken the mask and its mind control alarm chip with him.

"This won't hurt," Milgram tells me, in the gentle tone of a pediatrician.

"It better hurt a little," says Card, massaging the nearly healed burn I left on his hand.

"At least, not tonight," continues Milgram. "And you're of course welcome to stay, Mr. Mayor, but I would appreciate a mood of contemplative quiet. Now, Miss Kline, how much have you been told about my particular ability?"

"You can control minds," I say, my heart thrumming so violently in my throat that I can barely squeeze the words out past it. "Make people do things."

"You couldn't be more wrong," says Milgram, pleasantly. "I can't force anyone to do anything. All I can do is selectively remove certain barriers of conscience that might otherwise prevent them from acting."

"You forced good men to kill a good man. Someone they respected."

"You mean Quentin Julian." Milgram nods. "People always harbor a particular resentment toward those who've helped them.

A polite sense of obligation usually holds any acts of retribution at bay, but we never truly forgive being saddled with that obligation in the first place. Julian obligated a lot of people in his life, and when I lifted that obligation from a few of their minds, when I allowed them to exact their revenge for it and leave the responsibility to me, they jumped at the opportunity."

"Quentin helped people because he could," I say. "Because he *cared*. He never asked anyone for anything in return."

"But he could have," says Milgram. "You understand? That was the cruelty of Julian's lifestyle. Everyone who knew him had to live with knowing that if he were ever to ask them for a favor, they would have to grant it."

"Like people are totally free to say no to *you*." I yank against my restraints with a futile desperation that wobbles my chair.

"When I indebt someone, I always offer them ample opportunities to equalize our relationship," he continues. "Julian never allowed anyone that relief. Do you see yourself in him, Miss Kline? Does it bother you to realize how many people's hatred you've personally earned, under the pretense of their gratitude?"

I'm suddenly a different kind of furious than I have been since waking up to this twisted intervention, not with these conspirators who want my cooperation to rob innocent people of what little they have, but with everyone else I've ever met, because I don't understand what they want from me.

I have that feeling again that I had in the sanitarium, the feeling that something's very wrong with me, that I can't trust my own feelings and urgently need someone else to tell me what to do, and I realize Milgram's power is already taking effect. There are important parts of me missing, or inaccessible.

As soon as I get out of this chair, I'm going to set fire to the curtains.

I make this decision on the spot, trying not to think too much about why. It's just what I'm going to do, the first thing I'm going to do, no matter what else I do afterward.

"Does it bother you that you'd be just as easy to send a mob against as he was?" asks Milgram.

I don't answer. I can't answer. I can't speak, because I can't think. I won't know what I'm talking about and everything will come out wrong.

Milgram observes this and nods to himself, as if checking off a symptom on a mental clipboard.

"This is what's going to happen. You're going to go home to Juniors Ranch. You're going to find each one of the ignorant kids who co-enabled your bubblegum heroism and then wrote you off so easily to avoid having to grow up with you, and you will slaughter them, quietly, in their sleep."

His voice is like a dripping tap, a harmless and delicate sound that grows in my ears until it's all I can hear, though I know its volume and rhythm haven't changed. I picture my friends in their beds, content without me and smugly satisfied with another day's work protecting photogenic people who barely need them. The tears begin to run down my cheeks because I can already feel their necks snapping in my hands when my strength returns, and I know that I'm going to do this, because I'm so angry, so angry, but mostly because I need this dripping in my head to stop.

The tears make it impossible to breathe through my nose, and the air makes a wet, sobbing shudder through my mouth. Card closes his eyes and rocks into the sound like the crescendo of a goosebump-worthy symphony, then places his hand on my thigh and leaves it there.

Milgram doesn't comment, and I lack the power or wherewithal to respond with anything but more tears. I don't know why I'm surprised.

Why am I surprised?

"You will then report back here, at which point you will have two options," Milgram continues. "Either Solar Flare will publically swear vengeance on the WPC street villains who murdered her former teammates, and proceed to fight for that vengeance in precisely and exclusively the ways we tell her to, or she will be exposed and discredited for turning supervillain herself and killed in the Guardians' heroic attempt to apprehend her, and the devastated but innocent Erickson-Kline family will be forced to find a new heir after all. Do you understand the opportunity you're being offered?"

I try several times before I vocalize audibly.

"Is it . . . is it . . . is it the same opportunity you offered the rest of my family?"

"No," says Milgram softly. "No, it's not. You can't build an empire one hard sell at a time. I prefer to align myself with like-minded people whose loyalty comes easily. Believe me, I would never bother with such a cheap last resort if it weren't so important to your uncle to try and salvage you. Imagine, if you'd had a brother or a cousin, we wouldn't be in this uncomfortable situation. We could have been negotiating with him right now, while you partied your way across Europe with all the exotic boy toys you could handle, free from any particular purpose or expectations. What do you think, Miss Kline? Would you have preferred it that way?"

I think I'm drowning, one droplet at a time, in my sinuses and in my brain.

I think the Juniors are continuing to breathe for too long.

I think Card's hand is holding on so hard that my leg is bruising, and I can't remember what I'm supposed to be doing.

Someone needs to tell me.

Milgram doesn't make me wait long.

"I'm going to remove the Jovium," he says. "When I do, you will complete your mission, and you will not hurt us. You don't have the right to hurt us. You'll need our guidance when you get back. Do you understand?"

I nod.

"Answer."

"Yes," I croak.

Milgram retrieves a shielded hermetic crate from under the table and places the glowing stone inside.

Card withdraws his hand and slides his chair away from me, looking equal parts disappointed and wary.

Milgram sets the crate to seal and, little by little, the strength returns to my body, leaving my mind ransacked.

I pull at the restraints again, and this time the back of the chair splinters and breaks away, allowing me to stand.

I can't hurt the men in front of me, and I have to kill the Justice Juniors.

There's no choice in that.

That's how it has to be.

But there was something else, too. Something important.

Right.

With a measured burst of firework energy, I set the curtains at the other end of the room ablaze.

The men both look at me in momentary confusion.

I don't remember why I'm doing it, either, until the smoke detector activates, a siren that could wake the dead shrieking through the room.

I move toward the pain of the sound instead of away, sighing with relief as it purges the dripping of Milgram's voice from my ears, just like Dissident's earpiece.

Realizing what I've done, Milgram reaches for the hermetic case, but I'm faster than he is now and pick it up first.

Card's fingers are in his ears and he doesn't seem to understand what's going on even when I clamp one hand over his thick neck and reach the other into the pocket of his grotesquely tented pants, just long enough to relieve him of his phone.

The kitchen door opens in response to the alarm, and powers or not, I have to get out of here before—

Pinnacle reaches the doorway first, and looks right at me.

I can't beat him in a fight. I know his stats by heart. He's much too strong. But I'm a shade faster. My only chance is to lose him before he can start one.

Carrying the case of Jovium, I put on every ounce of speed that's returned to my body, escaping the first beam of his heat vision by millimeters, smashing through the window before I can feel it break, and rocketing halfway out to sea without looking back.

I hover for a moment, listening to make sure I'm alone, testing control of my limbs, my altitude, my temperature, and it's only when the sensation of utter helplessness has passed that the sting of it catches up and the shudders set in.

I don't want to go back to land. I've only just arrived here in this safe bubble of solitude where nothing wants to use, hurt, or lie to me, but I know I can't leave Milgram, Card, Pinnacle and my family to carry on with their plans, Jovium or not. I can't keep flying away whenever something happens that I can't stand to be close to, because someone needs to do better, and I meant what I said.

I choose me.

Finally, I look down at Card's phone. My recovering fingers don't want to cooperate, but I manage to turn the screen on without dropping it into the waves.

Numeric lock.

Worth a try:

11111.

It unlocks.

If my uncle and the rest of them are really pretending to each other that they're all equal partners in this, then Card's almost certainly got something on here that can tell me where that file is before it's too late.

On my last day as a guest at the bad guys' table, I can finally do what I went back to them for.

But first, I dial Eddie's number.

CHAPTER 21: THE DETECTIVE

When the world's a dangerous place and everywhere you ever considered safe has burned to the ground, sometimes you have to find safety in the least likely of places.

This is why we chose the now abandoned Snyder Sanitarium for Lost Souls as our rally point after the conspiracy's hit campaign. Ever since Kline and Dissident cleared the place out and the subsequent police investigation, the hospital has been empty, and it's about the closest thing we could find to a sanctuary.

After all, Milgram wouldn't come looking for us at his old home base, would he?

Dissident is already there when Petting Zoo, Kaley, and I arrive. She's in the entrance rotunda, still decked out in Milgram's Christmas decorations, which now look dim and tattered from the police investigation, faint memories of a better time that never came for the people who used to call this place home.

Her costume shines with sticky blood. Some of it hers, no doubt, the way she's limping, but not all of it. The moment she sees us, she limps over, pulls off her helmet, throws her arms around Petting Zoo, and kisses her passionately.

Though surprised, Petting Zoo quickly welcomes it.

When they're finished, Fadia grabs me by the shoulder and pulls me into a hug.

"Glad you're still alive."

"Same to you. You make it out okay?"

"Better than Milgram's guys."

"They're not all Milgram's."

"I know."

I mean to introduce Kaley, but she's gone invisible on us again. She fades into existence only long enough to look at Fadia and go back to hiding behind Petting Zoo.

"You up to date?" I ask.

"Yes," Fadia says. "We're going after them, right? We're going to tear them the fuck down for everything they've destroyed, *right*?"

"You really think that's an option at this point?" Petting Zoo asks.

"You really think there's any other option?" Fadia snaps back.

"Look, I've never once backed down from a fight in my life," says Petting Zoo, "but there's a first time for everything, and I think this might be it. Pinnacle City isn't safe for us anymore."

"Not an option. I've fought too long and hard for the people of this city. You don't want to fight, fine. But I'm doing this with or without your help."

"I didn't say I wasn't gonna, I just wanted to, you know, throw out all ideas."

"Well, throw out better ideas."

Fadia looks to me like I'm going to be the one to throw out this fabled better idea, but I've got nothing. I want to make them pay every bit as much as she does for all they've done and all they will do if nothing stops them, but Petting Zoo's not wrong either. No matter what we've done or how hard we've fought, Milgram and Card and their kind have always been two steps ahead of us, and likely always will be. If we keep fighting like this, there's a chance we'll be able to make some kind of difference, but there's an even greater chance we'll all die.

So, instead of coming up with a plan now, I say, "Let's wait for Kline first."

"The hero?" Fadia asks.

"Like it or not, she's a part of this. She got hit tonight too."

"How?"

"Milgram."

"And she got away?"

"Yes."

"On her own?"

"Yes," I say, with greater irritation.

"And you still trust her? With his powers . . . ?"

"I don't think he's in her head, but if he is, I've no doubt you got something in one of your belts that'll take her out."

"That's beside the point," she says, pulling a small dark vial from the back of her utility belt, where she keeps her collection of superhero weaknesses. "I'm just upset because you didn't tell us everyone you invited to this little party, and I need to know these things before—"

The doors swing open behind us.

Glowing slightly from her flight, Kimberly Kline stands with her arms splayed wide, bracing herself against the doorframe.

"We need to—Why is award-winning field reporter Fadia Bakkour here?"

*

Once she's mostly done goggling at Fadia's secret identity, Kline lays out the true scale of how utterly fucked we are in slow, painful detail. That there were superheroes involved in this isn't much of a surprise, because, hey, what *aren't* they involved in?

That the entire starting lineup of the Pinnacle City Guardians is in on it gives a lot more credit to Petting Zoo's "run away" idea.

Kline doesn't seem to have even considered that possibility.

"We have to sneak into the Card mansion and stop this, *tomorrow*," she says, motioning to Mayor Card's cell phone. With the loss of Collingwraith's laptop, this phone is all we have, but god bless Card for having shitty security, because Kline was able to break in and get all sorts of necessary info. "Well," she corrects herself, looking at the early morning hour on the phone's screen, "*tonight*, technically."

"Why tonight?" Fadia asks. I know she's especially irritated with being outed to Kline like this, but at least she's being professional and hearing her out.

"Because, going by the texts on Card's phone, that's when it all goes down. Mayor Card, Milgram . . . my family, all of them will be there for a big meeting where they're going to destroy Quentin's file. If we can sneak in and steal the file before it's destroyed, then it's game over for them."

She says it so confidently I seriously consider what Fadia was suggesting, that Milgram may have actually compromised her and that this is all a way to lead us into a trap.

I rule that out quickly, because if she'd been programmed to kill, she could've blasted us with energy from the skies the moment she got here, and there wouldn't have been a damn thing we could've done to stop her.

Even so, her plan just doesn't jive with me. I know she's proposing the sneaky approach because she thinks that's what Fadia and I would prefer, but this time I just can't agree.

"No."

"No?"

"No," I repeat. "We've done the sneaking thing, and it's time for a new tactic. They've been raining down hell on the Crescent and WPC the way they have because they know nobody'd dare doing stuff like that in EPC. I think if they're expecting us to attack, they're gonna expect us to try and sneak in and they'll be prepared for that . . . so why not try something different? Something so crazy they won't know what hit 'em until it's too late?"

"I don't know if you remember basic training all that well, but frontal assaults are generally considered suicidal for a reason," Petting Zoo adds.

"I'm not suggesting one, exactly."

"Then what are you suggesting?" Fadia asks, intrigued.

I wasn't really suggesting anything, but now I have to come up with something. I think of the few things we were able to salvage from the Lineup, and an answer comes to me.

"They get away with all the sneaking around *they* do because no one notices it over the noise of the rest of their shit on the airwaves. Well, how about we take a page from their playbook and fight fire with fire? This time, we won't bother trying to hide. This time, we'll be the ones making the noise."

✳

We've got a day to plan and set our affairs in order before we make our move on the Card mansion. Kline's knowledge of the grounds is invaluable, especially in figuring out just which spots would be most vulnerable to a breach. I have to hand it to her, she knows that this is going to be career suicide (*possibly literal suicide*), and she's ready to go in without the slightest hesitation.

The plan we come up with is simple and brutal.

Kline and I break into the compound from opposite sides and raise all sorts of hell, taking out as many goons and henchmen as we can while making sure none of the big bads behind the meeting can escape (Fadia's getting her hands on a teleportation jammer to help with that) and, god-willing, attract as much police and media attention as we can. If the mayor and the Guardians are seen conspiring with Milgram and his goons, it'll be pretty hard for anyone to ignore, and even harder for Card to talk his way out of it.

This is the showier part of our plan, the blunt force portion we've got in place for if anything goes to hell.

The real core of the plan rests on Dissident. While Kline and I tear down the house of Card and distract all the heavy hitters, Dissident's gonna sneak inside and steal the Julian file. Once found, it's her job to get the hell out of there and protect the file with her life until she can make the story of all stories and tell the world everything that's been going on in Pinnacle City.

We know we might not all make it out alive, but, not being able to speak for the others, I'm okay with this. I ain't led a life worth remembering, and god knows I've fucked up more than I've done right, but this . . . this is a chance, I think, my one chance, maybe my last chance, to do something good.

Maybe I'll be a hero, maybe I'll just be that nutcase who took a shot at the mayor, but whatever legacy I get out of this, I'll have done it for the right reasons.

And at least I know one person's gonna come out of this safe who otherwise wouldn't have.

Right now little Kaley Mendoza's on a bus to Amber City with Petting Zoo, going to lie low with some of our old army buddies until we see how tonight pans out. In the end, Petting Zoo didn't really want to run. Nothing would have kept her from joining in the attack, if we hadn't needed someone to keep one little girl away from the hell we're about to unleash.

With that out of the way, there's just one last piece of business I have to attend to, but compared to storming the mayor's mansion, this is much more difficult.

✳

Kline and I kill time in a mansion owned by some family friends of hers who're out of town for the holidays. I like this place because it's warm and has a fully stocked bar, and because they're not good enough family friends of Kline's that she minds me going through their stuff. We're here because it has a good view of the mayor's mansion, which we can actually see tonight due to a break in the rain.

We don't talk, much, which I'm glad for at the moment. I need to psych myself up for something I've been afraid to do for far too long.

Fear and me, we don't have much of a relationship. Oh sure, I've been afraid for my life, and that's an excellent survival mechanism, but cold sweat, wake up in the middle of the night sorts of fear I'm a lot less familiar with. I don't fear spiders or snakes or clowns or anything like that, just real things—things that oughta be feared.

The closest I've known to bump-in-the-night kind of fear was during my stint in the army. I just wanted to serve for a few years to help clear my name, and naturally got sent into combat with a superhuman platoon. I didn't see much action, but what little I did see, the few guys I did kill, was enough to bring its own nightmares. Being forced to do work behind the lines, "interrogating" the enemy . . . that made the nightmares even worse. Worse enough that when I woke up in the hospital with a mangled arm from an IED and was told I was being sent home, I said, "Good."

I haven't felt fear like that in a long time, but when I excuse myself from Kline to make a phone call, it's back again.

I know the number by heart. I assume it'll still work, even after twelve years, but I have a hard time hitting the send button. My heart beats so heavily I worry I'm gonna pass out. I have to close my eyes and take a few deep breaths to make this happen.

You're not facing down a pro-hero, you're not gonna watch Marco die again, this is just a phone call. Don't need to see his face, don't need to let him know he got to you, just say what you have to say.

Hand shaking, I press send.

The number rings once.

Twice.

Three times.

Four times.

Changed the number. Must've. He may be old, but even he knows how to—

"Hello?"

His voice has aged some, but it's still so familiar that it makes me feel like a little kid the moment he speaks. There's noise in the background, like a holiday party, music, people eating and arguing.

"I've got something to say to you."

"Who is this?" he asks, confused.

I take a deep breath, and continue, "You might hear a lot about me in the next few days, and if you do, I just want you to know it's because I'm doing something good this time. No matter what anyone says, I'm not a villain, alright? No matter what you want to think, no matter how much you want to hate me, I'm gonna be a hero tonight, not a villain this time."

A long pause. I can hear everyone in the background clearly.

"Eddie? Little Eddie?"

"Yeah, Dad. It's me."

Another long pause.

"Stop ruining our Christmas party," he says.

The line goes dead.

Fury boils inside me. Hasn't heard my voice for more than a decade, and that's what he says. I want to scream, I want to throw my phone, I want to destroy everything in sight.

Yet, after all this time, after everything I've been though. All I can do is let out a deep sigh.

"Family, huh?" Kline says, strolling into the room.

"Yeah." I crunch a pill, wanting to take the edge off both my arm and the call.

"I know I'm not the best person to talk about family right now, but if you want to . . ."

"I don't."

"Okay."

She's nervous. Maybe even almost as nervous as I am. I'm torn between old feelings; the feelings where I'm more than happy to see a superhero suffer no matter what and how I've come to feel about her in the time we've gotten to know each other. I can't say we know each other well, or are even what you'd call friends, but we're friendly, I guess. Friendly enough that I feel the need to fill the silence.

"So, what do you want to talk about?" I ask.

"What?"

"Ask me a question. Anything. Keep us distracted 'til we have to go in and kick some ass."

"Anything?"

"Anything within reason, I mean. Not giving up trade secrets or talking old flings or anything. Anything except about my family."

She smiles, a little. "You're not giving me a lot to work with."

"There's a lot still in there, trust me. I've led an interesting life, I think."

She looks thoughtful, trying to come up with a properly insightful question.

"Okay," she says. "How long have you—"

My phone vibrates.

Dissident.

Perfect timing.

"I'm in," she says.

"You have eyes on the file?"

"I do. And all the major players are here. Card, Milgram, Kline, Erickson, a few of the Guardians . . . Whenever you're ready to start your ruckus, it'll be much appreciated."

"We're on it." I hang up.

Wordlessly, Kline and I head to the roof. I retrieve the duffel bag I left outside and tightly cinch my trench coat shut. I've never tested how bulletproof the fabric really is, mostly because I've always hoped I'd never need to find out. While I trust what Fadia said about its strength, I silently vow not to let it make me lazy.

Finally ready, Kline grabs me under my arms and takes off, flying us over to the Card mansion.

I've never really liked flying—especially like this. It can be fun, especially when you're drunk, but when you're sober you're just being lifted and whipped through the air by someone who may or may not be strong enough to carry you. I'm glad that Kline's as strong as she is and can't be hurt by me hanging on too tight. Makes her a damn sight more comfortable to fly with than a lot of the guys I did this with back in the army. Even so, I'd have preferred to do this on the ground.

We pass through the protective shield without incident, Dissident's modifications to Kline's entrance code clearly worked enough not to set off any alarms, and though we see roving security patrols (can't tell if they're Card's or Milgram's guys, though there's not likely much of a difference), they don't notice us in the dark when Kline drops me off on the grounds.

"Be safe," she says.

"Back atcha."

She looks at me for a moment, concern in her eyes, and before I can wave her away to hold up her part of the plan, she flies off.

Now I'm kind of wishing she'd stayed. But we agreed, one of us takes the north end, one of us takes the south, and we both work our way toward the middle with Dissident.

I cling tightly to the duffel bag, unzipping it, reaching inside, ready to—

"Don't, fucking, move," a voice says from behind. He doesn't need to, but he cocks his gun for emphasis.

This is it. There's no going back from this, and no getting out of it without violence. I'm gonna be killing people tonight, the greatest sin of all, my old Sunday school teacher would say, and unlike my army days, here the killing's going to be all my choice. I know this is a bad man, and I know I'm doing this for the right reasons, but it still conflicts me to know that in a moment, he'll be dead because of me.

Best do it quick. Like tearing off a Band-Aid.

I whirl on the man.

Two quick, loud pops, and the feeling like I've been hit twice in the gut with a sledgehammer. It hurts, a lot, but I'm used to pain, and this passes faster than most.

The goon and his two partners look surprised that I'm still standing.

I take advantage of that surprise to introduce them to what we dug out of the Lineup.

Tragedii's massive Genentech Model 39-27b Flesheater gun unfolds in my hands as its multiple barrels whirl to life, and though the gun is ungainly and enormous, its future technology makes it pleasantly light. Light enough that I can barely feel the recoil of the first volley of plasma shots while Milgram's thugs, or what's left of them, very much do.

And like that, the deed is done. I feel guilt for killing these men, somewhere, and if I make it out of here alive I know it'll haunt my dreams, but for now all I feel is a great exhilaration.

The first, and worst, part is done.

Now to do what needs doing.

The roar of the laser cannon makes the compound come to life. There's shouts, confusion, people running toward me.

To focus their attention, I switch the weapon to its "low" setting and fire another long volley at the mansion itself, blasting holes in its gleaming golden exterior, shattering numerous windows.

There's an explosion on the other side of the compound, followed by more screams, and I know Kline has begun her part of the plan. I may not be as powerful as her, but armed with the Flesheater, Harriet, and the chunk of Jovium she gave me in case Milgram compromised her in my pocket, I'm feeling pretty unstoppable.

With this in mind, I run for the mansion.

CHAPTER 22: THE SUPERHERO

I hold out both hands and let the power of the shockwave vibrate through me on its way to set the topiary on fire.

The boxwood renderings of Ace, Anastasia, and Mayor Card himself explode under purple fireworks, heads and arms scattering across the yard in flames.

I remind myself to go slow, go loud, go big. Hovering closer at the pace of a drifting carnival balloon, I count out ten seconds before my next blast knocks the diamond-shaped door off its hinges.

Can you hear me in there, Mr. Mayor?

Mom?

Uncle?

Are you here, Guardians?

Yeah, I'm coming in.

The foyer is empty, and I make it past three sitting rooms, shattering ornamental columns and gaudy jeweled vases as I go, before security makes an appearance.

A dozen of Sergei's team rush into a rough circle around me on the ground, weapons aiming up.

"Hey, guys. Which way to the meeting, please?"

A few of them look vaguely embarrassed that we're no longer on the same side, others annoyed by the reminder.

One of them squeezes his trigger, and my stomach drops into my shoes.

Reflexively, my hand rises to catch the bullet, and I'm almost surprised when it flattens against my palm in that familiar, harmless way.

It's just ordinary lead.

Did I really believe for a split second that my family would trust the Cards' entry-level hired protection with Jovium weaponry?

I'm jumpier than I thought.

I can't keep worrying about it like this. The bad guys have control of the lab, and I could get knocked down with another dose at any moment, turned into a helpless puppet or hostage. But if I let the possibility stop me from trying, then I already am one.

And if I learned anything from seven years on the Justice Juniors, it's that when people come together to fight for what's right, no matter how hopeless it looks, things have a habit of turning out okay.

I've just never had a chance to test the theory on quite this big a scale.

"Sorry, which way did you say? I totally spaced," I ask the guard with the itchy fingers, jerking his gun out of his hand and crushing it in mine.

He's stuttering too much to answer me now, but luckily, Card's voice carries.

"This is my house! I don't care how they got in, get them out! What the fuck do I pay you for?"

I consider staying to disarm the rest, but I have to close the net, meet Eddie and Dissident in the middle to make sure none of the major players get to escape before we hit the evening news.

Oh yeah, Dissident, who happens to be *Fadia Freakin' Bakkour.*

When I offered the hermetic case of Jovium to the two of them today, just in case my earpiece fails and Milgram gets his claws into my brain again, she handed it to Eddie with a casual mention that she already has a piece, and wouldn't say how. I can't get over this vigilante who's been teaching me how to root out mob hideouts being the same person as the sweet, funny reporter who used to show up at my family's charity balls and poke gentle fun at the guests whenever they tried to suggest that their life stories were worth her professional time.

But here we both are.

Blasting a few more guns out of hands on my way, one at a time, I follow the sound of Card's tantrum.

I find Card standing in the TV room where I watched the announcement of Quentin's murder, shouting his face purple at Sergei and Jacob.

"This is unacceptable! You! Why didn't you warn me?" he demands of Jacob, whose face is still black and blue from its introduction to Eddie's bat. "What kind of a psychic are you?"

Jacob taps impatiently on his tablet, which answers for him. "Jeez, tell the world, boss."

I hover silently down the hallway toward them, close enough to realize that his jaw is wired shut.

"It's just a sixth sense for stirring up drama," says the tablet with an awkward, computerized cadence. "I can't predict what that drama's going to be. I'm starting to regret telling you."

"Damn right, you regret it!" says Card. "Because if *In the Cards* goes off the air, you better believe the DSA's getting a call about an unregistered super."

"It's illegal to knowingly employ an unregistered super," Jacob's tablet notes.

"Not as illegal as it is to *be* one!"

"Well, good—"

"Just keep the cameras off!"

"Sure, yeah, that could work," Jacob nods, like it's a brainstorming session over donuts. "We'll pick back up tomorrow with some tragic footage of the aftermath, tearful confessionals from Ana and the girls when they get back from Rome, while they're still in shock from the news—"

"Keep them off!" repeats Card. "And don't let that scientist box slow you down." He points at the tablet. "If you didn't do so much coke, you'd be able to afford the app to make you sound like a real person!" He turns back to Sergei. "And you! Get this situation under control, *now*."

There are gunshots, breaking glass, the chesty *whoomp* sound of Tragedii's future gun, evidence of how far from under control this situation already is.

Eddie and Dissident are getting closer.

I land in the TV room, announcing myself by touching down hard enough to splinter the hardwood.

"There!" Card points at me. "Take her down!"

Sergei lifts his walkie. "Need some super-backup in TV room four."

"I said *you* take her down!" demands Card, his face heating up to that shade that means he's hearing even less of reality than usual.

Sergei looks at me, expressionless, then raises his gun and fires.

The bullet ricochets off me and breaks a window.

Staring at Card, as if to demonstrate the futility of his assignment, Sergei lazily empties the rest of his clip in the direction of my invulnerable chest.

But in spite of Card's brilliant strategizing, Sergei's call for backup has been heard.

Bear Man and Hedgehog march down the opposite hallway, the acid spines on the back of Hedgehog's arms standing on end, poised to fire.

I don't know if those spines can penetrate my skin, but I'd rather not find out.

"Hey, Glitter Girl!" says Bear Man. "I was the first one to know that you weren't going to make it!"

"Dream on," says Hedgehog. "*I* knew first!"

"So, everyone knew about the selling out to the mob thing before I did, huh?" I ask, flattening myself to the ceiling to avoid a volley of quills, which skewer the jewel-encrusted couch and begin eating through the upholstery.

Bear Man takes a flying leap, grabbing my leg with the claws of his gauntlet and swinging me into the floor, snapping floorboards beneath me like twigs, then back into the ceiling, raining plaster down around us from the hole my head makes.

"Watch the furniture!" Card scolds, while Sergei braces himself in the nearest doorway and Jacob takes shelter behind the console cabinet.

I charge up and send a blast through Bear Man's hand. He jerks it away and then swings it back at me with all his oversized strength and weight, sending me rolling into a cabinet, spilling tacky figurines down over my head.

"Where's Pinnacle?" I ask. "At the evidence-torching party without you guys?"

"Pinnacle protects the city," says Hedgehog, like he's explaining why the sun rises. "He trusts us to make sure the job gets done tonight."

He fires his quills and I lift myself off the floor just in time to see them eat a hole through the curtain and window behind it.

Crud. Okay, no problem. Pinnacle may not be here in person to get caught, but he still has to be implicated in the file.

Bear Man takes about a quarter of the couch, now severed from the rest of it by Hedgehog's acid, and uses it to shield himself against the firework I send at his feet, then slams me into the floor with it, loading his full weight on top.

I can send both it and him sky high with one blast, but maybe not before the quills already leaving Hedgehog's forearms embed themselves in my face. It's a race of neuro-impulses and nanoseconds, and the heat in my hands is a fraction of what it needs to be, what it *will* be an instant from now, when a boot crushes the quills back into Hedgehog's wrist.

A loop of cable trails behind Dissident as she descends from the hole my head left in the ceiling. She barely pauses to stomp on Hedgehog's other arm before swinging around Mayor Card in an acrobatically precise pattern while pulling the cable's loose end to winch him up in the air by his feet, like a piñata.

I let off my energy buildup, blasting not only Bear Man but the floor beneath me, finally shattering it open. Bear Man is propelled straight upward, knocking Card into a spin with one flailing arm as he falls straight back down toward the hole I've left in the floor.

I put on a burst of lateral flight to avoid interfering with physics in action.

Bear Man grabs for the edges of the hole as he falls into the basement, succeeding only in widening it, dragging more floorboards down with him and making the few security personnel—who've finally caught up with the noise—jump back again to avoid following him.

Another few bullets bounce off of me where I'm hovering and Card yelps as one of the ricochets embeds itself in his shoe.

"Sergei! Tell your men to aim, or you're done! You're all done!"

Sergei watches Card spin around like a tire swing. He reloads his gun and raises it toward Dissident's slightly less invulnerable armor.

She begins to swing the end of one of her bolas in a lazy circle, and I let my hands glow, ready to explode the gun in his hand if I have to.

Sergei looks between us, calculating his long odds and maybe the entire value of his career. He looks back up at Card, holsters the gun, and raises his walkie instead.

His instructions are relayed clearly through every other walkie in earshot.

"Vacate Card property. Our services are no longer required."

Card struggles to reach the cable suspending him and only manages to make himself rotate faster. "Stay where you are!"

Several guards from outside the room trip over each other on the frequency to request clarification.

"I said we're no longer contracting with the Card family," Sergei repeats. "Lower the security field and leave the premises."

The guards in the room glance at each other, holster, and run for the door before they can be called back. Sergei follows at a stroll.

Dissident and I do nothing to obstruct their exit.

"You do *not* have permission to leave!" Card rages from the ceiling. "I'll see every one of you behind bars! Do you hear me, you cowards!?"

More clearly outnumbered than ever, Jacob forces a grin onto his mangled face and bolts down the hall in the opposite direction.

"One down," I say, spraying a few sparks at Card to make him squirm as I land next to Dissident.

"He was already screwed for having the meeting in his house," she says. "We need to round up the rest."

"Where's the file?"

"On a laptop. Erickson had it last." She shows me her phone screen, displaying an aerial shot of the Card estate and a glowing dot marked at the south end. "I lost visual contact, but I got a tracker on him, and he hasn't left the building. There's a chance it's still intact."

We leave Card swinging from the ceiling and Hedgehog curled into a ball around his broken wrists. Bear Man continues to smash up the basement trying to climb his way back up. Dissident and I chase the glowing dot through the tacky labyrinth of the Card mansion, splitting up and rejoining whenever the corridors break into parallel rooms, to up our chances of catching a hint of Milgram on our way.

If we can't get our hands on the Julian file, we have to at least make sure Milgram doesn't get away, and that the others are caught red-handed meeting with him behind closed doors.

At one point, I barge in on Ace trying to work the door of a one-person panic room but unable to raise his immobilized arms high enough.

I set one leg of his designer pants on fire, but I don't have time to stop and watch how compatible those casts are with the stop, drop, and roll maneuver.

A few of Milgram's thugs, both super and not, take shots at Dissident and me as we pass, but they're scattered, panicked, not forming a trail to their boss's whereabouts.

"Back. The fuck. *Off!*"

We stop to listen to the distant shouting and look at each other, or rather, I look at her opaque faceplate and imagine that she's looking through it back at me.

I check the screen in her hand.

"Get the file. We'll meet you in the south wing."

With a small nod, she rushes on, and I take a left toward the pool, Eddie's voice, and the sound of something shattering.

The Cards' indoor pool is shaped like a spade, with a Jacuzzi as its little triangular handle. Normally, the room has the unpleasant, chemical humidity of a gym.

Now it's like walking into an industrial freezer.

Eddie's standing at the edge of the Jacuzzi, which is frozen solid, ice crystals clinging to his hair and clothes, trying to fire his future gun across the pool at my mom. He's shivering too hard to aim straight, and she's pacing like a stalking cat, covering both sides of the pool against his escape.

"Back off!" he shouts again, defiant.

With a sweep of her hand, the edge of the pool rises in a wave toward him, sharpening into jagged icicles on its way. He hits it in its path with the gun, scattering ice across the jeweled tiles and back into the liquid part of the pool.

"Stop it!" I yell, flying out over the water between them and turning toward my mother.

I knew she was going to be here. I knew it, but it still feels wrong.

No one should have to walk in on their mom and their . . . whatever Eddie is to me, trying to kill each other.

"Kimberly, call off your friends and plant your feet right here," Mom says, pointing to the ground next to her. "And I'll go with you when you apologize to your uncle and our colleagues."

"I don't want to hurt you," I say, though I no longer expect her to listen to me any more than she appears to expect the same of me.

She sends a wave of ice from the pool in my direction, but I'm ready this time to answer it with proportionate heat, melting it back down and then turning my flow of fiery sparkles toward the Jacuzzi, melting it as well and trying to bring up the ambient heat around Eddie.

"The day you saw me dancing with Quentin, were you already planning to kill him for his research?" I scream across the pool. "Or did you just not care when Uncle Ethan told you? Did he even tell you before it was done?"

"I honestly had no idea how important he was to you," she shouts back.

"So if I'd never met him, that'd make it okay?"

Eddie fires at her again, and this time he's on the mark—or he would be, if not for the ice wall she pulls up between them to take the blast for her.

"I hope you're happy!" she snaps at him. "You've utterly poisoned my daughter against me. Mission accomplished!"

"I didn't do shit!" he spits back through chattering teeth.

The pool water rises nearly to the ceiling at her direction, ready to crash down on Eddie's head and freeze there.

"Mom, stop!"

"Say goodbye, Kimberly."

I drop down onto the tiles beside her, reach out with both hands and shove her into the water.

"Goodbye, Mom," I mutter to myself, as I direct my full power into the pool after her in a stream of purple fire.

The column of water crashes back down into the pool. The outline of my mother under the surface is highlighted with spreading ice crystals as she tries to direct the water to push her upward, to form a solid floor beneath her.

The half of the pool on the other side of my jet of fire heats up until it steams, simmers, then boils.

Eddie starts coughing from the chlorine in the air and circles around behind me, trying to absorb the heat from a safe distance. The crystals keep forming around her, but I'm winning.

Her side of the pool turns from ice to slush to water, until the boil rolls over it, and she surfaces, gasping and hacking, her skin blistering a brilliant red.

I reach in, grab her by the back of her suit jacket, and drag her out onto the edge.

She curls up, wheezing, running her hands over herself, barely able to generate enough ice to form a layer over her burns.

"Don't look for me," I tell her.

Between his own coughs and shudders, Eddie looks uncertain whether he should offer thanks, condolences, or congratulations.

I don't know, so I'm glad he settles on an all-purpose nod, and silence.

I turn and offer him my back, more to impart warmth than to speed our transportation, and he wraps his still icy limbs around me.

"Dissident," he starts.

"I know. We'll catch up."

CHAPTER 23: THE DETECTIVE

for a brief, shining moment after Card's personal security forces decided to bail, I had this glimmer of hope that things might not be that difficult after all. A lot of guns were taken off the table, and with both Card and Kline's mom incapacitated, how bad could the rest of this fight be, really?

Stupid question.

Stupid, stupid question.

There may be fewer goons with guns, but there sure as hell aren't fewer corrupt superheroes and Milgram henchmen. If anything, they fight even harder than before.

And yet, while we may not be the best match for them, we're doing a better job than I ever would've expected.

Watching Dissident and Kline fight, two heroes in their prime, is something to behold. Dissident's years of training in gymnastics and mixed martial arts make her brutally efficient, incapacitating Milgram's men with quick, violent strikes—and gadgets when those quick, violent strikes aren't enough. I'm so used to watching her fight in the dark and grime of Pinnacle City's streets that it's disorienting to watch her do battle in the gaudy, bright lights of Card's mansion.

Kline probably hasn't had the same kind of training, but she's studied enough Cape Fu to look confident despite being a flying brick compared to Dissident. She uses her superhuman strength to utterly annihilate Milgram's sturdier thugs, while her speed and durability come in handy on those occasions when she dives in front of a shot to save Dissident or me. She's strong enough, fast enough, and powerful enough to take on several of the Guardians at once without even messing up her hair.

Compared to these two, I'm barely an amateur.

A big gun, a baseball bat, and a near-indestructible trench coat at least make me an amateur capable of bringing the pain.

I keep a heavy trigger finger on the Flesheater, as much to keep henchmen down as to tear this gaudy monstrosity of a mansion to the ground.

The only time this fails me is with a particularly large, bald henchman, completely covered in tattoos. I unleash the Flesheater on him, expecting a steaming henchman puddle, and am surprised when he just stands his ground, a large hole in his jacket the only sign anything happened. He slowly walks toward me as I unload several hundred laser shots to his stomach, chest, head, and even groin when I get really desperate.

Nothing works.

When he gets close enough to strike, I dodge out of the way. He laughs. I whip Harriet out of my jacket and crack him across the jaw with it.

He doesn't flinch.

"Foolish man. I absorb all energy, even kinetic, and gain nothing but strength from it. Go ahead, hit me. Shoot me. But it will only make me stronger."

"Thanks for the tip. DISSIDENT!"

"YEAH?" she calls from across the room.

"TRANQ DART!" I yell, dodging beneath another of this giant's clumsy attacks.

"IS IT REALLY NECESSARY? I'VE ONLY GOT TWO LEFT AND AM RATHER BUSY!"

The giant smashes a hole in the floor with one of his fists, tearing out a massive slab of concrete like a boxing glove.

"PRETTY FUCKING NECESSARY!"

I don't see her throw the dart, but I do see the giant grab his neck, confused for a moment, before falling down face-first onto the floor with a roaring crash.

"Thanks!" I call to Dissident, before shooting a volley at the group of henchmen she was fighting. I take two down, probably for good, and scatter the others enough to give her some breathing room.

"No problem!" she calls back.

A hole explodes in the wall next to me as Kline crashes through, followed quickly by Demigod, who looks to be the one who threw her through it.

"Would you?" Kline asks from the ground.

"With pleasure," I say, aiming the Flesheater at Demigod.

His eyes go wide, and I take more than a little pleasure when I find out how high he screams. The Flesheater doesn't finish him, but I've made him think twice about sticking around.

I reach down to help Kline up, but before I can, she's on her feet, catching a marble pillar Strongwoman's swinging like a club before it can turn me to jelly.

"Thanks," I say as I duck away from the pillar.

"Don't, mention, it," she says through gritted teeth. "But, if you want to, return the, favor . . ."

"I'll get out of the way and let you wail on Strongwoman?"

"That would, be, lovely!" she grunts, forcing the pillar back into Strongwoman.

I take this as my cue to exit. And keep shooting. And . . .

And . . .

And there she is. On a curving staircase leading upstairs. She means to look like any one of Milgram's generic, well-dressed goons, but she's far too nimble in climbing the ruined staircase. I'd know that body movement anywhere.

Bystander.

I run for the staircase, not fully sure what my endgame is. She appeared in such a place and in such a way that she had to know she'd get my attention and that I'd undoubtedly chase her, which means this is almost certainly a trap.

I go anyway.

Part of me wants to believe I can still get her out of this. She's a killer, and I can't stand by what she believes in, but I know that somewhere in there is the woman I fell in love with. I can't change who she is, but maybe I can get her to ditch Milgram before she gets killed.

It's a long shot, but I have to do this.

She's fast, darting from room to room upstairs, and I'm barely able to keep her in sight, but every time I think I'm about to lose her, she slows down, slightly. This further backs up my trap theory, but for a while I indulge her because I don't have a better plan in mind.

Then, when one comes, I stop.

The hallway is quiet for a moment, until I see *her*, not some face she's assumed, but Bystander herself, edge out and look at me.

"I know what you're doing, and I'm done playing your game!" I call out.

She says nothing. She doesn't move.

"I don't forgive you for what you did. I can't. I won't. You killed a lot of good people. But what I said, I'm still willing to do it. Back out now, ditch Milgram, and I'll go with you anywhere. We can start over. We don't have to be these people anymore."

She doesn't move from the doorway.

To show her how serious I am, I drop the Flesheater and hold my hands above my head.

"I've taken the first step. Now it's your turn."

"Touching," the voice says from behind me.

I shouldn't have dropped my gun, but maybe if—

I dart for the Flesheater.

Milgram doesn't need to dart.

All he needs to do is say the word.

"*STOP!*"

And like that, I'm falling.

Falling into an infinite black void of my mind, the real world now so far away yet so close, out of reach yet still in sight.

I've heard what Milgram can do, but experiencing a full dose of his power is another story.

Damn chlorine, must've fucked up my earpiece.

I am a statue in the dark, motionless and numb. Whatever part of me wanted to go for the weapon has long-since disappeared. Now I'm just here, waiting to be told by a greater power than myself what to do next. Milgram and Bystander loom above me, determining my fate with the uncaring gaze of ancient gods.

I am a statue being dragged into a nearby bedroom for further torment. In a faraway place his voice taunts me, telling me of his vast superiority and how I was a fool for thinking I could ever stand up against his might. It's the same old bullshit supervillains have been telling heroes for generations, so I ignore it. He can't tell me anything new—not anything that'll help me, and despite all his speechifying he's just a thug with delusions of grandeur.

Padre Peligro with more funding.

Bystander, for her part, looks impatient. She tells Milgram to hurry this along, but her voice says even more.

She doesn't want me dead quickly so I'll be dead, but just so this'll be over.

There's something more in play, too, that neither of them knows. Something that keeps me from completely being in the dark.

The pain.

The pill I took before our encounter began has kicked in, and the pain is no more than a dull throb, but it's still there, anchoring me to the real world. The anchor is weak, barely held on by a thread, but if I tug on it in just the right way, I can use it to bring me back to reality.

So, while Milgram and Bystander debate between guns, knives, and other horrible ways to end me, I reach out. I try to find something, anything in my body that I can still control. I have a little strength everywhere, and can move slightly, but no more than just sway a little. Having frozen mid-step, my balance is off. With a little effort, I can sway more, first to one side, then the other.

They're getting impatient. Bystander's not listening to Milgram and pulls a large knife from her suit.

I rock to the side with all the limited might I can muster, overbalance, and then I'm falling for real.

I land on my left arm, hard.

And the pain. The sweet, beautiful pain. It's there, exploding outward from my arm and wrapping around me like a comforting blanket of fire and broken glass. I scream so loud they can probably hear me in Amber City.

So loud I'm no longer in the dark pit, but on the floor of a bedroom in Card's mansion. It's pink and covered in jewels and posters of pop stars and pro-heroes, and in my madness of coming to it takes me a moment to understand that this room probably belongs to one of Card's daughters rather than the Conqueror himself.

Milgram and Bystander look down at me, surprised.

They won't be surprised for long.

The Flesheater's out of reach, their doing, but Harriet's still in my coat. Can't get to her the way I am now. Have to get on my feet.

That won't be fun.

I do it anyway. Force myself up, ignoring the fire, the glass. Stumble into a wall nearby, which gives me enough balance to stand.

A loud popping sound. Heavy impact to the back, stopped by my coat.

Milgram's shot me.

The weight of the blast is agonizing, but it's heavy enough to spin me around against the wall so I'm facing them. My legs feel stronger. Everything hurts, but I know now that this is how it's supposed to be.

This is what I'm meant to do.

I'm able to reach inside my coat and grab Harriet as Milgram gets off another shot. The side of my neck feels hot, my head ringing.

I charge him. He gets off three more shots—two missing, one hitting me in the shoulder but not penetrating the trench coat. I'm almost within swinging distance. I can end this here and now.

But I can't. Not when Bystander jumps in my way. She does this because she knows I won't hurt her.

And she's right.

Instead of barreling right through her, like I should, I angle my shoulder to push her off to the side. She stumbles, falls on her face, stunned.

I feel bad, but don't stop, slamming into Milgram with the entirety of my body weight and knocking him to the ground. On the floor in front of me, bloodied and not surrounded by his goons, he doesn't look like much.

And then he starts laughing. The pain and anger that's been fueling me is galvanized, given strength with each chuckle.

"That's a really neat trick you got there. Fighting off my powers. You're gonna have to tell me how you did that, sometime."

"Nah, I'm good," I say, taking a step closer to him.

He holds up both hands. "WAIT!"

"If that was a command, it's not working."

"No, not a command, a request, a simple, human request from one man to another asking you not to kill me. You can't be seduced, you can't be bought, fine, I won't ask you to be a part of my team again. But I want you to think about something. If you kill me now, what will that accomplish? Someone, from my gang, or from outside, will fill that void, and you'll be back to square one. Would you honestly chance having to deal with a devil you don't know when you can, here and now, spare the devil you *do* know? I know it's not ideal, but—"

I don't let him finish his argument. Nothing he says will undo the evils he has done or bring back the countless lives he's ended.

Julian.

The Mendozas.

Tragedii.

And so I introduce him to Harriet. I swing her in powerful, overhand arcs, never once missing his head. At first he's bloody, then he's broken, then he's not much of anything anymore but a red, chunky smear with the occasional hard white bit mixed in.

Over and over I swing the bat, and still he tries to scream, to plead even through the destruction of his skull.

Over and over I hit him until he stops making sounds and his body just shudders on the floor. In some faraway place drowned out by rage and pain I hear a woman screaming, and I don't care, because Milgram has to pay for everything he's done.

By the time I stop swinging, I'm exhausted, panting like I've run a marathon and looking like I've just survived an explosion at a slaughterhouse. There's almost as much of Milgram's head on me as there is on the floor and the walls, the bright pink room now streaked with dark red and points of white.

I smile, sincerely, for what feels like the first time in years.

Milgram is dead.

The Crescent, WPC, they'll be better off with him gone. No more terror. No more Milgram Territory. No more having to watch our step—at least, any more than usual.

He's right that someone'll come in and try to take his place, vultures are persistent that way, but that's just something we'll have to face when we get there.

Dissident and Petting Zoo and Kline and me and . . .

Bystander.

I'd completely forgotten she was here.

She lets me know that it's best not to forget her when, tears streaming down her cheeks, she calmly opens my coat and slides a very large knife into my belly.

I thought I'd known pain before. I'd always thought that pain and I were old friends who didn't keep any secrets from each other, that I knew everything pain had to offer.

But I'd never had a knife jammed so far into my stomach that I could feel it tenting the back of my coat before.

I know now there's a few secrets pain's been holding for a rainy day.

I drop Harriet, locking my eyes onto Bystander's. She's staring into my soul, silent and unblinking and sadder than I think I've ever seen another person before. This allows me a certain peace I wasn't expecting. I know that by all rights I should be angry, or betrayed, but knowing how bad this wound is, and what it means, I feel almost freed. There's no more worrying about that far off day, no more wondering how it's going to happen.

I know what this means, and I'm okay with it.

The pain is so blinding I'm almost numb to it. That can't last, so I say what needs to be said.

"I get it. I get it. It's okay."

"Why?" she demands miserably. "He was my shot."

"You know why."

"We could've owned this city. You and me."

"In another life."

"A better life."

"You honestly think we're meant for better lives?"

"No," she admits.

"That's where you're wrong. You *can* do better. Better than this," I say, eying the blade in my stomach.

"I'm a killer."

"You don't have to be."

She looks at me long and hard, and I think she softens. I can see a little of the old Bystander in there, the part that hadn't entirely been destroyed by the awfulness of this world.

She slides up beside me, tries to hitch an arm under my shoulders.

"Come on," she says.

"No."

"I can still get you to a hospital."

"You and I both know I won't make it that far."

"Well, we have to try!" She struggles to move me.

"No, we don't." I shake her off.

"Do you want me to stay with you? Until you . . . go?"

I shake my head. "You need to get out of here. The cops and pro-heroes who didn't attend this party'll be here any minute. You need to disappear before that happens. And if it isn't too much trouble?"

"Yeah?"

"Try to live a better life," I suggest, though the words come out weakly, barely a croak.

She doesn't say anything to this, but she does close the gap. We kiss for a moment, the fire of our one and only night together returning to me, almost making me think that this battle at the mansion must be some bad dream.

But the fantasy of us living a normal life together, that's the dream, and one that disappears the moment her lips leave mine.

"Would you believe me if I told you I still love you?" I say, trying to grin, trying to make the joke feel like a joke instead of some pitiful, almost-last words.

She smiles wryly before transforming into one of Card's security personnel.

"No. But when you get to Hell, save me a seat next to Marco?"

"Of course."

And with one last lingering look, she turns and runs off.

My feet barely hold me up and I'm so tired right now that I want nothing more than to crawl onto this teenage girl's bed, pull out this knife, pass out and bleed to death all over her pink bedspread.

But with everything going on downstairs, I can't do that. I still have some fight left, and I mean to use it.

Pulling the pill bottle from my pocket, I pop the top and spill its contents into my mouth. A lot of them hit the floor, but I catch enough to serve my purpose.

I crunch down and swallow what's left. Even after only a few seconds, I feel the slight swimming sensation of them kicking in.

Achingly, I bend over, pick up Harriet and the Flesheater, and start to make my way back downstairs.

CHAPTER 24: THE SUPERHERO

'Ve lost track of the others.

Dissident's nearby somewhere. I don't know how long Eddie's been out of sight.

The Milgram thugs protecting the south end of the mansion are second-stringers; gunmen with subpar aim and supers with low-level or unrefined combat powers with crippling recharge times, but there are a lot of them.

I'm striking to disable, not to kill, but I can't even tell if I'm succeeding or not. The moment I drop one, there are two more demanding attention.

Sending a shockwave at the floor in front of me, meant to break a wall of legs, I take shelter for a moment behind one of the fallen columns to check Card's phone.

Without my app, DistressFinder takes forever to load in the browser, but after six smashes' and two screams' worth of waiting, it accepts my login and shows exactly what I was hoping it would.

"Gunfire and probable super conflict at home of Pinnacle City mayor" is currently the top result across three counties.

All the Guardians except for Pinnacle and me are marked as present and in need of additional assistance, due to continuing non-containment of the situation.

I'm both pleased and a little nervous to see that Pinnacle has declared himself en route. He'll be a serious ringer for the wrong side of the fight right now, but it was always the plan for him to be here, standing in a crater of his own culpability when the dust clears.

Thankfully, he's not the only one who's responded to the alert. Heroes from six different surrounding cities are coming to offer backup. We'll have to hope that they're from far enough outside Milgram's network that when they get here, they'll realize who needs that backup most.

Even the Justice Juniors are on their way, making an exception to their usual policy of giving the official adults a wide professional berth.

If I'm imagining the sounds of news choppers through the chaos, reality will catch up with my imagination soon.

I'm definitely not imagining the sound of another door breaking open with a wooden *crack*, or Dissident's computerized yell.

"Kline! Get over here!"

I put the phone away and levitate up from behind the column.

The locked door she's breached leads down into a half-sunken study. I hear him before I see him, downstairs among the golden lighting and dark hardwoods and velour upholstery.

"This really isn't necessary," says Uncle Ethan.

I land at the top of the abbreviated staircase, blocking Milgram's people from coming to his aid, while Dissident charges on ahead, throwing one of her bolas to pin him to his floating leather chair.

Uncle Ethan looks down at the cable holding him to the chair he never leaves and raises an eyebrow at Dissident.

"Is this how the masked vigilante crowd typically treats crippled old men these days? Because in my day, they had a little more respect."

Dissident ignores him, shoving him and his floating chair aside and kneeling down to examine the laptop on the desk in front of him. A faded, peeling repair tag on the back identifies it as the former property of Quentin Julian.

"He's erased the evidence from the local hard drive," she says.

"It's *gone*?"

"No. Julian had off-site backups. Erickson's been using this to track down all the different accounts. Didn't get them all yet. Cover me."

She takes a flash drive from her utility belt, plugs it in, and begins the download.

"Serves me right for being such a perfectionist," Uncle Ethan sighs, thoroughly put-upon. "I thought we'd all overwrite the files together, share a glass or two of brandy, and possibly one of the more Neanderthal among us might take a heavy object to the remains of the hardware. But what is it that separates the truly evolved individual from the refuse of history? The ability to adapt."

I know what he's about to do an instant before he does it, even though it hasn't happened since before I could form memories.

I fly between him and Dissident, shielding her and the computer while she works, as a golden light radiates from Uncle Ethan, then flashes over into the blinding flame that won him the title he gave me.

His chair burns away in the Solar Flare heat, allowing the unbreakable bola to fall loosely to the floor when he lifts off.

The awkward way his paralyzed lower half hangs, his stated reason for giving up active heroics, is barely visible through the glare of his power.

The heat radiating from him is uncomfortable from this distance, even for me. Everything made of wood in this office begins to char and smoke around him, and Dissident has to retreat back upstairs into the fray with the computer to keep it from melting.

Uncle Ethan starts after her, and I move to block him. He pushes, and I blast him into the nearest wall. He rights himself with a chuckle of exasperation.

"It's time to move over, Kimberly."

I hover at his height and fold my arms.

"I'm beginning to lose my patience," he says calmly.

It hurts to look directly at him, but I do.

"Every hero and news outlet within fifty miles is on their way here," I tell him. "By morning, everyone in the country will know who was here tonight, and why."

"You expect me to believe you'd sell out your family for some childish excuse to play the hero? You took an oath, Kimberly."

"We both did."

"To family."

"To protect the people of Pinnacle City."

"The *good* people," Uncle Ethan corrects.

"I know the words."

"So you side with the bottom feeders over the strong, smart people who keep the city running," Uncle Ethan proposes. "What then? When you're formally expelled from the PCG, when your mother and I decide to remove your name from *our* accounts, assuming you don't succeed in destroying them completely, where will you go? To join them in the welfare line?"

"I don't need your money," I say, trying to keep the doubt from creeping into my voice.

What I do or don't need won't change what has to happen tonight, but I'm embarrassed to admit that I haven't actually thought that far ahead.

"I'm a Solar Flare, too. Once the story breaks, another team will take me in."

"Maybe," says Uncle Ethan. "Until you run off on a new crusade that their sponsors don't like. It's not different elsewhere than it is here."

"It has to be!"

Raising my voice doesn't make this desperate proclamation sound any better, but I can't keep it down.

"Something, somewhere, someday, has to be better than *you*!"

Uncle Ethan swallows his first response, then says, "Last chance."

I hover in place.

With the force of a cannon, he barrels into me, fully surrounded in flames.

My clothes char in an instant, flaking away from the Solar Flare leotard underneath, a precaution I adopted after all the street clothes I've burned through, hoping I wouldn't need it. My skin sends those unfamiliar, intense pain signals to my brain, demanding that I jerk myself away from the flames, so much hotter than even Effigy's, though no real damage seems to occur.

We tumble out onto the first floor. I can't see Dissident or Eddie, and the Milgram thugs make no move to interfere with us, backing away from the blazing heat.

Uncle Ethan lets me go for the purpose of flying around me, but I block him with the heaviest charge I can summon, taking a chunk out of the wall behind him.

"I put you in that suit!" he accuses, pointing at the swirls of red and gold showing through under my ruined shirt. "I paid for your education! I paid for your room and board, your clothes, your publicists, your training, and your expensive damned cosmetic surgery! Solar Flare is *my* investment! What right do you think you have to cut me out?"

"I am *not* an investment!"

There's a noise signifying a computer error above us, and we both look up. Uncle Ethan zooms toward the corner of the high ceiling where Dissident's hiding like a spider, protecting the computer with her armor while she works. I catch him by his limp but red-hot ankle and throw him back into the floor.

Words that meant so much to me once, words I thought I'd given up on in the past weeks, resurface as I pick up the fallen column in the middle of the room.

"I am the tooth of the guard dog!" I scream as I swing it at the back of my uncle's neck.

My armorer was right. Uncle Ethan may burn hotter than I do, but his invulnerability factor isn't a fraction of mine.

"I am the edge of the ax!"

Crack.

"I am the fulcrum of Justice!"

Crack.

I can't stop. I can't listen to another excuse. I can't be talked into being bought and sold again.

Crack.

He's not moving anymore, but I keep swinging.

Crack.

"I . . ." I'm out of breath. I'm never out of breath. "I *am* a Pinnacle City Guardian."

"Kimberly."

The voice behind me is more exhausted than my own.

I turn, and Eddie is standing at the foot of the stairs, a half-dozen Milgram thugs dead or unconscious at his feet. I didn't even hear the struggle over my own screeching.

"Put down the pillar, okay?"

I don't know why I'm still holding it, and I drop it next to my uncle's lifeless body.

I'm not sorry.

Shouldn't I be sorry?

"The heroes are coming," he says, limping painfully, lopsidedly toward the body, taking out his already bloodied bat, and dipping it in the trickle coming from the base of the skull.

He's dripping blood of his own with every step as well.

"You didn't do this. Understand? I did."

"What?" I don't understand at all. "What are you doing?"

Eddie opens the front of his trench coat and I take in a sharp breath at the knife handle sticking out of his abdomen, dripping steadily onto the floor.

"Well, dying, for starters."

As soon as I can force myself to move, I'm in front of him, examining the wound.

It's bad.

God, it's bad.

"No," I shake my head, not sure if I'm refusing his suggestion or his condition. "No. I can't let you do it."

"Kimberly—"

"Because before you can count to three, you're going to be in the best hospital on the West Coast, and when you're better, we're going to explain how *we* saved the city."

Eddie smirks sadly, and even though he doesn't believe me, he nods.

"Sure."

He takes my shoulder and turns my back to him, and in the same instant I realize he can't ride that way with the knife in him. Something then clicks open under his coat, and his other hand darts out to press the glowing piece of Jovium to my face.

I try to break away, to tell him that he can't, that I won't.

To tell him goodbye.

But consciousness slips away in a few wordless seconds.

✳

THE DETECTIVE

Knocking Kline out was a shit thing to do, but necessary. If I had a tomorrow to see her in, I know she'd be pissed at me, but since tomorrow's gonna be for everyone but me, I don't have any regrets.

Truth be told, despite the knife buried in my gut, I'm feeling pretty good right now, though that's more than likely due to my pills kicking in.

I stumble over to the ruined wall and peer outside. The compound's now surrounded by dozens of police cars. Setting a perimeter, not going to burst inside just yet, not until the area's secured. Then it'll be guns blazing.

The pro-heroes, though, they won't be held back waiting for the area to secure. As soon as they get here, that's it. No amount of holding paperwork over my head is going to save me this time.

I reach into one of my coat pockets, pull out a half-crumpled pack of cigarettes, place the most intact one between my lips, and light up.

"You know those things'll kill you?" Dissident says, dropping to the floor beside me and tossing a battered laptop into the wreckage.

"If you think smoking's bad, you should try one of these," I say, opening my coat enough to show off the knife in my belly.

She cocks her head to look, then says, "I'll take your word for it."

"Thought so."

"You're not going to try to get out of this, are you?" Though it's hard to tell with her digital voice scrambler, I know she's not joking anymore.

"No."

"I'm sorry."

"I'm not. I had a good run."

"It should've been longer."

"There's a lot of things that should be that aren't."

To this, she says nothing. Though I can feel the life draining out of me, there's a few things I have to take care of first.

"Tell me you got the file."

She shows me a flash drive.

"And it's good?"

"Julian collected more than we could have ever hoped for," she confirms.

"Good. Deliver it to whoever'll take it. FBI. DSA. Dump it all online if you have to, but people need to know what happened here."

"They will. They'll know everything."

"But they can't know *everything*."

She doesn't say anything, cocking her helmeted head again.

"Kline. She may be one of the only good superheroes out there. Her involvement tonight can't be known. No one can know she killed her uncle, or she *will* go to prison. Even if he's exposed, they'll never accept him as a legitimate supervillain target under her heroing license. Fill the gaps in the story however you want, just make sure she sticks with it. Say I killed them all. Private detective, vet, crazed ex-henchman, uncovered a conspiracy, and after being driven mad by the conspirators killing his friends took the fight to them. Kidnapped Kline at gunpoint as leverage or revenge or something along those lines. Killed Milgram and Erickson and however many others died here, before being killed himself. Taking advantage of this, the costumed vigilante known as Dissident, who has always had it out for both Milgram and Card, jumped in to take her pound of flesh."

"I like the part where you add me in. Might actually help my image," she says.

"Least I can do."

"You know, some people will hate you for this, but I think more will love you."

"Well then it's a good thing that I couldn't care less, don't you agree?"

"Not really."

A silence passes between us as we watch the lights and listen to the sirens.

"We're really surrounded here, aren't we?"

She nods. "Pinnacle's waiting outside for some backup; he's already got the Justice Juniors waiting in the wings, but from the chatter I've picked up it sounds like he's getting some out of town help, too. ATHENA, Helios, maybe even El Capitán."

"Huh. Pinnacle City's really hit the big leagues."

"It was bound to happen eventually."

"Do you need a distraction to get out of here?"

"No. But if you're offering, one could only help."

Hefting the Flesheater, I let my cigarette fall to the floor and smile. "You got it. Now get out of here before they're all over us."

She turns from me and begins to walk away.

With her back to me, she says in a low voice, "You always were a good friend, Eddie."

"You too, Fadia."

And in a swirl of her dark cape, she's gone. I don't want her to get caught, but there's a primal tug inside me that doesn't want to die alone, either. Having one friendly face by my side, even if I can't actually see that face, would've been nice.

I guess I'm just going to have to settle for doing the right thing.

I take one last, long look at Kline unconscious on the floor.

There'll be tough days ahead for her, but she'll make it through. She'll want to tell the truth, but her desire to be a true hero will ultimately kick in and she'll tell the lie that needs to be told. . . and if everything goes well, she'll be able to save this city from those who'd tear it apart without a second thought.

I meant it when I said she was one of the good ones.

Now I just hope she won't be alone.

A few weeks ago I wouldn't have thought that possible, but I have to think now that people like Kline and Dissident can't be the only ones. There are heroes in this city, some of them already in capes and masks, some wanting to do what's right but feeling beaten down by the world. If we expose this, let people know that there are those who'll fight for what's right no matter the odds, I have to believe those who've been waiting to step up will.

I laugh. A wet, bloody laugh.

Fucking Kline. Her optimism really is infectious.

"Let's do this," I mutter, ripping the knife from my stomach in a massive gush of blood. I can't last much longer like this, but no way in hell am I dying with that thing sticking out of me.

Lifting the Flesheater, I fire a long volley into the sky, blowing out more of the ruined wall and giving me a great view of the night sky. The gun and its smoking barrels finally die after only a few seconds, but it seems to have attracted the right kind of attention.

The silhouetted forms of a small group of flying heroes come my way.

I hobble over to the broken body of Ethan Erickson, original golden boy of Pinnacle City, and lift Harriet high above my head with my good hand.

The heroes hover by the broken open wall, looking down at us.

In the middle is Pinnacle, flanked by members of the Justice Juniors. At first Pinnacle looks down at me with that stern, angry gaze that only a disapproving superhero can really pull off, but when he sees Erickson at my feet, when the recognition hits, his face collapses into profound sadness.

"No, no, no, no, no," he repeats to himself, softly.

If you got any epic last words, now's the time to use 'em.

"I just killed Ethan Erickson and saved this city. What've you done today?"

So I probably could've put some more thought into them, but that doesn't matter anymore.

Pinnacle's face rebounds to stern anger before transforming into a look of pure, impossibly powerful rage. His eyes glow a brilliant crimson as he charges his eye beams and floats closer to me. The Justice Juniors try to hold him back, screaming and telling him that this isn't how heroes do things, but Pinnacle is far too powerful and too far gone to hear their pleas.

I can feel the heat from here, even before he unleashes his eye beams, but that doesn't last. Soon they are around me, through me, cutting through my near-indestructible trench coat and flesh.

And then, finally, the pain is gone.

CHAPTER 25: THE SUPERHERO

The cemetery in the Crescent is overgrown and a little cramped, but I like it better than Lilac Hills, where the Erickson family plot waits for me someday.

The perfectly trimmed grass and recirculating water features there remind me of my fake, dignified brave face when they lowered my dad into the earth, and my even faker sad face when they did the same with my uncle last winter, all part of the obligatory funerary pageant of pretending that everything makes sense.

The dandelions and clover patches that cover everything here may not be the most dignified accents to the faded tombstones, but they're real, and they grow without anyone telling them when, where, or how high, and make the bouquet of orchids in my hands feel just a shade pretentious.

There was no service to attend, no family to throw one, and even if there had been, in accordance with his wishes as Fadia relayed them to me, I wouldn't have been allowed to be seen there. She took care of the arrangements herself, such as they were.

I think it's been long enough now for me to risk a visit, though. If anyone catches me, I'll tell them I needed to see it, to make it real.

It won't even be a lie.

The grave is easy to find. All I have to do is follow the graffiti.

Edgar Enriquez

Detective
Soldier
Friend

Under this Spartan epitaph, squeezed onto the tiny grave marker, someone has spray painted "*and psycho.*"

In another color, the next visitor has crossed out "psycho" and replaced it with "hero."

This disagreement has been splashed all across the city in similar dueling scribbles.

Officially, Eddie is a criminal and I am a victim, and back home in EPC, this story goes more or less undisputed. I'm still getting about ten offers a day for exclusives on the story of my terrifying kidnapping. On this side of the city, though, his name and face adorn every reachable surface that paint can adhere to.

There are even a few murals of the two of us together. The details are all wrong. We're usually holding hands and gazing at each other with sappy-yet-daring Bonnie-and-Clyde-esque expressions, but better that than painting me as his hostage.

Fadia's work again. She broke the story that needed to be broken. I don't doubt she also leaked a few extra details that needed to be leaked.

I stand at the foot of the grave, staring at the engraved words and searching for a place to start.

A woman with dark eyes watches me from a few rows away, cementing my jaw self-consciously shut, but when I look back a few seconds later, she's gone. There's just a girl rolling in the clover a bit farther off, running her fingers through it, probably looking for the perfect four-leafed specimen.

"Hi. I brought flowers," I say, setting the bouquet down by the marker and sitting in the grass.

"Sorry if you hate flowers."

This is harder than I thought it would be.

Mom used to take me to Dad's grave and encourage me to talk to him, and when I was little, I took her word that he could hear me. I loved telling him every little thing I'd done that day, imagining the tombstone acting as a magical intercom, pretending I could hear him answering me through it.

When I was about twelve, I told her I felt stupid talking to a rock, and we didn't come back much after that.

I don't know what I believe now, about whether the dead can hear the living. After fifteen years of superheroics, fighting demons and soul-eaters and all manner of paranormal beings, it's hard to discount any possibility, but the idea that Eddie's chances of hearing me are somehow improved by my proximity to his bones, stored in a box under six feet of dirt that a living person couldn't hear through, feels like a stretch right now.

But I've come this far.

"So, that was a pretty dirty trick you pulled on me, you know?" I say, winding the long grass between my fingers. "Taking advantage of a weakness I trusted you with in case of mind control. Making me choose between lying to the world about who you were or destroying everything you died for. Brutal."

The grass tears in my hand.

"But you got your way. I'm still here. Sole surviving non-incarcerated heir to both the Erickson-Kline fortune and the Pinnacle City Guardians. I might actually be the most powerful person in the city right now."

I wish I weren't laughing alone at the strangeness of this phrase.

"Technically, I could claim the Pinnacle mantle now, being the senior member of the Guardians and all, but I'm sticking with Solar Flare. It's more mine to redeem, I think. I changed the outfit, though. And I'm rebuilding the team. Now it's me, Dissident, Petting Zoo . . . is it just me, or is there something going on between the two of them? Anyway, it's us and some of my old friends from the Justice Juniors. Gothique, Makeshift, Brisk Boy. We're working on a new name for him."

If Eddie were actually here, he'd probably be giving me a blank stare.

"You never met them, but they're good people. They've just been overdue to get out of the Junior zone for a while. It was awkward at first, kinda merging two cliques, but I think everyone's finally falling into a rhythm. We're thinking of starting a new Justice Juniors satellite team, get some new kids onboard. Right now, there's just Kaley. She's sort of our live-in apprentice. Our ward? I'm going to be officially dubbing her the new Glitter Girl this weekend. She's, uh, she's not okay. But she's doing good, considering. Better than when you last saw her. She's actually learning a lot more from Dissident than from me, but she wants the purple supersuit, and I can't tell her no."

We're all learning a lot from Dissident, actually. The Guardians have become more of a co-op these days, but if we had to name a leader, it'd be her, not me.

"Mason's still off the grid. I think I'm finally hoping it'll stay that way this time. I never told you about him either, did I? That's probably just as well."

The topics of conversation left open between Eddie and me comprise a shorter checklist than I thought.

"Let's see, what else? Um, Ace is in jail—for now, at least. So are my mother and the old Guardians. I don't visit. Card managed to weasel out of doing time, but he had to resign from office in the plea bargain, drop his senatorial campaign, and the mansion's in foreclosure. Apparently, he went way into debt gambling on the WPC demolition scheme, and most of his "investors" have filed lawsuits against him . . . so, I doubt he'll ever get back on his feet again. The new guy's okay, I guess. He won on a platform of police accountability, but we'll see how well that ends up working. Oh, and *In the Cards* is finally off the air."

I hope this gives him the same satisfaction it does me.

"Anastasia's filing for divorce and trying to get a new show started with her daughters and new ex-superhero fiancé . . ."

What am I doing? I didn't come here to talk sordid celebrity gossip. If there were ever a way to make Eddie roll over in his grave.

I take a breath.

"We've got our work cut out for us, still. There are a lot of people who still want everything from the Crescent to the docks purged and leveled, and some others who want to declare themselves the next coming of Milgram. Mostly, I've been working on resurrecting the Julian Foundation, setting up infrastructure repair and community outreach programs. And then the team has to come in to arrest whoever shows up to sabotage them or extort the people who show up for help. It's working so far, but the predators keep coming."

It occurs to me that I may have spoken more to Eddie today than I ever did while he was alive.

We had one drunken night and a few days of guerilla heroing together.

He helped me find a new way to be a Guardian when I was ready to quit, and he set me up to rebuild the city when I would have left it broken just to keep it out of the wrong hands. And in that time, we never watched one movie together, or shared a meal more substantial than dry crackers in the Well.

I don't know what TV shows he watched or what foods he hated, or what he believed about whether the dead can hear.

"I think," I brush away the pile of shredded grass I realize I've gathered in my lap. "I think I would have enjoyed being your friend."

My phone vibrates, and I check it.

Mutant bomber pigeon attack at the new free clinic.

I text Leah back, let her know I'm on my way.

"City in peril," I tell Eddie's grave, lifting myself off of it to hover in the air, removing my street clothes from over my full-length Solar Flare leotard. "You know how it goes."

✳

ACKNOWLEDGMENTS

As always, we'd like to start off by thanking our wonderful agent at Literary Counsel, Fran Black, for everything she has done, will do, and is always doing for us. There are times when being a writer is phenomenally taxing, and she has always lifted us up and kept us going as no other could. Thank you, as ever, for taking a chance on us and the crazy stuff we write.

We'd also like to thank everyone at Talos Press and Skyhorse Publishing who helped sculpt our raw words and occasionally half-baked ideas into something that could be called a book, especially our editor Jason Katzman. You approached us with the basic idea of doing a superhero noir story, and this is what came out of it. Thank you for your infinite patience and understanding, and for being cool with us when we wanted to argue on behalf of the content we really felt strongly about.

A special thanks to everyone who's ever put pen and ink to page to bring superheroes—good, bad, and otherwise—to life, and for making us believe that people can fly. Thanks especially to those who understand that true heroes come in every shape, size, and color, that not all of them wear capes, and that the good fight is always worth fighting.

And finally, if you've actually read this far, we'd like to thank you, the reader. Without you, none of this would be possible, because do words truly exist if they aren't read? Think about it! Oh, wait, they're still printed or encoded here anyway because that is the nature of multimedia publishing. Well, it's still great that you read this far. High five! Enjoy the post credits scene where we leave hints at the rest of our cinematic universe as well as the possibility of up to three Netflix series all tangentially related to this book.

❋

We've been informed we have run out of time and money for a post credits scene. High five!

ABOUT THE AUTHORS

Matt Carter & Fiona J. R. Titchenell are married sci-fi, horror, and YA writers who together have co-authored The Prospero Chronicles series. Matt has also written *Almost Infamous: A Supervillain Novel*, while Fiona has written *Confessions of the Very First Zombie Slayer (That I Know Of)*. They live in sunny San Gabriel, California, with their pet king snake Mica.